Taylor Swift for Adults

Taylor Swift for Adults

Taking Swift Seriously

Kev Nickells

WHITE OWL
AN IMPRINT OF PEN & SWORD BOOKS LTD.
YORKSHIRE – PHILADELPHIA

First published in Great Britain in 2024 by
White Owl
An imprint of Pen & Sword Books Limited
Yorkshire – Philadelphia

Copyright © Kev Nickells 2024

ISBN 978 1 39905 275 7

The right of Kev Nickells to be identified as
Author of this Work has been asserted by him in accordance
with the Copyright, Designs and Patents Act 1988.

A CIP catalogue record for this book is
available from the British Library

All rights reserved. No part of this book may be reproduced or transmitted in any form or by any means, electronic or mechanical including photocopying, recording or by any information storage and retrieval system, without permission from the Publisher in writing.

Typeset by Mac Style
Printed in the UK by CPI Group (UK) Ltd, Croydon, CR0 4YY.

Pen & Sword Books Limited incorporates the imprints of After the Battle, Atlas, Archaeology, Aviation, Discovery, Family History, Fiction, History, Maritime, Military, Military Classics, Politics, Select, Transport, True Crime, Air World, Frontline Publishing, Leo Cooper, Remember When, Seaforth Publishing, The Praetorian Press, Wharncliffe Local History, Wharncliffe Transport, Wharncliffe True Crime and White Owl.

For a complete list of Pen & Sword titles please contact

PEN & SWORD BOOKS LIMITED
47 Church Street, Barnsley, South Yorkshire, S70 2AS, England
E-mail: enquiries@pen-and-sword.co.uk
Website: www.pen-and-sword.co.uk
or
PEN AND SWORD BOOKS
1950 Lawrence Rd, Havertown, PA 19083, USA
E-mail: uspen-and-sword@casematepublishers.com
Website: www.penandswordbooks.com

Contents

Shout outs   vi
Introduction   vii

Part 1   Essays   1

Part 2   The Business of Swift   9

Part 3   The Swiftian Tropology   16

Part 4   Album Guides   47

Coda   191

Shout outs

Shout outs and thanks are accorded to:

The practical help: Russell Hedges for introducing me to Taylor in the first place, a terrifyingly long time ago. Dr Sam Cutting for his incisive generosity in reading drafts. Richard Fontenoy for giving me the space to develop my writing style and being an outstanding editor, despite his incorrigible opinions on serial commas. The literally very good poet Verity Spott (these thank yous: yours) for poetic consultations. Helen 'Finchpalm' Boobis for matters grammatical. Timothy Thornton for musicological knowhow and generosity therewith.

The ineffable help: those people who haven't contributed directly to this book but have contributed to making my life exponentially richer – Geo 'Wood Eyes' Leonard – an eternal font of generosity and patience; Georgia Jones, who is an eternal font of ADHD wisdom, Nu McAdam for being an eternal font of neighbourness/pal/activist/chaffinch; Tilda Fox for being an eternal font of piss-taking and affection since the dawn of time; Frances Donnelly, whose counsel and wisdom were hugely missed in the writing of this book. RIP Frances.

Shout out to family – Nickellses and Davises – for being family, and especially my mum, Eileen Nickells, for instilling me with a love of country music.

Top of the props go to my cats – Weetie, Big, Sznurka – who will be profoundly indifferent to these thank yous and claim not to have been fed. And most importantly of all, BGFE PPPCN Agata Urbaniak, without whom I would be just a worm looking for a leather jacket. Kocham cię najbardziej.

Trans Rights are Human Rights. Black Lives Matter.

Introduction

Taylor Swift is many things, in the public eye. She's a pop star, a frequent subject of gossip columns, an Internet subculture, a marketing machine, a media darling. Variously decried and exulted, according to preference. She also has, with her fanbase – known as 'Swifties' – a terrifyingly dedicated following.

This book is called *Taylor Swift for Adults*, but what is an adult? In this case it's someone who's less interested in who Swift is shagging and more interested in how Swift's art has captured so many hearts and minds. It's a book that talks about Swift as a musical and media polyglot – writer, producer, director and multi-instrumentalist – a serious artist, in short.

For all the writing about Swift in the public eye, much of it is concerned with her in terms of 'celebrity culture' – who was she seen with, has she had a falling out with X or Y? There's little that approaches her as an artist, and too much that churns out facile copy regarding whether her skirts are too long/short (etc.). So *Taylor Swift for Adults* aims to remedy that.

One of the other screws I'm turning here is that this isn't necessarily a book for the hardcore Swifties – though I'm sure they'll get a lot out of it. What I mean by that is that there's a huge amount of Internet space given to interpreting Swift's songs in terms of her personal life, and in terms of the self-generated mythology – tropes like the one about the fifth track on every album being the most personal and revealing one, how Swift's lucky number is thirteen, and so on. That stuff is fascinating and there's a real sense that Swift has a very sweet relationship with her fans. My aim here, however, is to perform something more 'death of the author' – interpretation and criticism which divests the historical, personal narrative in favour of a close look at how we might want to interpret Taylor Swift, as if all that was left of her was her art.

So far as that goes, I'll largely be avoiding the 'this song is about X' stuff, where X is an IRL event or person. I'll be drawing on Swift's sociological standing at a few points – difficult not to with regards to Swift's capacity as a businesswoman.

This is a book that's less concerned with reiterating all the gossip column personal biography flotsam and more interested to eke out what's made Swift a songwriting machine, how she's kept a consistent writerly voice from a terrifyingly young age, and how she's developed into someone who sets the pace for pop songwriting in the 2020s. Frankly, Swifties have mined the songs for autobiography to the point of desiccation, so there's no real need for me to append to that corpus. This is a book which hopes to show that Swift is a shrewd writer, musician, businesswoman and a step in the critical work of appraising Swift as a serious artist of historical note. If I might be so bold, the first act of Swiftology.

An important fact about adults – they are allowed to swear. So I hope to do a bit of that as well. Hope you enjoy as fuck.

Part 1

Essays

This is country music

> You're not supposed to say the word 'cancer' in a song
> And telling folks Jesus is the answer can rub them wrong
> It ain't hip to sing about tractors, trucks, little towns,
> and Mama – yeah that might be true
> But this is country music, and we do
>
>   Brad Paisley, 'This Is Country Music'

Of the United States' many musical products, it's probably country music which is its most insular. Plenty of musical genres are quintessentially American, yet internationally recognised and consumed – R&B, jazz, hip-hop, and so on. By contrast, country music has never quite garnered much more than occasional piercing of the popular consciousness. For all the international appeal of Johnny Cash or Dolly Parton, many figures remain unknown outside of the US – George Strait couldn't get arrested in most countries but is a household name in the US.

To an extent, this is explained by the jokes about country music. Typically the impression in the UK, where I was reared, is that it's depressing, morbid or just songs about trucks. We don't have too many trucks here. And, moreover, there's a sociological fact that the UK is primarily not agricultural. I'm not sure the US is, but the maybe the small-town, semi-agricultural speaks to the highly dispersed non-urban American. It's particularly white America too – prior to Hootie and the Blowfish's singer Darius Rucker making a country turn in the in the late 2000s, the most famous African American country star was Charley Pride, who didn't have a hit after his late-1960s heyday.

What Brad is saying above is that country music makes a virtue of the things songs ain't meant to be sung 'bout. For all the popular forays into the macabre or darker subjects in other popular music – from goth to heavy metal and your singer-songwriters of a Leonard Cohen type – I can't think of a genre that includes songs about stillborn pregnancies (Dolly Parton – 'Down from Dover'), songs about chronic alcoholism (Dwight Yoakum – 'Two Doors Down' and countless others), not putting up with someone's shit because of contraception

(Loretta Lynn – 'The Pill'), losing a parent (Hank Williams – 'I've Just Told Mama Goodbye'), songs about cancer diagnoses (Craig Morgan – 'Tough') and so on. To say nothing of the strong pro-military bent (Toby Keith – 'Courtesy of the Red, White and Blue') and, of course, the strongly pro-truck bent (Red Simpson – 'I'm a Truck', Lee Brice – 'I Drive Your Truck'). And in the truck category, Taylor Swift has an entry from her self-titled first album – "Cause I hate that stupid old pickup truck you never let me drive / You're a redneck heartbreak who's really bad at lying' ('Picture to Burn').

But we'll come back to Swift in a minute.

Harlan Howard, country legend and probably best known for co-writing Patsy Cline's 'I Fall to Pieces', famously described good country as 'three chords and the truth'. What that doesn't tell you is how restrictive country is – studio production may have moved on from the days of yore but the form is still principally about three-minutes, an absolute maximum of three chords. Like that other deeply American genre of hip-hop, country trades primarily on lyricism, the story being told by the singer. And even so, country's lyricism is way more spare than hip-hop, where the hugely variegated flow weaves complex rhythms around repetitive beats.

The formula for country music, then, is three chords and the truth, but that truth has to be within very conventional songform, and the subject matter should be familiar to its audience, ideally dealing with an extreme emotional situation, and if it could have a surprise denouement in there, that's a bonus. For my money the all-time master of country songs is Hank Williams – died at 29, left a limited corpus of songs which operate with a surgeon's precision on the wobbly bits of human emotion. Despite covering some brutally harsh territory in his songs – 'My Son Calls Another Man Daddy', 'Angel of Death' and a whole heap about heartbreak and loneliness – Williams was encouraged by his label to record his more dark material under the pseudonym of Luke the Drifter. And under that pseudonym we get songs about infant funerals ('The Funeral'), and an obsession with mourning and death – 'And to those who weep / death comes cheap / For men with broken hearts' ('Men with Broken Hearts').

But Hank's template for country music was less about difficult subject matter, and more in his capacity for pithy, sharp, succinct lines. 'There was a time when I believed that you belonged to me / But now I know your heart is shackled to a memory / The more I learn to care for you, the more we drift apart / Why can't I free your doubtful mind and melt your cold, cold heart?' ('Cold, Cold Heart'). Note the prosody here – 'There *was* a *time* when I be*lieved*' – Hank's words were strongly rhythmic, often strong-weak paired syllables. Da DA, da DA, da DA. This is the opposite of rap's lyricism above, where the flow is an improvisation of a rhythm on a rhythm – the country songbook written by Hank is a lesson in terse, unambiguous writing that brings the story front-and-centre with precise rhythmic attention.

Swift's best *writing* is nakedly country – terse, taut and unambiguous. The best writing doesn't, however, correspond to her most country-*sounding* record, her self-titled debut. It's certainly thematically country – lyrics about 'My old faded blue jeans', 'Your stupid old pickup truck / You never let me drive it'. But really the country songwriting is in those clipped, unrelenting couplets that are the match of Hank, such as this from album number three, *Red*: 'You were an expert in sorry / in keeping lines blurry ... All the girls that you've run dry / Have tired lifeless eyes / 'Cause you burned them out' ('Dear John') – stress unchangingly every other poetic foot, just like Hank, who also had a song called 'Dear John'. Later '...Dropped your hand while dancing / Left you out there standing / Crestfallen on the landing / Champagne problems' ('Champagne Problems') – the stress of tight rhyming scheme that's given a jolting release but without the rhythm changing (*cham*-pagne *prob*-lems).

In some ways, Swift's themes vary wildly – this book is full of reviews to get to the bottom of that – but at a certain remove she's really the current queen of break-up songs. As the music gets further from the realms of trucks and banjos, heartbreaks and God, Swift's capacity for writing becomes more laser-focused. Inheriting St Hank's capacity for breaking your heart ten times in twenty minutes and, without steering too far into hyperbole, being the millennial generation's finest songwriter. Swift's paradox, perhaps, is that she's *always* very country: hers are traditional songs with traditional arrangements (usually) about classic country themes – heartache and how men are bastards – and the further she gets *musically* from country orthodoxy, the more her songs sound like the saddest God-damned thing you ever heard. You're not meant to break your listener's hearts on the regular – but this is Taylor's country music, and she does.

Taylor and colours

Synaesthesia describes people who have an atypical relationship between different senses. Typically this means certain sounds will conjure colours in the person's mind. Taylor Swift apparently doesn't regard herself as a synaesthete – though it has come up in interviews:

> The quality that really confounded me about Aaron [Dessner]'s instrumental tracks is that to me, they were immediately, intensely visual. As soon as I heard the first one, I understood why he calls them 'sketches.' The first time I heard the track for 'Cardigan,' I saw high heels on cobblestones. I knew it had to be about teenage miscommunications and the loss of what

could've been. I've always been so curious about people with syn[a]esthesia, who see colors or shapes when they hear music. The closest thing I've ever experienced is seeing an entire story or scene play out in my head when I hear Aaron Dessner's instrumental tracks.[1]

It's difficult to properly cite, but I'm pretty sure in the 2014 show I saw in London, Swift introduced the song 'Red' (from *Red*, 2012) in terms of seeing colours in sounds and instruments. Cue the 'Red' intro just at the moment she says '…and this one reminds me of an emotion that was just… red'.

Colour appears as a theme fairly regularly in her work – plenty of workaday blue references – blue jeans, blue eyes, blue skies. But there's plenty of using 'blue' in a fairly atypical way; rather than a nominative 'blue', the abstract designation of 'feeling down', there's a fairly precise, apparently literally descriptive 'blue' – 'Losing him was blue like I'd never known' ('Red'); 'Don't want no other shade of blue but you' ('hoax', *folklore*).

For the first, the blue isn't 'I feel' blue but a syntactically deadweight '…*was* blue' – the kind of literalism we'd expect of poetry. '…no other shade of blue, but you' is designating a person as blue – parsed another way (and taking liberty with the scansion), the lyric might read 'don't wanna feel any other shade of blue but you'. Without a descriptor, blue has a sense of being literal.

Elsewhere red gets a look in – 'loving him was red' (from the song 'Red', on the album *Red*). Not 'loving him felt red'. Not anything more typically, clichéd, metaphorical or idiomatic like 'I felt the red mist' – loving him *was* red. And that it's the terminus of the chorus's lyrics makes it more elusively peculiar. Whether Swift herself is synaesthetic is not for me to say and it's clear she doesn't use that term to describe herself. Swift's lyrics do definitely have a strong synaesthetic quality, though. But it's perhaps more appropriate to view the function of colour in Swift's narratives as mnemonic:

> *The burgundy on my t-shirt…*
> *…the blood rushed into my cheeks*
> *So scarlet, it was*
> *Maroon*
>
> 'Maroon', *Midnights*

Here the colours are used like running through a reddish colour swatch – the reds of being flushed, which are scarlet-maroon. If colours are mnemonics here they are also very specific – it's not enough to say 'off red', the colours

---

1. https://uproxx.com/pop/taylor-swift-synesthesia-aaron-dessner, accessed 26 February 2023.

are described very closely. Perhaps mnemonic is a preferable way to describe Swift's narrator's relationship with colour – it's not so much that emotions and colours are some sort of parallel internal dictionary but rather that each colour conjures a time and a place. This seems entirely plausible, given that certain things can immediately conjure places and times – a certain smell brings to mind your mother's cooking, a certain song brings to mind a party from when you were young.

> *I once believed love would be (Black and white) But it's golden (Golden)*
> 'Daylight', *Lover*

The 'black and white' of the first line here is a typical usage – the idiomatic English sense meaning 'plain, easily distinguished'. Followed by a contradiction, a re-interpretation – 'it's golden'. This of course pushes a listener to a reading like 'ah, it's shiny and high value'.

> *You showed me colors you know I can't see with anyone else*
> 'illicit affairs', *folklore*

Elsewhere in 'illicit affairs', the narrator speaks of 'a secret language I can't speak with anyone else'. The colours and language are part of a private vernacular – experiences that don't happen with other people. So whether or not those colours are synaesthetic to the narrator, they are symbolic of exclusivity. It's peculiarly *private* – there are experiences which are relatively public, there are ideas that are relatively private, but here the sense is that the antagonist invokes exclusivity in the narrator's most private realm – her own mind. It's an intensive magnification of the way in which we give parts of ourselves to our significant others, that they might influence and invoke a private, exclusive neurological state. Whether metaphor or not, the colours are used to indicate an extreme intensity.

> *you painted all my nights*
> *A color I've searched for since*
> 'Question…?', *Midnights*

Similar to the preceding – here the colour of the nights was *unreal* – a colour that's remained unmatched, a colour that is exclusive to the association with the antagonist. While there's a strong association with a very particular, and unavailable, colour, there's also the idea that the narrator's memory is intimately linked with that colour; that the embedding of memory relies upon recognising that colour.

It's difficult to pin down all of Swift's use of colours in too specific a way because sometimes colours are just descriptions. Nevertheless, there's plenty of instances where colours are given a place within the emotional-memorial dictionary of her narrators. Swift's lyrics are brilliantly colourful (in at least two senses of 'brilliantly'). It's perhaps also the problem that as soon as a colour gets invested with meaning, as well as mnemonic qualities, it becomes harder to pin it down specifically. Colour is slippery and splattered all over, appropriately enough.

Swift for Swifties

Throughout this book, I've almost piously refused to interpret Swift's lyrics in terms of those lyrics being about Swift *herself*. There are a few reasons for this. Primarily, I'm keen to invoke the 'death of the author' idea of Roland Barthes – that is, that the artist themselves is not the primary guarantor of interpretation. The author's 'intention' is not definitive of the interpretation of a work of art.

While this may seem outrageous to some, it's a fairly commonplace methodology for a lot of critical work. Interpreting a work of art means to consider a lot more than just what the author intended to say. Linguistic arts (poetry, songwriting, literature) in particular are *social*. What this means is that to use language, to communicate with another person, brings with it assumptions about its audience. We must both speak the same language, we must understand the same thing. If the audience for a work of art is public – as Swift's surely is – then its interpretation is substantially broadened. What the author intended to say becomes secondary to how a work is interpreted.

A simple example: The Police's 1983 tune 'Every Breath You Take', with its refrain of 'I'll be watching you', has a fairly substantial rift between the author's intention, and how it was received by its audience. Sting had intended that the song be understood as being written from the perspective of a stalker; the more typical interpretation is that it's a love song. It's arguable that the *reason* Sting's intended interpretation is less popular is because where he had intended satire and irony, he didn't telegraph that sufficiently to the song's audience; couple that with a fairly bouncy, jaunty arrangement and the typical listener is likely to miss the subtlety.

Now the question of which is the 'correct' interpretation of that song is kind of moot; Sting can repeat it till he's blue in the face (and he has, for some forty years now) but the song is still 'read' as a simple love song, one that accompanies people down the aisle and one that commemorates plenty of relationships. There's a lot of interpretive work we could do to eke out potential interpretations – love song/stalker song/humiliation-kink sub song – but given, mercifully, I'm not here to interpret Sting's lyrics, the key here is that a work of art may have multiple interpretations. A general interpretation of a widely known work of art is not singular, the 'interpretation' *in toto* is an amalgam of many interpretations. This isn't to say that all art is *absolutely* interpretable – that there would be a million interpretations – but rather that the language's function rests on a *limited* but not *unitary* set of interpretations. In language, the individual is of less value than the community of users, so the author's intention is of lesser value than the interpretation of the community which uses the language-object-thing (in our case, a song).

So given all of that, I've made a decision to *not* interpret Swift's songs as being autobiographical; to assume that they do not convey personal information, rather that each is a self-contained narrative – as such, I've leant on terms like 'narrator' or 'protagonist' to talk about the characters Swift occupies as the singer of the 'I' of the narrative. In a complementary sense, the 'others', or subjects, of her songs, are usually termed 'antagonists' or similar.

There's a small problem with this approach, though – it is, in fact, pretty ridiculous. Taylor Swift consistently invites and encourages that the characters of her songs be considered as 'herself'. When a songwriter does the rounds of press – interviews in various places – there's usually a PR 'line', a narrative that they will push for those interviews. This is tied in with the branding of an artist. Swift's branding relies massively on the notion that her songs are deeply personal, that they have a literalism that is atypical even for singer-songwriters. More on that literalism in a moment.

Swift's fanbase – known as 'Swifties' – are a formidable presence in online spaces. The fans are notoriously loyal – ensuring her album and singles dominate pop charts, and ensuring that Swift is well-defended in any open comments section. They are, at least potentially, a political force – Forbes reported on 6 December 2022 that the group has taken legal action against Ticketmaster for anti-competitive behaviour. Swift in many interviews has referenced the way in which her fanbase excise personal detail from the songs. The depth of reading and capacity for interpretation in Swiftie communities is most impressive, and it would take another book to detail it.

There's a strong sense that Swift's work is more personal than regular songwriters. For the first two albums, there's a raft of characters whose names are given as their actual names: 'Drew looks at me' ('Teardrops on My Guitar', *Self-titled*), 'Cory's eyes' ('Stay Beautiful', *Self-titled*) 'Abigail gave everything she had…' ('Fifteen', *Fearless*). Typically a song would have an abstracted pronoun – he, she, they – but Swift's songs eschew that self-protection. Self-protection because it's more typical for a songwriter to use the theatricality of songform as a mask to obscure the 'real life' details.

It's key to Swift's songs – for Swifties at least – that the usual divisions between song and songwriter, the abstractions which lend the songs a quality of *personal distance*, are removed. Or if not removed, then at least challenged.

And if this book is working towards establishing Swiftology, then it's not important to resolve whether we should read personal details into Swift's work. My take is that there's plenty enough in the way of poetic detail and elegant lyricism such that personal details are not adding much more. It may well be the work of other writings to establish the ways in which Swift engages her audience by revealing part of herself. And, for that matter, the ways in which Swift *doesn't* reveal parts of herself.

One of the keys to hermeneutics (that's a fairly academic/theological term for 'interpreting texts') is that there be many interpretations of a work. Whole religions grow out of different ways of reading a text (see, for instance, the huge number of denominations of Abrahamic faiths). So my point here is that if Swiftology becomes 'a thing' then part of that thing will be having different ways, different techniques of interpreting works. Well-known details – like Ye's stage invasion – surely have an important bearing on Swift's work. Finally, then, my point is that there's lots of ways to skin a Taylor Swift-shaped cat (though obviously don't touch Swift's actual cats. That way lies certain doom).

Part 2

The Business of Swift

I said in the introduction that I didn't really want to talk about Swift's personal life. This is primarily because it's well-covered; she's a gossip column regular. Speaking personally, how a person operates within celebrity culture is of less importance to me than their art. This inexorably draws out a discussion on 'separating the art from the artist'; given sufficient time, references to French literary critic Roland Barthes's concept of the 'death of the author' abound. For those averse to critical theory, you may want to skip the next couple of paragraphs.

Barthes's concept has been used many and multifariously – to summarise it brusquely, the artist's own perspective on their art is not defining of that art – rather that the art exists to be interpreted by a community, that community being the art's audience. From this we move to the idea that the author's biographical details are not imperative to thinking about their art. It's not absolute – biographical details frequently furnish us with context for a piece; but the point is that the art is more than merely a reflection of an individual's experiences. In the case of Taylor Swift, there's *such* a glut of writing about her personal life that her actual skills as a songwriter are usurped by scurrilous gossip.

Primarily in this book I've tried to avoid bringing personal biographical detail to bear on the interpretation of Swift's work – which is at odds with a lot of pop culture readings of Swift. However, there are *some* biographical details which are important. The principles of dialectical materialism – an early twentieth-century school of philosophical thought – are many and diffuse, but a very rough rule of thumb is that 'the richer you are, the easier it is'. Put another way, a person's socio-cultural standing – the wealth and cultural conditions of family, friends, and sociological cohort – strongly influence a person's capacity to succeed.

Taylor Swift's parents are both in the realm of high-paid financial workers. Her dad, Scott Swift, is the founder of the Swift Group – a wealth management consultancy associated with Merrill Lynch; Forbes listed the Swift Group as number twenty-three in 'America's Top Wealth Management Teams: High Net Worth' in 2022. Andrea Swift, Taylor's mum, is a former mutual fund marketing executive. Without going into vulgar detail about the Swifts, these are a long way from impoverished or downtrodden backgrounds – they are solidly well-off.

Swift received a lot of parental support in her early career – parents moving from Pennsylvania to Tennessee to allow Swift to pursue her music career.

This isn't to push a trite truism that 'Swift owes her career to family money'. It's usually the case for most people in the public eye that there's some support network, social privilege and money which plays into a person 'getting their break'. Swift has been at it too long and too consistently and, in songwriting terms, too well to be a flash in the pan. What I do want to emphasise, though, is the ways in which Swift has learnt sound business practice and ownership of her own work, presumably from her dad's early investment in Big Machine records (her first label):

> Swift's dad, a Merrill Lynch stockbroker, was a minor investor in [Big Machine] … 'Scott Swift owns three percent of Big Machine,' [Scott] Borchetta says. 'But I hear people go, "Oh, well, he funded the whole deal, and that's why Taylor's Number One." It's like, "Please, people." Everybody wants to say, "Well, there's a reason." Yeah, there is a reason. 'Cause she's great. That's the reason.'[2]

The deal with Big Machine is critical in two senses – the obvious one, that it was Swift's first proper deal, the deal that pushed her initially to the echelons of country fame, then to the general pop consciousness. The other important thing is the split with Big Machine – Swift's BigMachxit, if you will.

First of all, though, the influence of Swift's parents has been their presence and support, and their presence within the music business itself, with Scott Swift's share in Big Machine records. It's not so much the typical parental role of personal investment in terms of driving to and from, bigging up their kid, but the concrete business investment coming from someone whose day job is to make investments that make other people richer. Every parent is convinced their kid is special; not many of them have the capital and social standing or knowledge to make a concrete difference.

There's plenty of places for rich parents to sink money in order for their kid to get the feeling of being a pop star – the notorious meme 'Friday' by Rebecca Black is an example of that. In that case, ARK Music Factory would take a few thousand dollars from the parents and produce a music video and song that was the definition of shoddy – and if you think 'Friday' was bad, it's worth checking out Alison Gold's 'Chinese Food'.

Big Machine is not ARK, though – it's a joint enterprise between Scott Borchetta and Toby Keith. Borchetta's pre-Big Machine experience was with DreamWorks Records, MCA Records and MTM Records – of the three, only

---

2. https://web.archive.org/web/20160731171417/http://www.rollingstone.com/music/news/taylor-swift-in-wonderland-20121025, accessed 21 November 2022.

MTM was 'independent' and even so it was ultimately subsumed by RCA. Incidentally, latter-day country star Trisha Yearwood got her pre-fame break as the receptionist at MTM. Toby Keith is a businessman and country music star (also DreamWorks Records) – probably better known outside the US as one of the few musicians who'd play Donald Trump's rallies. His music is very close to the negative stereotypes of country music – nationalistic, pro-gun, pro-military, pro-ol' timey real men. For what it's worth, with a pinch of salt Keith is a great down-home songwriter and his 'Beer for My Horses' (a duet with Saint Willie Nelson) is absolutely peak country.

All of this is to say, Big Machine is by no means some vanity project. Scott Swift's investment has likely paid massive dividends, with or without his daughter as the label's biggest artist – in 2022, the label had a mix of new (Callista Clark, born 2003), old (Wanda Jackson, born 1937) and dead (Glenn Campbell, 1936–2017). It also provides a home for John 5 – former Marilyn Manson (and Rob Zombie, Mötley Crüe...) guitarist.

Most musicians are relatively passive, and limited, in terms of their engagement outside of their given role: stick to the one instrument. Songwriters may have two roles – performer, writer. There's a few – especially within a lot of hip-hop or dance music traditions – who double up; think of Missy Elliot, producer and performer, or Dr Dre, producer, performer, musician, label magnate. It's worth noting that a lot of US hip-hop culture has a tendency to keep matters 'in house' – keeping legal rights over the music, running the label, owning the studio. This is typically reflective of the kind of exploitation that is endemic to the music business in the US – that is to say, there's a long and ghastly history of exploitation of black musicians; the turn for a lot of black musicians to take ownership of as much of the industry as possible is a clear response.

So in those sorts of terms, it's worth noting the ways in which Swift has taken responsibility for parts of her career which have an extensive material value. For *Taylor Swift* (2006) and *Fearless* (2008), her credits are musical – writer or co-writer, acoustic guitar, and vocal harmonies. On *Speak Now* (2010), she's listed as producer, and additionally is credited with 'art direction'. These are likely the green shoots of her taking full control over the Swift brand – notable also that her younger brother Austin Swift is listed as 'tour photographer'. *Red* (2012) lists her as producer for a number of tracks; it's also the album where the songs turn from 'live band' (guitar, drums, etc.) arrangements to more pop productions. Following this, *1989* (2014), with its Max 'Hit Me Baby One More Time' Martin productions is maybe the first shiny electro-pop record, and also the first to list Swift as the executive producer. And Swift is executive producer on all her subsequent albums up to *Midnights* (the most recent album at the time of writing).

In itself, this isn't perhaps atypical; it's a pattern for musicians to go for the more lucrative credits as they mature. Similarly to how actors will take an executive producer credit later on in TV shows, or turn their hand to directing (see: Johnathan Frake's brilliant *Star Trek: The Next Generation* directorial turns). But my point here is that it's of a piece with other ways in which Swift has wrested control.

Several of Swift's videos have been self-directed – earlier on, live footage collage 'I'm only me when I'm with you' (from *Taylor Swift*, 2006) and home video collage 'The Best Day' (from *Fearless*, 2008). Both are fairly perfunctory efforts – I don't think anyone would regard them as breaking new ground, but they are significant in terms of Swift's attention to different areas of her brand. The album *Lover* (2019) is really the point at which Swift starts to show signs of having a grasp on most areas of her music. Her label changes from Big Machine to Republic. And with it we note that the majority of videos subsequent to then are directed by Swift herself.

Wedged in there is the 'Spotify issue' – that is, between 2014 and 2017, Swift's music was not on Spotify, the largest music listening platform worldwide. Plenty of ink was spilt over this but the core issue – and one that is still the case for legion other artists – is that Spotify represents a poor deal for the musicians hosted on there. Regardless of the profitability of the Swift brand (and we'll see in a second – it's massive), in business it's predictable that provider may withhold their services or labour in order to negotiate better pay. Taylor Swift's Spotify strike seemingly resulted in a more equitable payout for her music. A shame that Spotify can't find a way to share its enormous profits more equitably with the other musicians who provide content for them.

In terms of Swift's business impact, it's telling that articles about her proliferate in non-pop outlets. Forbes has a series of articles – relating to her impact on Spotify, to her being the most well-paid celebrity, to a snafu over ticket sales with Ticketmaster (seemingly a problem of volume-demand infrastructure). Elsewhere, reports have circulated that Swift's use of a private jet exceeds that of any other celebrity. I'm not able to assert the veracity of that but it's certainly worrying, and emblematic, that Swift is so far into the realm of prodigious personal wealth that even speculatively it's easy to assert that her lifestyle is likely damaging in a world of climate meltdown. She may be a shrewd businesswoman – and clearly I'm asserting she's an exceptional songwriter – but the trappings of global capitalism do not avoid pop songwriters, no matter how much I squee over them.

Legacy squared

Notoriously the music business is mired in murky ethics; for all the guitar-shaped swimming pools, plenty of people have been royally shafted by the industry. Shafted by bad publishing deals, shafted by lack of copyright, shafted by the stresses of touring. There's not much new insight to be given by exploring that. In business terms, though, it's worth saying that the advent of streaming has pushed the industry in different directions – expressly, varied revenue streams. With the atrophy of revenue from record sales that accompanied Napster et al. came the need for different revenue streams. The industry is typically diffuse in its revenue streams, and reactive to changing culture – twenty years ago, mobile ringtones were selling like poorly rendered hotcakes. Look at the average pop video on YouTube in 2024 and you'll see a raft of buy-ins – corporate sponsors who recognise that the video can be a platform for product endorsements.

Typically pop music has been taciturn about its relationship with financing. For the indie sector, less so – there's a kind of cultural clout from musicians' labels being financed solely from music. The insinuation being that major labels are involved in 'dirty money' – and typically the bigger record companies have investment in a number of less-than-salubrious areas. That isn't to say that there isn't a degree of exploitation in the indie sector – it is still a business, and business is dirty – but the smaller the company, the easier it is to trace its financial ethics.

But even so, indie music has rarely been purely transparent about what goes into producing a record – musicians will gripe about bad deals and will sometimes set forth on bad business, but typically actual financial discussion isn't sexy. Some very left-wing musicians – British anarcho-punks Crass, for instance – may have had included some business details on their sleeves but it's fairly unusual. To bring finances front-and-centre is typically regarded as a kind of fourth-wall-breaking, ungainly thing; if not expressly forbidden then at least profoundly uncool.

In 2021, Swift released re-recorded versions of *Fearless* (Big Machine version first released in 2008) and *Red* (Big Machine version first released in 2012). It would be remiss of me to insinuate that this was an act of abject transparency; it did, nevertheless, generate headlines about the nature of recording contracts. Atypically for a pop singer, it generated a lot of press in the business world – at the time of writing, the second-to-top link I found when searching for 'Taylor Swift re-recording' is an article on CNN business.

The back story to this, in short, is that the re-releases were a means of Swift reclaiming copyright for material that she didn't have control over, due to her shift from Big Machine records to Republic Records, the sale of the masters by Swift's *persona non grata* ex-manager Scooter Braun.

What's *unprecedented* in this situation isn't so much that Swift fought for a means of owning her own material; it's the lengths to which she went to do so. Having apparently ceded the rights to a tranche of her early career (the six albums from *Taylor Swift* to *reputation*) she elected to re-record the albums.

Typically legal arguments in the music industry (as with the legal world in general) are resolved in favour of the person with the biggest purse, and in many cases brutally swerving a just outcome. Notoriously, James Brown's drummer Clyde Stubblefield received no money from being one of the most sampled drummers in dance and pop music, from hip-hop through to drum'n'bass – and Stubblefield is by no means alone in not getting his due recompense, especially with regards black musicians.

So what makes Swift's decision to re-record *radical* is that it quite precisely circumvents the legal situation; there are now two versions of her songs available for the various streaming platforms and radio to play. And, given that Swift is no longer a Big Machine recording artist, well, there's a lot less promotional money behind pushing old material. Given that Swift is actively promoting the re-recorded albums, there's a sudden drop in interest in Big Machine capitalising on the recordings they own. But there's an important factor to this – the recordings should be indistinguishable. I'll avoid saying 'identical' but suffice it to say, the re-recordings are typically as near as damnit to the Big Machine originals.

If the re-recordings are indistinguishable then the radio will presumably prefer the newer ones – which from an engineering perspective will seem like they're re-masters, listener-imperceptible tweaks to the existing sound. A lot of press mileage is made out of 'the resurgence of vinyl' and it should be known that that resurgence is clouded by re-issues of heritage music – a new generation buying and the old generation re-buying Pink Floyd and David Bowie with 're-master' stickers. Swift's re-recordings, as well as being a shrewd political fiat against Big Machine, also nominate those re-recorded albums as heritage works (although they're a great deal more spry than the half-century-old canon of most heritage albums).

So that is to say that the re-recordings are a sharp and ingenious *political* and *business* move, but what are they in recording terms? Well, there's a lot to observe about them in terms of detail; they're not *cheap*. One of *Red*'s (2012) big singles, 'We Are Never Ever Getting Back Together', has a couple of details that are by no means necessary but also are surprising in that they feature on both. The opening guitar motif – which forms the base for the verse – opens with the guitar figure and then a sound like two small fingertip taps on an acoustic guitar; the motif is reversed and played again, and second time around there's a single, quieter tap. In terms of the minutiae of arrangement, these are the kind of subliminal reaffirmations of the rhythm, which itself is highly articulated with a bass drum following the pulse, á la disco. It's something of a moot point as to whether they are necessary to the arrangement; nevertheless, these taps are present in both versions. Swift's re-recorded version (from *Red (Taylor's Version)*, 2021) is very subtly different to the earlier version. For one, her vocals have matured, are not so much deeper as *rounder*, and for another there's a bit more emphasis on the aforementioned bass drum with a slightly roomier recording. Re-recording an album *precisely* – same mics, same rooms, same ambient temperature, same room moisture levels, etc., etc. – is nigh impossible, due to the plenitude of factors. Anyone who plays an instrument knows that the same instrument is slightly different sometimes for no discernible reason, no matter the care you take. But given that, the fact that the re-recorded version is functionally identical – as in, the core and periphery of the arrangement are equivalent – is reflective of a superhuman attention to detail.

A sceptical reader may scoff at the superlative 'superhuman' there and I should be clear to say that I'm happy to attribute that assiduous attention to detail to 'the Taylor Swift machine' – the community which forms and defines the brand of 'Taylor Swift' – as much Taylor Swift 'the person'. Regardless, to leverage that attention to detail for what is effectively a record to spite a spurned record label is quite the undertaking and all the more impressive for the end result being – so far as radio listeners at large are concerned – as near as damnit identical.

Part 3
The Swiftian Tropology

Tropology introduction

It may be overwrought to describe this book as the opening salvo for a tradition of Swiftology (i.e. the study of the words of Taylor Swift). Nevertheless, this is called *Taylor Swift for Adults* and there's a lot of critical work done on pop culture figures – a whole modern academic tradition of media studies devoted to unpicking the appeal and complexities of popular culture. So why not also Taylor Swift?

This is partly predicated on a suspicion I have about the nature of 'canonicity' in popular culture – canonicity referring to the way in which popular culture decides on what the imperative examples of an artform are. The boundaries of canonicity are typically ill-defined – we would definitely describe J. S. Bach, Mozart, Beethoven as canonically part of 'classical' music. We'd less keenly turn to (say) C. P. E. Bach or Kaija Saariaho in discussing the canon. The boundaries between 'definitely part of the canon' and 'probably not part of the canon' are not clear by any means (and for what it's worth, Saariaho is very much worthy of more investigation than she currently gets from the classical realm).

There's a sense in which the figures who are frequently most vaunted as 'serious' pop musicians are those ones who most closely resemble the status quo of power within society in general – straight, white, able-bodied men. The list of great songwriters – the likes of John Lennon, Bob Dylan, Leonard Cohen – are conspicuously male (though also two of those I cite here are Jewish, so not exclusively WASPs so much as white or white-passing). When 'greatest songwriter' conversations arise, there are plenty of people who are sidelined despite absolutely fitting the bill. Her imperial majesty Dolly Parton being a great example – on paper she's got a formidable, indomitable body of work spanning several decades. But she's not the first name that comes to mind when it comes to 'greatest songwriters of all time' (though she was inducted into the songwriters' hall of fame in 2001) and I'm not convinced the fuzzy boundary of 'canon' for 'greatest songwriters' would intuitively include her.

There's a sense in which the makeup of music industry institutions like the songwriters' hall of fame are changing – more figures like Missy Elliot (2019) and Mariah Carey (2022) are included, rightly recognising the contributions of black women to popular music. These examples are pointed – Elliot has turned out a raft of hugely atypical yet compelling work; Carey is little recognised as a songwriter despite being one of the more storied songwriters of the 1990s and 2000s. Their induction – and veneration – within songwriter canonicity is on the back of a long history of those figures being primarily male, primarily white. And a sizeable number of those being questionable – I don't think anyone doubts the impact the Rolling Stones' Mick Jagger/Keith Richards (both inducted in 1993) have made on pop music in the twentieth century but I'm also pretty sure their most recent relevant, innovative, impressive material was half a century ago.

Swift was given a Hal David Starlight award in 2010, cementing (in industry terms) her maturing talent as a young songwriter. So it's not so much the case that female songwriters go unnoticed; just that the emphasis of industry recognition still lists heavily towards people who resemble the powers that be in the music industry, or the wider political or business landscape.

This is all to say – canonisation is tricky to pin down and a big part of the process of recognising the value of work is that we take it seriously, and treat it similarly to how we do the classics. Affording it the same dignity regardless of its context. It's difficult to imagine in the twenty-first century, but the recognition of jazz as 'serious' music in popular culture is in part due to the commitment of a narrow few academic works, such as Gunther Schuller's *Early Jazz: Its Roots and Musical Development* (published 1968). Despite a distinct change in demographics – that is, despite the fact that adults now listen to pop music without embarrassment – there's still a sense in popular culture that pop music is facile. There's an aside here that some pop music being facile is precisely part of its appeal – but here isn't the place for me to valorise Happy Hardcore or Disco Polo.

Part of the process of 'taking pop music seriously', finally, is to establish what are the themes, the tropes which establish the art as self-consistent. To an extent this is tricky to pull off while the artist's 'canon' is still under construction – the themes established by James Joyce prior to *Ulysses* would be very different to those established afterwards. But also Swift's body of work *is* substantial at this point – ten albums as of late 2023 – so there's plenty of work that can be done to eke out those tropes that form Swift's lyrical style.

Building a picture of what someone's art *is* is tricky – if that artist is well known then there's the danger of missing something that the audience strongly relates to; if the artist is lesser-known then there's a danger of misrepresenting them such that no one bothers to investigate further. Swift is massive such that the tropology in this book will likely frustrate some readers – *mea culpa*, but this is not a comprehensive tropology so much as it's a speculative outline, a kind of academic first draft.

With all this in mind then – what are the elements that make up a Taylor Swift song? As I've noted elsewhere, it's very easy to pull at the thread of her music which is the gossip column fodder – figuring out which song is about which boyfriend, and so on. I'm suggesting it may be more compelling, in forming a picture of *why* she is strongly regarded as a songwriter, to examine those themes which draw folk into her songwriting. Plenty of people have had relationships or not with famous boys – not all of them are ten albums into a career of writing to and for, perhaps, a generation of younger people. So without further ado…

Lipstick

The musical world of the 2020s is as much defined by visual branding as it is radio performance. It's something of an 'it is what it is' proposition – the consumption of music is split across multiple mediums and the advertising even more so. Hearing the song on the radio and seeing the reel on Instagram and seeing the popularity of the dance on TikTok (etc.) all feed into the decision to stick our hands in our pocket and buy the record/ticket/branded towel. Check out Swift's webstore – more branded items than you could shake a Swift-branded stick at.

The nature of that advertising is complex. But suffice it to say for now that Taylor Swift as a *visual brand* is a critical component of her popularity. So each of the album covers features Swift's face, with the exception of *evermore*:

- *Self-titled* – young woman facing the camera, lots of wavy blonde hair, peachy lipsticked lips prominent.
- *Fearless* – had a few different sleeves, but the more popular design was Swift facing left, long blonde hair strewn above her, porcelain, pale skin almost shining, peach lips in the centre.
- *Fearless (Taylor's Version)* – Swift facing right, hair in the air in a less artificial fashion than the original, slight sepia yellowness over the golden background, lips still visible and central to the image.
- *Speak Now* – distance shot, purple sparkling gown that perhaps looks like a pastry, prominent red lips and wingtipped eyeliner (this one has always made me think of horses and I've no idea why).
- *Red* – Swift's face mostly in shadow, save for the prominent red-lipsticked lips.
- *Red (Taylor's Version)* – more homely. Nice brown winter jacket, red felt sailor's hat, prominent silver ring, prominent red lipstick.
- *1989* – polaroid cutting off the top of Swift's head – red-lipsticked lips prominent.

The Swiftian Tropology 19

- *reputation* – black and white image of Swift looking dead casual, lots of pseudo-newspaper print half-obscuring the right side of her face, prominent lipsticked lips.
- *Lover* – dusty pink background, Swift facing forward with 'messy' hair dyed blue at one end, glittery pink heart circling her left eye, prominently red-lipsticked lips.
- *folklore* – Swift looking like a black and white candid, 'oh, are you taking pictures?' pose, is holding her lipsticked lips with her left hand, face mostly in the shade, hair tied up messily, exposing much of her back.
- *evermore* – the outlier, the back of Swift's head done in a ponytail against a blurry woodland background, nice warm-looking jacket again.
- *Midnights* – Swift half-obscuring her face with her left hand, purple glittery eyeshadow and red-lipsticked lips exposed.

Just to emphasise the sense in which red lipstick is an integral part of the Swift brand, there's a graphic associated with the Christmas single 'Christmas Tree Farm (Old Timey Version)' where a screengrab of a very young Swift from a family video has surprisingly crimson lips for a toddler. It's *quite* uncomfortable, to be honest, but that's the nature of advertising.

Lips make plenty of appearances in Swift's lyrics also. It's not perhaps as key to her lyrical identity as it is her visual identity, but it's there. There's a frequent meeting of the visual brand with the lyrical brand, where the prominent, usually red lips are directly referenced – 'I got that red lip classic thing that you like' ('Style', *1989*); 'Cherry lips, crystal skies / I could show you incredible things' ('Blank Space', *1989*); 'Red lips and rosy cheeks' ('Wildest Dream', *1989*); 'Crimson red paint on my lips' ('I Did Something Bad', *reputation*). 'So here's the truth from my red lips' ('End Game', *reputation*); 'Standing there in my party dress / In red lipstick' ('The Moment I Knew', *Red*). It's interesting to note that the majority of these *self-conscious* references to red lips appear after the country period, in Swift's adulthood. That is to say, having the confidence to reference her own appearance and visual brand takes a while to germinate as a notion.

'Cardigan', from *folklore*, has a more intractable reference:

> *Sequin smile, black lipstick*
> *Sensual politics*

This is mildly counterintuitive – 'sequin smile' would presumably mean sequin lipstick; the 'black lipstick' is contraindicative to that, so the 'sequin smile' then describes the *effect* of the smile – glimmering wildly. The conjugation with 'sensual politics' turns it into a comment on the function of makeup, presumably in the context of being female. This might also be a comment on the centrality of lipstick to the Swift visual brand.

Elsewhere lips are invested with a more direct 'sensual politics' – 'Put your lips close to mine / As long as they don't touch' ('Treacherous', *Red*), suggesting a kind of foreboding, forbidden, charged sexuality. 'The taste of your lips is my idea of luxury' ('King of My Heart', *reputation*) which is pretty transparently sexual (or sensual, according to preference).

Synecdoche is a rhetorical device where a part is used to represent a whole – closely related to *meronym*, a term for something that is part of something else. Think how 'wheels' represent a car, or moving within a car. There are a few instances in Swift's writing that use lips as synecdoche: 'Loose lips sink ships all the damn time / Not this time' ('I Know Places', *1989*) – this playing on the US wartime propaganda-catchphrase 'loose lips sink ships', whereby people were discouraged from discussing wartime matters for fear of exposing state secrets to spies. Swift's use here is exaggerated, if not hyperbolic – it's unlikely that 'loose lips' (talking unguardedly) will have a catastrophic effect comparable to marine collateral damage; this is, however, in line with Swift's capacity for being very *extra* – dramatic to the point of excess.

'False God' (*Lover*) has this sharp dual metaphor playing on the meronymous sense of lips: 'Religion's in your lips / Even if it's a false god'. This deliberate ambiguity drives two non-contradictory potential interpretations – a person speaking of religion, even if it's a false god (that is, they don't really believe); the lips are the source of religion-like, devotional ecstasy, even if that sexual devotion is a false god (irreligious).

On the same album we also get: 'Your name on my lips, tongue-tied / Free rent, living in my mind' ('I Forgot That You Existed'). It's a neat extension of the common metaphor ('Your name is on my lips', meaning someone's name being spoken of easily and frequently). This is establishing the 'name on the lips' but then problematising that with 'tongue-tied' – where 'tongue' is a comparable meronym for speech in general. The 'name on the lips' is less a case of willingness or affection, more impediment – hence the reference to the very millennial 'living in my mind rent free' using metaplasm – rearranging the typical order of words for emphasis. The next line establishes that 'one night … I forgot that you existed' – these lines are establishing a kind of pre-revelatory paralysis of tongue-mind-affections typical of the aftermath in relationships.

Earlier in Swift's career, this synecdochal use is more simple: 'Your name, forever the name on my lips' ('Last Kiss', *Speak Now*) – using the repetition of name as a rhythmic device.

Elsewhere, lips are used in a more peculiar but perhaps also more powerful sense – investing lips with a sense of being a home, a centre or a physical anchor.

'The lips I used to call home' ('Maroon', *Midnights*); 'Pushed from the precipice / Clung to the nearest lips' ('long story short', *evermore*); 'Now you hang from my lips / Like the Gardens of Babylon' ('cowboy like me', *evermore*). To speak again of sensual politics, this is a compelling metaphor where the primary indicator of the significant affection which is 'partnership' is typically (in typical Western relationships at least) indicated by kissing. It's not merely that kissing is a sexual or affectionate act but also that it is the one thing we don't do with non-partners (kissing family or younger people is usually described as 'pecking' so as to differentiate it from its relationship/sexual function). It's an exclusive act and one that is therefore invested with a description more significant than those denoting sexual impact, it's *home*. 'Clung to the nearest lips' is a gorgeous exposition of the sense in which, in moments of severe destabilisation, we seek affections haphazardly in order to ground ourselves, to give ourselves a sense of home. 'Now you hang from me / like the Gardens of Babylon', implicating a kind of worldly eternity, stability, solidity to the way that this labial commingling grounds and centres us.

Love/drugs

If we're spending time talking about tropes we should probably talk about the weaker ones. Pop music is very permissive of the underbelly of well-considered, poetic language which is cliché. Swift's clichéometer is arguably a lot lower than average but she's not entirely blameless.

> *Oh, Lord, save me, my drug is my baby*
> *I'll be usin' for the rest of my life*

This is Swift's main contribution to the canon of 'metaphors that are clunky'. The song's dressing is a kind of pseudo-gospel piece that might work as a song in isolation, but feels incongruous in Swift's usage. The temptation to use the metaphor is compelling – it brings with it a lot of bandwidth to explore the social opprobrium on drug use. While the 'forbidden' drug use varies from country to country, and culture to culture within those countries, it's a fairly common socialised principle that some drug use alienates a person from 'regular' society. Swift isn't using the love/drugs metaphor to leverage an argument for decriminalisation, sadly. Rather it supports a later citational line, 'She's gone too far this time.'

It may be seem overwrought to introduce the politicisation of drugs as a theme here but there's a reason for it – the association of love with drugs insinuates that drug users have an extreme affection for their drugs. This is where it's an iffy metaphor, because drug users rarely 'love' the drugs (with the exception of epiphanic weed users) – rather they use the drugs for their effects. The metaphor is, at best, slippery insofar as the heightened drug use associated with 'addiction' only really shares the quality of being *compulsive* with affection; it's a metaphor that lacks sympathy for the general way drug habits develop, and the complexity of addiction as a social phenomenon.

> *gave up on me like I was a bad drug*
> 'Death by a Thousand Cuts', *Lover*

A more appropriate love/drug metaphor here – whereby the antagonist abandons the narrator suddenly and dramatically. This comes closer to fitting with the general state of addiction whereby some heavy users can only stop their habits by 'cold turkey', a severe cessation of all intake. It shares characteristics with some romantic relationships where the person can only detach themselves by a dramatic volte-face in order to pull themselves away from compulsive behaviour.

> *A dwindling, mercurial high*
> *A drug that only worked*
> *The first few hundred times*
> 'illicit affairs', *folklore*

This use of the love/drug metaphor is exquisite – and possibly indicative of a Swift who's experienced drugs more directly, or at least put more consideration into the metaphor. This 'dwindling mercurial' pairing has a gorgeous euphony. Mercury has the chemical associations of drugs, and the physical association of expanding with heat. 'Dwindling' brilliantly describes the habit of drug use whereby tolerance grows with increased usage. 'The first few hundred times' is a great use of a kind of off-hand hyperbole – leading the listener to expect 'the first few times' but to cement the longevity with the 'hundred', atypical usage; it's a kind of iterative habituation, a pattern that only emerged after it happened consistently for a period of time. The way that illicit affairs become damaging and habitual, and also the way in which most drug users don't start off their problematic usage but rather notice it at a point when the drug is firmly part of their life.

Metaphor abuse

Metaphor abuse is a kind of tongue-in-cheek way of identifying the way in which Swift's writing can really drill into a metaphor. Swift is in many ways one of the defining songwriters for millennials, and being dramatically *extra* is surely part of that. Metaphors are a key part of songwriting and by no means does Swift hold dominion over them; she does, however, have a particular talent for holding onto a metaphor, stretching it, or exploding it dramatically.

It's one thing to use a somewhat tired romance/drugs metaphor (see love/drugs in tropology). Frequently, though, Swift will extend a metaphor over a whole stanza, or longer:

> *A string that pulled me*
> ...
> *Something wrapped all of my past mistakes in barbed wire*
> *Chains around my demons*
> *Wool to brave the seasons*
> *One single thread of gold*
> *Tied me to you*
>
> 'invisible string', *folklore*

This stanza operates on the 'string' metaphor in several ways – a string has the property of pulling, wrapping, pinning, heating, coupling; a string made of barbed wire, chain, wool, gold. The string's 'string-ness' is appropriately frayed by its multiple applications. The string retains the quality of connectivity but sometimes that connectivity is hazardous (barbed wire) or restrictive (chains… demons). It's not so much that the metaphor outstays its welcome but it's so rapidly mutated that it's ultimately a surprise that it's returning to a normative string function of tying something together. The string-metaphor itself is a complex tangle – the overriding metaphor occupying string-like qualities itself, if you'll forgive the meta-analysis.

> *I guess it's true that love was all you wanted*
> *'Cause you're giving it away like it's extra change*
> *Hoping it will end up in his pocket*
> *But he leaves you out like a penny in the rain*
> *Oh, 'cause it's not his price to pay*
>
> 'Tied Together with a Smile', *Self-titled*

This is to illustrate that the quality has persisted from Swift's earliest work. Here the money metaphor is stretched – it's surplus, fortune, unwanted, price. That is to say the work done by the metaphor takes on a property that's akin to enjambment, bridging gaps between song sections.

> *I'll show you every version of yourself tonight*
> *I'll get you out on the floor*
> *Shimmering beautiful*
> *And when I break, it's in a million pieces*

The metaphor only occupies one stanza here; another instance again where the properties of the metonymous object are stretched over the whole section. The multiplicity of reflections from a mirrorball, its social function as dancefloor architecture, the oddity of light striking it shimmeringly, the exceptionally messy manner of when it's damaged. Mirrorballs are typically signifiers of dancefloors, passive and incidental to scene-building; Swift's assiduous eye finds them expansively expressive of a plethora of properties.

On 'long story short' (*evermore*) we encounter the opposite – seemingly every line in the first verse/chorus a new metaphor subverting a common idiom:

> *I tried to pick my battles 'til the battle picked me*
> ...
> *The knife cuts both ways*

It's a very witty and dextrous approach; overloading the listener not with extended metaphors but rather a profusion of metaphors. Each adding narrative content to a cliché or commonplace idiom and delivered at a rate such that it's not necessarily apparent what's happening at the speed of listening. 'Knife cuts...' a witty malapropism indicating the mutual destruction of breakups. 'Pick your battles...' using the spiky plosives for sonic balance and marking the nature of power – picking our battles is the privilege of the one with most power and the unexpected battle is always debilitating, especially if (again) it's mutually destructive.

That principle of highly feminised detail expressed in adroit near-incidentals reappears a lot in Swift's writing; here's one of the more subtle incidences:

> *Now I'm begging for footnotes in the story of your life*
> *Drawing hearts in the byline*

'tolerate it', *evermore*

It's another break-up song (Swift has a reputation for that theme for a reason) and it's a kind of humiliating confession – 'begging for footnotes' is one level of humiliation but the 'drawing hearts' is compounding – not only is the narrator subjugated to being incidental but she's also infantilised. 'Drawing hearts' is most typically associated with teenagers, particularly teenage women, relegated to naïve atavism. It's taking the metaphor and really hammering it for an effect that's substantially *extra*.

This metaphor abuse is lightly dusted over a great deal of her material, so it suffices here to just allude to it – isolating all the areas of *extra*-rity might take in the whole of her work (depending on the reader's preference), but one more for luck:

> *you stabbed me in the back while shaking my hand*
> ...
> *And so I took an axe to a mended fence*
>   'This Is Why We Can't Have Nice Things', *reputation*

The brilliance of this – in the sense of being vividly preposterous for dramatic, or comic effect – lies in the excessiveness applied to the metaphor. 'Mended fence' in itself has a lovely rhythm from the half-stop of the repeated nasal 'n' (meNded feNce). The setup of being stabbed in the back is pedestrian, almost understated – but with a view to the visceral image of swinging an axe at a mended fence – the weight and heft of an axe as the particular instrument dictating the force of desire. It's not a moderate image and the fact it's a 'mended' fence intimates that it was already frail. Taking an axe to a mended fence is vividly OTT, a well-timed payoff for an otherwise plain verse.

Bri'ish

Swift's writing is typically situated in the US. Not necessarily specifically this street or that town. But it is possible to read a subtext of that setting – the trucks and semi-rural values of *Self-titled*, for instance. Upping sticks to speak about the UK, then, is an odd trope.

It's also a fairly outlandish trope (with apologies for the pun on 'outland'). Each reference to the UK is significant insofar as they stand out to me, a British listener. They're usually incongruous but no less charming for that – sometimes a sore thumb is what draws your attention to a lyric. Without drawing too heavily on Swift's personal biography, it's easy to see a correspondence between Swift spending more time in the UK and her British-influenced lyrics. And not merely London, given that the Windermere peaks (in the Lake District, a long old way from London) get a mention ('lakes', *folklore*).

The earliest reference I could find was in *reputation*, where we get two songs using specifically British slang. 'Say you fancy me, not fancy stuff'. The use of the word 'fancy' to mean 'attracted to' is surely an adoption of British slang. Difficult to say authoritatively – it's a term that appears every now and then in unusual places, such as in the song 'fancy' by K-pop group TWICE (2019). It's difficult to imagine that it's *not* being used as a consequence of exposure to British usage, though.

Also on *reputation* we get 'My baby's fit like a daydream' – possibly playing on the shock inversion value of using 'fit' to mean 'attractive' rather than the more typical (in American English) 'my baby fits like a daydream' – the sort of language that appears elsewhere in Swift's lyrics (e.g. 'Back when you fit in my poems like a perfect rhyme' – 'Holy Ground', *Red*).

The most clearly British-influenced song in Swift's canon is 'London Boy' (*Lover*) – it has an intro accredited to Idris Elba and James Corden. It cites Camden Market – home to a raft of food stalls, the industrial-culture clothing Mecca Cyberdog, plenty of market tat. There's a very touristy crowd of goths, punks, Asian tourists, bewildered Americans, shifty students and exasperated natives. It also cites Highgate, presumably because Swift went to Highgate Cemetery to show her respects to the grave of Karl Marx.

> So please show me Hackney
> Doesn't have to be Louis V up on Bond Street
> Just wanna be with you

There's a small irony here – Louis V(uitton) is used to here in contrast to Hackney. We are (correctly) led to believe that Bond Street is high end and fancy. But the contrast with Hackney is not as pronounced as it might be – Hackney being an area that is home to some complex sociology. While parts of it retain its impoverished, council-housed rough edges, it's also an area notorious for suffering the effects of gentrification. By contrast to Bond Street, it's not 'simply' posh but it's also an area that regular Londoners, by and large, can't afford to live in.

Other areas mentioned in the song – Brixton, Shoreditch, both relatively touristy areas and, in the case of Shoreditch, notorious home to London's gentrifying hipster crowd. Brixton is not too far away from that but it also boasts some of the finest Bangladeshi cooking I ever experienced in London.

What this is all pointing to really is that there's a sociological picture drawn of London where Swift's experience was largely of rich London. Which is fine; who can imagine her camping out in a Peckham squat and getting a bag in?

The song 'London Boy' is some of Swift's most *specific* writing – while places are referenced, they're usually used as staging rather than the subject itself. We also get a few smatterings of the word 'fancy' (as in find attractive), which is a charming affectation still.

For *Midnights* we get another couple of references that feel like nods to the British:

> *At teatime, everybody agrees*
>
> 'anti-hero', *Midnights*

That use of 'teatime' is peculiarly British – its use here may well be leaning on a US picture of the British as a bunch of stuffy and classist nose-looker-downers. Not an inaccurate image, in fairness. So the 'teatime' potentially does the work of conjuring a judgemental audience for 'the problem' who has just introduced herself.

It's maybe fanciful to say but I'm often inclined to read, from US pop culture, that one of the ramifications of the American Revolution is that the British are viewed as *the perennial* older, condescending figure of US culture. The snooty English man in a top hat who Homer pulls out of his mound of stolen sugar in *Lisa's Rival* (season six, episode two of *The Simpsons*) is archetypal of the way that English or British people appear in popular US culture – the very model of superiority.

From 'Question…?' on *Midnights* again: 'She was on your mind with some dickhead guy' – the insult 'dickhead' is typical as to be asinine in British culture; I'm by no means an arbiter of US culture but it certainly *feels* atypical for someone from the US to use it; and regardless of whether its provenance is British, it's characteristic of the expansion of Swift's lyrical métier in her later work. It's a jolting and atypical word that brings focus to its intent, which in context is the wrath of her antagonist towards some fabricated other woman, suggesting it's a quotational 'dickhead' rather than an assertion of Swift's own – hence, perhaps, the less Swiftian voice.

Midnight

There's an interesting thing that happens to an artist when their canon is of a certain size – it becomes possible to refer the work to itself, to use earlier parts to shed light on later parts. It isn't so much that that artist is regarded as an oracle (although there are plenty in the Swift fandom who are happy to go down that avenue) but that their artistic light is refracted in different ways, at different times.

In Swift's case, with her tenth album *Midnights*, the title and album concept – broadly, songs whose stories take place at midnight – shines a light on her own previous usages of 'midnight'. In focusing a whole album around 'Midnights' it elevates preceding uses; we are inclined to look at midnight as a significant time and, if we're keen to read Swift's personal biography into her work, we take more seriously previous mention of midnights in light of that album's stories all being set around midnight.

There's a sense in which this is complicated, though – midnight is a time pregnant with romantic promise, the intersection of two days. So some uses are mere setting – such as 'the last great american dynasty' (*folklore*): 'Pacing the rocks, staring out at the midnight sea' – the midnight is not so much invested with narrative weight as it is indicative of a kind of madness, the witching hour – the protagonist is already on one precipice between worlds (the shore is where the land meets the sea, known as littoral space) so using midnight is doubling up on that conceptual in between-ness, its liminality.

This concept of a midnight which is *the wrong time* – an oddity of not one or the other – is elsewhere leveraged in a cutesy way: 'It feels like a perfect night / For breakfast at midnight'. That is, the 'madness' or *joie de vivre* of inverting norms encapsulates the carefree life of a 22-year-old.

'New Year's Day', from *reputation*, has a line about wanting someone's midnights. Midnight is invested with the power of intimacy – the time when we're most exposed, asleep or preparing to sleep, those moments of domestic intimacy only shared with romantic partners, family, or very close friends. It's easy enough to brush over what midnight means in Swift's usage until the album *Midnights* has caused us to re-examine it – the sense in which Swift the writer draws midnight closer to the centre of the conceptual universe of her writing.

The line itself is also a lyric of plain domestic fealty – about cleaning up bottles together. It could be parsed as 'we'll do the fun social stuff, but we'll also have the intimate bits'. Midnight is a precarious time and a time of protection, given to our most intimate partners, midnight is a time of love.

> *From the dress I wore at midnight, leave it all behind*
> *And there is happiness*
>
> 'happiness', *evermore*

Here again the midnight is off-hand but invested as a symbol of intimacy and precarity. The significance is in neither dress nor midnight per se but the fact of wearing a dress at midnight. What is being left behind are those moments of intimacy; relinquishing that emotional proximity is the condition of happiness in the break-up being described. Knowing as we do, as a result of *Midnights* the album, that midnight is a precious and intimate hour, the midnight-dress that is sloughed is to let oneself go on condition of happiness. It's worth noting that exposing oneself to another is *uncomfortable*, and that Swift has discretely drawn a midnight which is a metaphor for exposing oneself rather than the more typical witchy/hinterland interpretations.

Midnights are of course the focus of the album *Midnights* (if you'll pardon the tautology) and that's dealt with in the review of that album, but the status of midnight in general is contorted by dint of its exposure to the Swiftological conceptual apparatus.

Self-referential

The idea of self-referentiality has been covered in brief already in this chapter (under the midnight section) but it bears repeating here. Postmodernism is a theory of cultural products which is… well, complex to say the least. Viciously decried in many quarters but held in some regard elsewhere. Without exploring that hornets' nest, it's a theory which describes the (then-) emerging themes in art and cultural products in the mid-twentieth century. One might think of it as a way of describing culture as TV comes to dominate life in Western societies. The properties that are most commonly associated with it are usually scepticisms about modernist notions – grand narrative, how we come to and assert knowledge, the problems of relativism. All of this is relatively incidental to our current project, but one of the key things that art under postmodernism is said to do is refer to itself. It is said to be self-referential.

That is to say, prior to postmodernism (whenever we say it began and whether we say it's ended) art was not typically in the habit of referring to itself. It's easy to see how self-referentiality came to have a central position in arts, especially pop music, TV, film. The age of international celebrities brings with it a state where celebrities see only themselves; it's difficult to imagine a Michael Jackson, Madonna, Elvis, etc. getting away from their own reflection, whether in papers printing pictures or in the interview process of endlessly talking about themselves. And if this seems too much like celebrating vanity, consider the realm of hip-hop, emerging from black communities that are largely belittled in the wider sphere – bigging yourself up seems like a natural response to that social depredation.

Swift's form of self-reference is perhaps more diffuse than writing songs directly about herself. Although there are detractors who'd certainly disagree with that. Rather the Swiftian approach is more tightly knit, to use her own material to refer to itself – let the material do the work of creating a more tightly bound lyrical universe. We've looked at how this happens with the concept of 'midnights' and how it invests midnight with the weight of intimacy, let's have a look where else it happens.

> *I once believed love would be (Burning red)*
>
> 'Daylight', *Lover*

The brackets indicate where the words are sung in a kind of backgrounded chorus of Swift's voice – sort of antiphonal, except the chorus is more emphatic than responsorial, as if amplifying the sentiment. It's the kind of trick that a writer with a smaller body of work would be less inclined towards – the 'burning red' is a direct reference to 'Red' (*Red*): 'When I still see it all in my head / In burning red'. The line is reflective of maturity – *Red* was released in 2012, *Lover* in 2019, a difference of seven years. The effect of the difference is to moderate a juvenile experience of love – red, flamey and hot, intense and embattled – to the more opulent but static gold. It's a work of interpretation that commands self-reference – it's just an odd line otherwise. It's also demurely self-referential – while the Swifties were all over it in seconds, the general, non-invested, commercial radio audience likely didn't pass it a second thought.

Similarly in 'invisible string' (*folklore*) we get:

> *Bad was the blood of the song in the cab*

This line references the song 'Bad Blood' from the album *1989*. While that song was rich in animosity and venom, 'invisible string' is much more pacific, talking about the ties that bind couples. It's a cute reference in that it succinctly intimates the whole semantic world of 'Bad Blood' – and 'invisible string' is doting on a kind of reflexive calm. Accepting one's own lot, and resisting the animosity which characterises 'Bad Blood', is a circuitous reference to support the song's narrative.

> *Standing in your cardigan*
> *Kissin' in my car again*

This line from 'Betty' (*folklore*) – sits on a faintly hilarious pun (cardigan/car again) – it's also providing a thematic link to the song 'cardigan', from earlier on the same record. The album *folklore* isn't quite a concept album but it's certainly got a self-reflexive maturity that is comfortable with talking about itself. And again, the cardigan is now invested with the characteristics and narrative identity that we acquired from listening to it earlier. It's also slyly referencing a trope of Swift's where clothes are symbolic of a relationship – the scarf in 'All Too Well' (*Red*): 'And I left my scarf there at your sister's house / And you've still got it in your drawer, even now', which is a narrative pivot in that song.

Earlier in Swift's corpus there are some less subtle self-identifying pokes. In '22' (*Red*) we get the ad-lib 'who is Taylor Swift anyway?' used to indicate that Swift is not part of the 'cool kids' who don't know who she is. It's a well-timed poke, insofar as it was probably the last time the world at large could feign ignorance about Swift; it's also mildly ironic insofar as the *folklore/evermore/Midnights* triumvirate strongly cements Swift in the world of hip, 'proper' songwriting that cool kids are, in the 2020s, all over.

Earlier still – 'Mean' (*Speak Now*) has an antagonist criticising the narrator – 'Drunk and grumbling on about how I can't sing'. Which is once again irresistible to not point it towards Swift herself. Similarly, 'Hey Stephen' (*Fearless*) has 'But would they write a song for you?'. It's sometimes the mark of a juvenile songwriter to write *about* the process of writing and while I'm not comfortable going that far, it's certainly the case that the earlier self-referentiality is less semantically complete or narratively complex than the 'mature' works.

Internet Culture

'Internet Culture' is perhaps tricky to pin down as a concept – in the early twenty-first century, most culture is, in some way, online. Or at least reflected there. One of the defining factors of millennials is that they've spent most if not all of their lives being online – the Internet is not a *new* thing but just a commonplace.

It's worth outlining what being online was like in the early twenty-first century, though. There wasn't so much of a domination of a limited number of sites (Facebook, Twitter, TikTok, Instagram, etc.) and socialising online was frequently more anonymous, and substantially more haphazard. It wasn't quite the Wild West of the 1990s, but there were also a lot more non-technical people coming online.

What we now know as meme culture wasn't quite *everywhere* in the 2000s. Without delving into the full historical emergence of meme culture, sites like 4chan, Encyclopedia Dramatica, Know Your Meme, I can has cheezeburger (etc.) were critical in providing platforms, often anonymous or pseudonymous, to capture and express Internet Culture. In the 2000s and 2010s, these are the kind of places that English-speaking younger people would piss about, share memes, talk shite. It's difficult to express it any other way. Important sidenote – I'd recommend avoiding any of those sites if you're of a sensitive disposition; 4chan in particular has been rightly described as the 'armpit of the Internet' and strongly leans towards right-wing libertarianism in the 2020s.

Swift is certainly of an age for Internet Culture. But she's also referenced it plenty in her songs.

There's an image that's fairly well-heeled in Internet lore of a grey cat with the text 'this is why we can't have nice things'. For a number of years, it was a mainstay of the 4chan board. It doesn't really express much more than what you've just read. Its typical usage was when 4chan users were expressing something horrendous, it's like a self-effacing statement of 'yeah, we're terrible'. The album *reputation* has a song called 'This Is Why We Can't Have Nice Things'. It's difficult to imagine that Swift dropped the reference to that meme without knowing the image, given her age (the album was released in 2017, when Swift was 27). The song doesn't, so far as I can tell, reference any other memes but its title is certainly a nod to Swift's awareness of Internet Culture.

Similarly, 'I Forgot That You Existed' (*Lover*) features the line 'Got out some popcorn / as soon as my rep started going down down down' references the meme of a gif (a short animated loop) where someone is eating popcorn. This is used in forums to indicate that something dramatic is happening. The inference is that the audience is sitting down to watch a show, as one might dig into the popcorn during a film. Initially the gif used was of Michael Jackson, a still from the 'Thriller' video (1983/4), but later any gif of a person eating popcorn was used to indicate that drama was happening. And again, this is indicative of Swift's age and position within millennial culture. It's an indirect way to illustrate the scenario, an oblique narrative device that is well known to her audience.

It may well be the case that memes are always oblique, insofar as their semantic use is not always clear. Sometimes the response to a meme is just 'it's funny' or 'it's cool'. The notion of 'rick-rolling' has led to a situation where Rick Astley's career has been revived, and a generation who otherwise wouldn't be aware of Astley know who he is.

One of the more ineffable memes is Africa's 'Toto' (1982), a song that was revived by means of a series of covers and parodies. It's a song that wasn't well known to younger generations, but it came to be repeated, covered, and referred to online. The line 'I bless the rains down in Africa' from the song is used as a kind of ultra-dry non-sequitur, reaching for profundity but failing. Consequently, the song is lowkey one that is enjoyed, ironically or not, by a whole generation who weren't born when 'Africa' was originally released.

Swift references this in 'Cornelia Street' (*Lover*) – 'we bless the rains on Cornelia Street'. The song dotes on the nostalgia of Cornelia Street. Somewhat ironically, the song is probably more nostalgic for millennials than the gen X/ baby boomers who were its main audience. Swift is using it to invoke a kind of generational shared experience. It's a sense that people of a certain age will immediately understand the idea of how the song brings back memories of a specific place and time. Referencing the meme in itself is enough to bring its audience into the realm of nostalgia.

The difficulty with memes is that they can be fleeting – this year's hot meme is forgotten the next. Any references have a diminishing audience – while someone my age might recognise (for instance) Boxxy, generations above and below are liable to be lost. Swift is careful not to overload her songs with meme references. She's also careful not to spend *too* much time setting her songs in the realms of Internet Culture, and what Internet Culture tropes are in her songs are sparing or very well known.

> *Say it in the street, that's a knock-out*
> *But you say it in a Tweet, that's a cop-out*

At the time of writing, Elon Musk has failed to destroy Twitter but it's easy to imagine a generation for whom referencing a Tweet is liable to have the same sort of currency as referencing the top friends of MySpace. It's a curious line, insofar as Swift is not of the generation to intuitively prefer fleshworld interactions over online, but also this succinctly evokes the kind of behaviour known as subtweeting – indirectly referencing someone in a message without mentioning them directly – which is seen as cowardly and bitchy.

Love's architecture

We move now into the core, foundational metaphors of Swift's writing. And appropriately enough, these tropes are the ones that are most revealing of the psychology of Swift. I don't want to intimate that there's any great revelation about her foundational being here but rather that we're proximal to Swift's methodology – her way of thinking about and orienting her inner-world and the tropes and metaphors which most keenly define her writing style.

This section is called love's architecture, partly for that overwrought poetic vibe, but also because the trope at hand is related to the foundational architecture of our identities. One of Swift's more common devices is to use the concrete buildings or entities which constitute home, as in where we live – our nation, the buildings we live in, the cities we occupy – as a metaphor for our bodies. *Where* we are, in geography and architecture, is a core part of *who* we are.

Possibly the most transparent example of this is 'exile', from *folklore*:

> *You're not my homeland anymore*

This, incidentally, is counterposed with another of Swift's most popular devices, that of filmic visions ('I think I've seen this film before'), which we'll come to in the cinematic section of tropology.

Here the core concepts are homeland/defending [that homeland]/hometown/feelings of exile. These are powerful concepts, ones that cut to the core of who we are; despite latter-day reticence by appalling political machinations, the displacement of people by war and famine is pretty universally empathised with. A more diffuse understanding of alienation from our core identity comes with the notions of excommunication or disenfranchisement – to expressly be irrevocably alienated from something that operates as 'home' (whether religion or nation).

These are powerful metaphors and they are very dramatic, very *extra* in a Swiftian sense. 'You're not my homeland' is a hyperbolic device; it's not merely the mutable fealty of a romantic coupling but is elevated to that of national identity. There's a sense of humiliation in the 'what am I defending now' – leaving aside any anti-war sentiments we may have around the fatuousness of defending nation states – the principle is that the narrator is somewhat preposterously defending a state to which he no longer belongs. The metaphor ultimately is that the relationship had the solid, immutable properties of a homeland, hometown, with all the compulsive defences we might feel for that; in the relationship's ending the process is comparable to exile, no less immutable and exorbitantly tragic. And that 'exorbitantly' is key to Swift's visceral metaphors – the depth of feeling is escalated beyond the interpersonal bounds of 'sadness' and transubstantiates into a sympathy with displaced peoples. It's profoundly effective; for the Swift detractor it's doubtless ridiculous but that interpretation potentially misses that the lyricality dotes on exceeding the typical metonymy of 'mere' devastation.

> *Our songs, our films, united we stand*
> *Our country, guess it was a lawless land*
> 'Death by a Thousand Cuts', *Lover*

There's a cute pre-emption here – the 'united we stand' belongs more to the 'our country...' strophe but it's apropos for the metaphor at hand – our songs/films are critical parts of our identity. Especially when we're younger, the art we consume is worn as a badge of identity, a demarcation of our 'self' within society. We stand united within our cultural associations; they don't have the heft or political bearing of a national identity (or a religious one, for that matter) but they still strongly represent and reflect who we are, in our core being. The 'united we stand' is a cohesive aspect of our identity-within-culture – intimating that the stronger, more trenchant part of the relationship orbits those cultural associations; the country-as-relationship metaphor is more 'lawless', which works towards evoking mess, disorder (presumably Swift is disinclined towards anarchist visions of the problems with carceral justice).

Key to Swift's use of these powerful homeland/country metaphors is their capacity for containing a lot of discrete information. These lines invoke the relationship's schema, its broad outline of correspondences and disjuncts, succinctly expressing the fault lines and disagreements while explicitly saying little. It's not merely that these are powerful metaphors, but that they can manifest a lot of self-identity information without express verbosity; whether it's uniquely Swiftian as a lyrical method, it's certainly core to Swift's identity as a writer.

> *My barren land*
> *I am ash from your fire*
>
> 'hoax', *folklore*

Here again the break-up is embodied in geographical terms. The word 'barren' is not typically applied to people; when it is, it's most typically a euphemism for being infertile, as in 'barren womb'. I don't want to intimate anything here about Swift's reproductive capacity – not least because that would feel phenomenally invasive on my part – but there's a particular power and association for a woman using the term. The 'barren womb' in itself is easily viewed as a failing on the woman's part. This isn't so much direct interpretation of the lyrics as it is associations with the terms but it's difficult to avoid it – the two most common uses of the word 'barren' are describing areas lacking in vegetation and infertile women.

It's much simpler to interpret this in the sense of barren meaning sterile, lacking in vegetation. Land which is useless. Given the following line saying 'ash from your fire' it's tempting to pick up on the sense in which 'barren' land is desiccated, dry – in the extremes, deserts are profoundly barren. But the 'ash' of a fire is the product of *use*.

There's a neat aside here that the pejorative British English term 'slag' describes (in a boring, sexist, dated) the way a woman is 'overly' sexually active. The slag is also a hard waste product of vitrifying – that is, it burns hot and is useless when cold. It's over-reading Swift's words to infer this but it's an interesting structural parallel that Swift here is implying her cold remains after being used are dry and undesirable.

Land here is again nidification, the nesting and establishment of our core selves and its destitution or radical destabilisation in breakups; this time the land is rendered useless rather than re-territorialised. That is to say, the metaphor is consistent but its contours are manipulated by Swift.

Establishing this city/land/territory-as-bodily-metaphor gives us the chance to view earlier lyrics in a slightly different light. 'Dear John' (*Speak Now*) features the line 'I'm shining like fireworks over your sad empty town' – and while the context there points more strongly to the notion that this town is the one the protagonist has moved away from, if there is a more strongly drawn town-self correspondence then that 'sad empty town' is more directly redolent of the passed over antagonist. Similarly, the lines 'You put up walls and paint them all a shade of gray' from 'Cold as You' (*Self-titled*) takes on a quality where the 'walls' are more directly reified as metaphors for interior architecture.

'Afterglow' (*Lover*) has this peculiar line: 'I lived like an island, punished you with silence'. Reading here 'lived like an island' as continuous with the city/land/territory-as-bodily-metaphor trope it becomes markedly less peculiar. It's not a complex metaphor – living like an island is pretty transparently intimating disconnection. But it's also uncanny – it's unusual to compare oneself to a large geographical body, to say 'I *lived* like an island'. How does an island live per se? Because the more typical thing to say would be 'I *was* like an island' – implying the geographical-personal disconnection. Having drawn this into a trope of Swift's, it's at least contiguous, if not coherent with that trope – living like an island is to re-construct the self-as-territory metaphor and this time to frame it as a body disconnected by something external (water is presumably the matter of that self-isolation).

We see in 'Daylight' (*Lover*) a kind of inverse embodiment, where the territory is given human characteristics: 'My love was as cruel as the cities I lived in'. Cities aren't cruel, or it is at least atypical to describe them as such; it's odd to make that *metaphor* of cruelty to be the *subject* of comparison. And of course cities are cruel, insofar as there are innumerable effects which make city living unbearable – top of the list being something like rampant landlordism driving up rents and therefore driving down quality of life. But they are not directly cruel, they have no direct agency for self-awareness. To say something is 'cruel like the city' is to impute secondary qualities to the city. It's by no means the most outrageous thing ever said in verse but it's perhaps a more significant as a result of being part of Swift's city-self characterisation.

> *You're a flashback in a film reel on the one screen in my town*
> 'this is me trying', *folklore*

This is once again a relatively simple metaphor which is bolstered by the town-self characterisation – the '…film reel on the one screen in my town' evokes a sense of the pedestrian, parochial forgettability; but again the town being a person means that it's less saying 'you are insignificant like…' so much as 'your part in my life is insignificant'. It's a subtle difference, and one that's achieved by positing a trope within Swift's writing, but it's also one that makes the comparison more acidic and withering.

There are plenty of other instances where places – especially cities – are referred to in Swift's work but I'm keen for this not to look like stretching – my point is that the town (or 'geographical setting' most generally) is rendered as coextensive with the self in the Swiftian schema; this isn't so much an act of psychoanalysis as it is a tropological assertion. Metaphors for Swift can be highly *extra*, can be supremely embodied and thoroughly holistic (if that's not too much of a tautology). It's important to read her metonymy in the sense of whole-ness, to recognise that from at least one perspective the 'self' is *always* referred to in Swift's music, by contrast to the notion that her songs are sketches of 'real' narrative events.

Cinematic

Filmic references are probably the second-most used device in Swift's lyrics, after the monsters we'll deal with presently. It's worth immediately separating what I'm referring to here, though – there are a few instances in Swift's writing where she refers to cinema indirectly:

> *Got out some popcorn*
> *as soon as my rep started going down*
> 'I Forgot That You Existed', *Lover*

> *Combat, I'm ready for combat*
> *I say I don't want that, but what if I do?*
> *'Cause cruelty wins in the movies*
> 'The Archer', *Lover*

These sorts of references aren't the ones that form the core trope for Swift – in these examples the cinema is a (potential, alluded to) setting or a narrative simile. Rather the trope that is most prevalent in Swift's work is the private film reels, the narrativisation that Swift performs whereby events in her life are imagined as moving images in her head (or rather, the head of her narrators).

'We were both young when I first saw you / I close my eyes and the flashback starts: / I'm standing there / On a balcony in summer air'. This opening stanza from 'Love Story' (*Fearless*) is possibly the most pellucid exposition – the narrator establishes that the scene ('standing there...') takes place in their head, is a mental scene. As a personal aside, this is perhaps more astonishing to some people than others – I am aphantasic, meaning that I don't experience mental images; the idea of being able to see something in my imagination is beyond my ken.

This stanza isn't perhaps the most striking, but it is exemplary of the device that Swift leans on time and again. Every album has an example of these internal films. Swift's *Self-titled* has 'And when I got home, 'fore I said, "Amen" / Asking God if he could play it again' ('Our Song'), in which the 'play it again' intimates the filmic quality of the memories to recapitulate on. 'Midnight Rain' (*Midnights*): 'My boy was a montage'. Principally the notion is that Swift's characters frequently rely upon strongly eidetic recall.

The appeal of describing memories in terms of moving pictures is powerful and very twentieth/twenty-first century; while poetic devices have long used visual imagery, the specifically 'filmic' nature of those memories is one that's intensely familiar to latter-day listeners, young listeners. It's sympathetic to how younger people experience things – in pop culture, many more people are familiar with film-as-memory than they are other devices. But there's another acutely sharp resonance – the 'screen' which is the cinema is an opulent, prestigious form of viewing the moving image; the screen is also the mediating device for a lot of the sociality of Swift's generation of listeners. Everyone's watching the world through their mobile devices or computer screens – so while the cinema is the prestigious form the individual still is able to strongly sympathise. Put another way, it's important that the 'screens' upon which those memories are projected are *cinematic* rather than phone screens – it affords a width and gravitas to the memories, which by the time they reach the listener have been mediated through several different screens (an additional screen being the speaker, should we want to go that far).

It's important also that these aren't purely visual associations, but rather that they are a dissolving of a boundary between visual and emotional – that is, the visual *is* the emotional; the lines are not (always) 'you are *like* a flashback' but rather 'You're a flashback in a film reel on the one screen in my town' ('this is me trying', *folklore*). The antagonist here isn't a character in a play but rather is a visual *function*, inseparable from the emotions connoted. This is coming back to the idea, once again, that Swift's writing is often *extra*, that she exceeds typical similes or figuration for dramatic effect. Reifying the emotional by exceeding its description.

The phrase I used there – eidetic memory exceeds the figurative – is perhaps obscure. So let's explore it some more, with a view to re-phrasing. When a lyric uses visual cues, it's typically as a setting, as a way of establishing a visual image. The listener sympathises, is able to imagine (this word shares an etymological root with 'image') what's happening. 'Eidetic memory' describes an acute capacity to visualise internally. 'Figurative' is describing the kind of abstraction, the poetic way of speaking. And what happens with abstraction is that there's a conceptual distance between the original object and the abstraction. The metaphor, the figure of speech, address something *indirectly*. And that indirect address can be *intensive* – improving or emphasising some aspect of it. But there is still an assumed distance in that indirect address, a wider focus. The 'shortfall' of rhetorical devices in general is that they impute a distinction between 'the thing in itself' and 'how that thing is described'. Swift's 'excess' of the figurative is in bringing the abstraction closer to the object itself – defying the 'it was like this' and asserting 'this is what it was'. In another (mildly haughty) expression, we could say that Swift's metonymy is reifying, not abstractive. Or we could cut our losses and say simply that Swift makes a lot of effort to intensify her metaphors such that they *feel* less like an intellectual distance between the audience and the thing that's being described.

One of the key appeals of Swift is that she is quite intense, lyrically. I've frequently referred to it as *extra*. It might be simple – in the sense that it's pop music, not high modernist poetry – but the exceptionally visual schema, the mode of description, all point towards an intensity that is particular to Swift's style, as well as descriptive of the way in which millennials tend to think about the world.

And these filmic descriptions are everywhere in Swift's lyrics – 'I think I've seen this film before' ('exile', *folklore*); 'You know I adore you, I'm crazier for you / Than I was at 16, lost in a film scene' ('Miss Americana & the Heartbreak Prince', *Lover*); 'And you *flashback* to …' ('Forever and Always', *Fearless*) – and so on.

It's worth mentioning, finally, that Swift's exceptionally visual mnemonics are more substantial than merely being a poetic device – latter-day Swift videos are typically self-directed so it suffices to say that her visual-centrism in the lyrics is due to a strong affection for, and deftness with, visual culture.

The monsters turned out to be just truths

The actual theme of this trope is difficult to pin down in a single concept. Broadly speaking, the notion is that Swift makes reference to magic, or the spirit realm, very frequently.

It's not so much that the idea is one of fantasy – there are minimal references in her lyrics to, say, fairies or goblins. But it is quite a particular set of 'magical' ideas – monsters, demons, ghosts, haunting. That is, ideas from 'that realm' which are strongly coupled with twentieth/twenty-first-century anxieties. The sort of stuff that Freud would be talking about if he was alive today and not creepy and sexist.

Haunting

The most common of these terms to appear is 'haunting'. And it's a particular usage – it's not in the sense of an apparition of a person who's died; rather it's in the sense of the marking of an absence. Haunting for Swift is used to intimate that there is a *presence* retained of something that is no longer here. In a fairly poetic sense, that's what a ghost is – some indicator, some representation of something that is no longer here.

There's a sense also that haunting is the term Swift often uses to indicate the *spite* of bad partners:

> *Wondered how many girls he had loved and left haunted*
> 'Ready For It', reputation

In this instance the 'haunted' is something that the antagonist actively *does* to his partners – he leaves them haunted. That is, he comes into their life, vacates and leaves his traces behind. This is a metaphor which quite strongly resonates with sexuality, the idea that when we share our bodies with another person we take a part of them. That haunting is something Swift's antagonist here has agency over. Likewise in 'my tears ricochet' (*folklore*), we get 'You know I didn't want to have to haunt you' – whereby haunting is wielded as some sort of retributive force.

> *Can't breathe whenever you're gone*
> *I can't go back, I'm haunted*
> 'Haunted', Speak Now

This haunting is gesturing towards a sense of paralysis – in leaving, the narrator cannot move forward or backwards (figuratively); the antagonist's absence is felt in paralysing effect. This haunting necessarily speaks of paradoxical relations, which is at the core of what 'haunting' articulates – it's an absent-presence, something which is felt and not seen; paradoxical also because of inhabiting two contrary states – in traditional terms, the ghost is both here and not here. In Swift's lyrical cosmology, haunting is the paralysis of absent-presence or present-absence, impossible states.

> *Get me with those green eyes, baby, as the lights go down*
> *Give me something that'll haunt me when you're not around*
> *'Cause I see sparks fly whenever you smile*
> 'Sparks Fly', Speak Now

This is to illustrate that the paradoxical state of haunting isn't purely negative; here the haunting is the felt presence of a person in their absence – and in fact Swift's haunting here is economical. It's *given* to a person, as a gift; the logical opposite to what I spoke of earlier as *spite*. In our coupling, in our relationships with others, we inextricably leave our presence with and on that person. This is the stuff of philosophers, really – and I'm not declaring Swift as this century's foremost Derridean but there's a definitely sense that one of her gifts as a writer, and the crux of this trope, is in succinctly articulating these paradoxical states of haunted-ness.

> *I knew you'd haunt all of my what-ifs*
>
> 'cardigan', *folklore*

This is a less embodied sense of haunting, the sense that to be haunted is to be visited by lost possibilities, dead ends. A rumination on 'to linger', or the way in which much of our own personal understanding of relationships *in themselves* is coloured by those relationships that didn't happen – and this idea could just as easily apply to non-romantic relationships – friendships that never quite got off the ground. There's a Swiftian take that would likely say that we are haunted not just by people who were part of our lives, but also those who were not. Here, at least, haunting is about the potential to influence and impact upon another person's life.

> *Tryna find a part of me that you didn't touch*
> ...
> *Now I'm searching for signs in a haunted club*
>
> 'Death by a Thousand Cuts', *Lover*

Given that we've recognised Swift's application of haunted as something we *do* to people around us, this seemingly innocuous line – '…signs in a haunted club' starts reading in a different way. The body is haunted ('tryna find a part of me that you didn't touch'). The simple reading of the final line in this extract seems perhaps off-hand or only tangentially related; but the temptation now is to read the 'haunted club' as the narrator's body. Not least because we might want also to apply the earlier trope of buildings being embodiments of people. We might want to speculate on how a club-person could be haunted by another person – what marks they leave. A severe reading might suggest a transgression of bodily autonomy; a lighter reading might suggest trying to rediscover those signs of intimacy long after the 'haunter' has disappeared.

> *And I've been meaning to tell you*
> *I think your house is haunted*
> *Your dad is always mad and that must be why*
>
> 'seven', *folklore*

This is articulated in a register of childish innocence – it seems like a stretch for the house to be a body in this instance; but the haunting works in a dual way. If the child's voice is abided to, the dad is mad because of simple ghosts; with the adult understanding, the house is still haunted. The dad is still marked by undeclared absences, his madness has an imprecise cause. As well as being a neat concept for songs, haunting is also a kind of conceptual Swiss army knife of undisclosed torment. A Swift army knife, if you will (sorry).

Ghosts (and grace)

Ghosts haunt people but not all haunting is done by ghosts. If haunting is an absent-presence then to be a ghost is to be a present-absence; no less uncanny but the ghost is the *occupied haunting*.

> *I wake in the night, I pace like a ghost*
> *The room is on fire, invisible smoke*
>
> 'The Archer', *Lover*

It's also noticeable that the theme of the bridge is 'they see right through me', alluding to the translucent state of an apparition. The narrator's ghost-ness here is her transparency, the self-pitying; but it's also the futility of walking up and down. It's also the tell-tale signs of fire which is also a ghost, and a person who can't keep hold of something. The making-incorporeal of things that were corporeal.

> *Stand there like a ghost*
> *Shaking from the rain*
>
> 'How You Get the Girl', *1989*

The ghost here is the presence on the doorstep – the old flame who reappears out of nowhere. The vision that reappears from the past. Things that *should* be absent and are not.

> *You say sorry just for show*
> *If you live like that, you live with ghosts*
>
> 'Bad Blood', *1989*

There's a kind of popular dialogue, perhaps a post-Freudian cultural commonplace, where we talk of the psychological realm in spiritual terms. Catholics replacing the confession box with the therapist's couch (other traditions vary in the centrality of confession, you see...). Catholicism also continues the practice of exorcism (albeit in a limited sense). Why do we confess? In a sense it's an exorcism; it's to divest our sins. It's God's problem now. And that's mirrored in the sense of 'if you don't get rid of your sorrow, you live with ghosts'.

It's worth for a second taking a quick diversion in Swift's personal religion. It's never, to my knowledge, been declared, but her brother goes to a Catholic university, so... I don't want to steer into the theological evidence of Swift's Catholicism *but* it's definitely worth noting that her relationship to the spirit world bears the very real *presence* of ghosts in a way that's uncommon to other denominations. And Catholicism is the biggest denomination in the US. And frankly, it's been far too long since we've had anyone to be proud of on team Catholic. So, with my MA in Theology, I'm claiming her for Catholicism. Hands off, apostates.

It's worth also talking about the centrality of grace to Swift; this is peculiarly Catholic (insofar as Protestant traditions tend to believe in salvation by faith alone, *sola fide*). There's the song 'State of Grace' on *Red*; there's 'I didn't have it in myself to go with grace' ('my tears ricochet', *folklore*). There's 'I would fall from grace' ('Don't Blame Me', *reputation*). There's 'All I know is a new found grace' ('Everything Has Changed', *Red*). The concept of grace is poetic and common enough that these aren't dead set professions of Catholicism; these aren't Swift's nailed theses, but they are conspicuously and particularly *Catholic* in a way that most pop writers are not. To say nothing of the aforementioned sense of *extra*-ness in common with sacraments that are literally about drinking blood.

Adding to the list of peculiarly Catholic affectations in Swift's lyrics – 'Make confessions and we're begging for forgiveness' ('False God', *Lover*). 'Confession' in and of itself isn't specifically a Catholic matter but it's worth noting that Protestant traditions (which loosely describes the other popular denominations in the US) don't have confession as a part of religious practice.

There's an excessive version of this where we replace 'ghosts' with 'the Holy Spirit'; let's not go there, but it is important to note that Swift's rendering of 'ghosts' is very much as presences, things which manifest and have effects but also things which are alienated from the fleshworld. Ghosts and hauntings are *everywhere* in Swift's music.

> *You know I didn't want to have to haunt you*
> *But what a ghostly scene*
>
> 'my tears ricochet', *folklore*

The line isn't 'ghastly' or 'gross', it's *ghostly*. Whatever 'ghostly scene' means, the signs here are that ghosts are tightly coupled with Swift's writerly imagination, if not psychic being. And ghostly scene presumably means a scene which is littered with unresolved emotions, present-absences.

> Your kiss, my cheek, I watched you leave
> Your smile, my ghost, I fell to my knees
> When you're young, you just run
> But you come back to what you need
>
> 'This Love', *1989*

It's maybe worth dialling back a second and observing that 'ghosting' is quite a common term in the last decade or so – meaning to completely disappear from a person's life without communication. The song 'This Love' operates on a series of oppositions, contradictions: 'This love is good, this love is bad'. The stanza follows that pattern – it's not entirely clear why 'my ghost' (if it means 'to run') precedes 'I fell to my knees'; falling to one's knees is an act of subjugation or an act of falling over. Perhaps consistent with running, either way an act of humiliation. But if we think of ghosts as present-absences, 'my ghost' is someone staying yet leaving, a ghost which is non-commitment. It's certainly vague enough that it fills with any number of readings we might want to impute. A ghost of the writer's intention, even – not a gap or ambiguity but a narrative ghost.

It's worth noting briefly that the magic in Swift's songs becomes more sophisticated and introspected as her career progresses – earlier on, in 'Hey Stephen' (*Fearless*) we get 'Come feel this magic I've been feeling since I met you'. It's a relatively unspecific but explosive sense of shared, incoherent *feelings*. By the time of *Red*, the magic has a typology, names and archetypes: 'And you've got your demons, and darling, they all look like me' ('Sad, Beautiful, Tragic', *Red*). But further yet, those 'demons' are self-directed – not a name for an antagonist's failings but full acting agents of the protagonist's interior narrative: the 'Chains around my demons' of 'invisible string' (*folklore*), those archetypes paralysed by the 'invisible string' of affections.

Swift's relationship with feminism, which is spattered across this book, is either complex or circumspect. There are a few gestures in the magic realm that are common to the millennial trope of Tumblr witches – young feminists who associate the persecution of witches with contemporary feminist issues; the name 'Tumblr witches' is derogatory but really there's only good things that come from arming young women with spells and a strong female-led empowerment narrative. 'I Did Something Bad' (*reputation*) has: 'They're burning all the witches even if you aren't one'. It's in service of Swift's self-affirmation ('They say I did something bad / Then why's it feel so good?') in the face of criticism; it's a narrative that resonates well with teenage women and the sense in which, after all this history, women still get dealt a shitty hand in life (and women of colour, outside of the global north, a shittier hand still – a story for another time).

> *I wish to know*
> *The fatal flaw that makes you long to be*
> *Magnificently cursed*

This is a really piquant, extravagant use of curses. It's not merely that they're a warning or to the detriment of a person, it's that her antagonist *actively seeks* them. It's a relatively plain strophe and one that push-pulls with the tension of short lines (first/third) and a long line (second). All of the descriptive work goes into emphasising *magnificently* cursed – magnificent relating to magnification, forestalling the tendency to view the curses as detrimental. Which pivots the lines back to the narrator's affection, love despite great flaws; flaws which are impervious even to curses.

Monster

And finally for the tropology, onto Swift's characterisation of monsters. Monsters is a broad definition for a terrifying creature, something extra-large. It's a great opportunity to wheel out this quote from twentieth-century French philosopher, Jacques Derrida: 'Monsters cannot be announced. One cannot say: "here are our monsters", without immediately turning the monsters into pets.'[3]

Derrida is notoriously a pretty dense writer, so let's not lean on him too heavily here; we can read this quote as saying that the act of calling something 'a monster' undermines that 'monstrosity' – domesticates it, in his sense. Derrida's writing comes from a world that's super aware of psychological theory, so there's a context where that process of naming the monster is part of the unburdening oneself. Derrida's use is broader than that, but let's focus on that idea – that the naming of the monster, the declaration that something is 'monstrous', has a consequence of domesticating, mollifying the effect of that monster.

---

3. Jacques Derrida, 'Some Statements and Truisms about Neologisms, Newisms, Postisms, Parasitisms, and other small Seismisms', *The States of Theory*, ed. David Carroll (New York: Columbia University Press, 1989), pp. 63–94.

> *Remember when we couldn't take the heat?*
> *I walked out, I said, 'I'm setting you free'*
> *But the monsters turned out to be just trees*
> *When the sun came up, you were looking at me*

The monsters turned out to be just trees; having applied sufficient perspective, the monster ceases to be horror. The solution to the monster, the tension (heat) of the freighted relationship is distance. Just as a child is haunted by looming figures, monsters, on the horizon.

The monsters trope is a profoundly psychological subtext for Swift – monster appears as the mendacious presence of denial.

> *…running wild 'til you fell asleep*
> *Before the monsters caught up to you?*

'Innocent', from *Speak Now*, has an instance of nostalgic memory – remembering fondly the time 'before the monsters caught up'. The innocence of childhood is a state of monsters in abeyance. The antagonist of the song is 32, and the state of adulthood is one of present monsters. The payoff of the chorus is that the dread, the monsters of adulthood, are of no consequence – he's still innocent.

'Anti-Hero', from *Midnights*, features the line 'I'm a monster on the hill'. Here monster is more grotesque, out of character – the lumbering, lurching oaf of the narrator is opposed to the childlike 'sexy baby *voice*'. Unlike previous monsters, this one is impenetrable – not so much the presence of denial as the presence of the disgusting or out of sorts. It's redolent of fairy tales but it's unspecific – the kind of figure that could easily reference the epic of Gilgamesh as Grimms' fairy tales. Looping back to the notions of monsters and domestication, this monster is the narrator's self-doubt, her self-repulsion; resistant to the naming. It's an odd character, insofar as it's much more coarse, dense than Swift's usual hauntings, ghosts, monsters. It's perhaps the case that this is a monster which is also a ghost – it's certainly one of Swift's more depressive tunes.

Part 4

Album Guides

Taylor Swift

Self-titled is a surprisingly mature work, considering Swift's age at the time of writing – much of it written when she was just 14 – but it's a work of largely standard pop country; it's got the birthmarks of an astonishing songwriter, but is encumbered by genre. The songs are good, but not outstanding, and very much in keeping with pop country of the time. Three chords and the truth, but more a truth of well-worn sentiments rather than the particular, singular voice of the 'mature' Swift in its successor *Fearless* – itself written more than a half a decade away from her being a legal drinker in the US.

What we do see, though, is a songwriter who knows how to get herself noticed – such as where she references country royalty: 'When you think Tim McGraw / I hope you think of me' ('Tim McGraw'). However, this isn't a cheap record, and even if it's not a musical area she stayed in it, it remains a charming instance of a great songwriter wrestling with a genre's norms while finding her own voice.

'Tim McGraw'

The opening track of the opening album sets the store for Swift's writing in general. Observe the opening line:

> He said the way my blue eyes shined
> Put those Georgia stars to shame that night
> I said, That's a lie

Swift was a precocious freshman (14/15) when she wrote this, clearly already well-heeled in songwriting form. Already we have an A/B/C form, consistent metre, using phonemes for thematic material (said/shine/shame/said), a kind of volta or lyrical false turn with 'I said that's a lie'. It's the sort of suspense-building that's common to country music: sentimentality – some would say cliché – with a sprinkle of contradiction.

The song draws the outline of a former relationship, and how country music legend Tim McGraw songs will remind the ex-boyfriend of her. It's a fairly pointed debut single – country fans know Tim McGraw well so leveraging his name to push Swift's is doubtless a sound promo technique. It sits with a bunch of country themes – the boy has a truck, Swift talks about her old faded blue jeans. There isn't much that directly situates it as about *teenage* romance – key to a broad appeal, heartbreak is ageless – but there is a hint of the way teenagers are so motivated, paralysed by shame – 'September saw a month of tears / And thankin' God that you weren't here / To see me like that'.

Possibly most interesting, in terms of the songwriter Swift became, is that there's plenty of ambiguity here – the only shot we have of the relationship's dialogue is the '…that's a lie', we never learn when the relationship ends: 'And I was right there beside him all summer long / And then the time we woke up to find that summer gone'. 'Summer' here is supposed to be a kind of synecdoche, that the relationship ended with it. Show, don't tell. Summer couldn't hold the relationship but the songs of Tim McGraw are the reminders.

It might be very business-as-usual for country songwriting; what is probably most precocious is the modesty of teenage Swift-as-spurned lover – the passive, modest 'I hope you think of me' or 'it's hard not to find it all / a little bittersweet'. In terms of her songwriting voice, we're yet to see the 'don't fuck with me' side emerging – which is also to say this has all the hallmarks of Swift's breaking into music, rather than 'Swift's personality' being central to her songwriter identity.

'Picture to Burn'
By this point in music history, the distinctions between country music and bluegrass are not well known; so much cross-pollination has happened between the 'country' and 'Western' that it's difficult to pin down exactly. Nevertheless, bluegrass tends towards being banjo-led and with lively 8th-note rhythms. 'Picture to Burn' isn't perhaps the purest exposition of bluegrass but it's firmly within the musical modes that say 'country music' more than the 'pop' of 'country-pop'.

Country music is expansive but it can be typified with broad strokes. There's particular instruments, particular styles that put us in its realms. Perhaps most importantly, it's a lyrical style with a range of subjects (see 'This is country music' for more on country in general). Key themes with country music are small towns (concomitantly, an opposition to urbanity), traditional living, agricultural norms (shotguns, trucks, intense labour), Christian values (no shame in talking about God here), small, well-connected communities with strong family values.

Unfortunately, those themes strongly intersect with small-c conservativism, so 'Picture to Burn' includes one of Swift's more regrettable lines:

I'll tell [my friends] that you're gay!

Later versions of this song quite rightly change it to 'you won't mind if I say' – which has a lot less bite as a lyric but has the bonus of not being palpably homophobic. This isn't something that should be held over Swift in perpetuity – and there's a sense that later on she's not so much liberal-tolerant of gay folk as actively pro-gay (see: 'You Need to Calm Down', with its explicit valorisation of gay folk).

Also, even if this lyric were extant in later versions of the song, Swift was still a teenager when she wrote it; people can and do change as they get older.

But the lyric *is* worth isolating in terms of what it connotes – where pop music is typically anodyne in content, country music *does* appeal to a more conservative base. The Brad Paisley notion that country music is more expansive in its subjects brings with it the notion of regrettable expositions – see also Paisley's 'accidental racist', a well-meaning but clunky attempt to exonerate himself from wearing a confederate flag that's often associated with revisionist, white supremacist conservativism in Southern US.

Further into the notion of a family-focused country music is a kind of oppositionalism: the line is about winning points in a social battle. It's very teenage to break up and draw the lines heavy and thick between the two adversaries; zooming out a bit, small-c conservativism has a tendency towards nationalism, which is them-and-us mentality in another form.

It's not so much that Swift's music is conservative, no more at this point than any other, but rather that in embodying a genre it lists towards the political norms of that genre.

Given that this song is a form of lyrical retribution, it's worth noting the nature of that retribution – one of the put-downs is the notion that the narrator will 'go out with all your best friends'. Again, because of the norms of country music, that retribution takes the form of social humiliation. The family-first mentality, and the small-town, tightknit social community thrives on the strength of social bonds; hence the humiliation here isn't the antagonist's failings as a partner (their romantic impotence, broadly) but rather that the narrator intends to infect his social being. Going for the jugular here means to stymie their ability to exist smoothly in the social fabric.

A common country technique where sung lyrics are swapped out for spoken lyrics – the notion being that these lines are more effective because they're more human, 'real' (although that 'real' is heavily embroiled in the performance of the song). The spoken verse typically carries the most weight in country music – think Dolly Parton's annunciatory verse in 'I Will Always Love You' (and if you don't know Parton's original then you should probably put this book down while you look it up). It's a technique Swift uses sparingly on this tune to accentuate lyrical sections.

The *way* the verse is spoken is important as well – while later Swift tends towards a more neutral accent, at this point the spoken verse clearly illustrates a 'regular' country US accent – marked by the rhoticity of the 'r' in speech patterns (whether the 'r' sound is sounded or not).

> *There's no time for tears*
> *I'm just sitting here planning my revenge*

One of the themes that persists through Swift's lyrics is the notion of self-assertion; certainly a large part of her appeal to a lot of young (and not so young) women is the sense that the narrator (assumed to be Swift herself) is affirming her own identity and not taking it lying down, etc. Here the affirmation is that the protagonist isn't going to cry because they're planning revenge. It's importantly couched in the combative, familial terms (per country norms) but it is also a resistance to a narrative of a shrinking wallflower.

> *Burn, burn, burn, baby, burn*

While Swift's music is rarely referential to any great degree, her first album is an exception. Building popularity is tricky and sometimes the 'hook' for new listeners is to use concepts that are already familiar. For the opener we had Tim McGraw, and for here we have a line so familiar that it's difficult to remember where we heard it first – I *think* it's The Trammps' 'Disco Inferno' but it's such an evergreen sentiment it's difficult to say authoritatively.

'Teardrops on My Guitar'

> *Drew looks at me*
> *I fake a smile so he won't see*
> *That I want and I'm needing*
> *Everything that we should be*

This phase of songwriting is perhaps Swift finding her feet but it's remarkable how clean and clear these lyrics are; there's no awkward compromising of pronunciation to fit scansion. What's noticeable here is a dramatic use of a rest in the final line of the verse – so the subject ('everything') is delayed just a little to build tension before the shift into the pre-chorus. It's consistent across all the verses of the song – the enjambment and a rest married to sustain just enough of a pause, a break, for the listener to have their interest piqued.

One of the keys to Swift's lyrics – and a point I'll come back to a lot – is in her capacity for a very filmic, very visual setting of the stories in her songs. Her writing is storytelling, which is to say very country, but it's also very much like the kind of teen drama of *Dawson's Creek* or *One Tree Hill* (two popular early 2000s dramas that were likely in Swift's field of vision). But linking back to earlier forms of teen drama – *My So-Called Life* particularly – there's a particularly compelling technique where some scene is given to the viewer, and then more context is given by way of the lead characters' monologue. That's the pattern this song follows – we're given scenic details of (e.g.) people walking by, and we're given the narrator's emotional perspective.

Further on this kind of multi-perspective allows for some hugely insightful lyrics on Swift's part; for now it's a method to give more depth to a story as well as to intimate that these aren't merely *selfish*, self-centred songs about boys and breakups.

> *only one who's got enough of me to break my heart*
> *He's the song in the car I keep singing...*

Here in the final chorus, we have something that's verging on clichédly 'country'. The association of country music with its effects – in this case, guitars and crying – is pretty strong but it's also a rare area of music which tends towards non-anodyne responses – that is, honesty about crying and emotional upset. The poignant part of this chorus, though, is the sense of emotional attachment which is built upon exceptional intimacy. 'The only one who's got enough of me to break my heart' – that is, the romantic connection is only afforded to the person who knows the person intimately enough. Thus we have an irony, contradiction which is an observation on our most intimate relationships – to reserve love for someone we give ourselves to entirely is also to reserve heartbreak to those few people.

The terminal line in the chorus 'he's the song in the car...' is the kind of everyday observations – broad enough to be familiar to everyone yet specific enough to avoid platitudes – that characterises Swift's capacity for expressing intimacy. It's to speak of that holism-affection connection again – the reflexive, autonomous reactions we have (singing a song, being in love) are the ones that form and inform our own self, our 'wholeness'; their destitution is our devastation.

And speaking of holism – the closing line draws the story full circle by repeating the opening line. As if the exposition within the song is all an aside to the 'real' scene which is the narrator faking a smile; insinuating that the actions of the song were merely an aside, the intensely churning thoughts of the person whose love-object is blissfully unaware of the turmoil they're causing. It's the stuff of classic poetry and it's equally the stuff of low-brow teen drama, to forge a symmetry to the whole.

It's fair to say this is one of Swift's A-game material from the first album – it was added to the international version of the next album, *Fearless*, as a kind of bonus track, with a mix more in keeping with that record. Which is to say it's a song that was considered strong enough to represent the 'teenage country' of the debut and the more established pop country of the sophomore album.

'A Place in This World'

Questions of identity and belonging are critical ennui-isms for teenagers. For adults as well – that's the crossover appeal of this era of Swift – but more critically for teenagers because their identity tends to be more in flux and being shaped all-too-slowly. This song's refrain of 'trying to find a place in this world' is strongly in that domain.

This being Swift's first album, we haven't established at this point what her songs are going to be about; while there's already a majority of songs about romance and romantic conflict, there's a notion that these existential questions can propagate. Unfortunately, there's not a great deal of content to this song – it dotes on a simple question of that 'place in this world'.

We do get the country standard tropes, though – 'Got the radio on, my old blue jeans' – that sense of familiarity and constancy which is clothes and media.

> *And tomorrow's just a mystery, oh yeah*
> *But that's OK*

One of rock 'n' roll's greatest contributions to popular discourse is the idea that everything's going to be all right. It's a very Lou Reed sentiment. It's a very individualistic idea – if we can assert ourselves, our individual identity, then it's all going to be all right. The vibe is that we chill. It's OK. It's louche and it's carefree. It's odd to hear Swift saying it but insofar as pop music in general goes, a line saying 'it's OK' is OK.

> *I'll be strong, I'll be wrong, oh but life goes on*
> *Oh, I'm just a girl, trying to find a place in this world*

We do get this slight shadowing of the female-centric narrative of Swift – it's important to recognise that the problems of teenage people have a specific quality for women, not least women in conservative areas. Unlike her usual unspecificity, though, it's difficult to read this song as much more than platitudinal.

'Cold as You'
The extent to which Swift is 'purely' country is sometimes contested – given there's a transition such that her later work is simply pop, for some quarters this calls into question whether the earlier work is all that country. It's difficult to draw too precise a circle around something and declare it country – typically the arrangements for pop or country songs are built around some fairly simple chord progressions (this is also true for a lot of rock, metal, punk, etc.). What I mean is that the qualifying criteria that 'make' something country tend towards a few effects – which you could split into two larger groups: instrumentation, lyrical content.

A banjo doesn't make a piece country, but it's strongly associated with it. 'Cold as You' features a very prominent violin. Violins feature across Swift's work but they are typically supporting – lending an air of class to the supporting chords of a song. The violin here is much closer to the kind of leading fiddle work one might associate with bluegrass or Appalachian traditions – passing double-stops accentuating the chords while also developing a distinct melodic line. It's a lovely sound and it's a shame that there aren't more Swift songs with prominent violin, even during the country era.

One of the common tropes to Swift's lyrics is using physical places as metaphors for bodily states – where the 'self' of the narrator is considered as a city, a town (see 'Love's architecture' in tropology). 'Cold as You' has something in that ballpark – perhaps not as sharp a metaphor but certainly doting on inverting expectations. 'I've never been anywhere cold as you' works in a few senses – I've never been intimate with someone as emotionally distant as you; I've never been to a place that is as cold as you are; finally, with an assumption about abridged words, I've never been anywhere (near as) cold as you. It's fairly open, vague imagery but it's all pointing at the same place – a barbed description of the antagonist's emotional negligence.

> *You put up walls and paint them all a shade of gray*
> *And I stood there loving you and wished them all away*

Again, a theme that pops up in other forms elsewhere in Swift's lyrics – the antagonist's monopoly over the colours, operating as mood indicators: 'paint me a blue sky / then go back and turn it to rain' ('Dear John', *Speak Now*); 'you paint dreamscapes on the wall' ('peace', *folklore*); 'And all my walls stood tall, painted blue / And I'll take 'em down/ ... And open up the door for you' ('Everything Has Changed', *Red*). The figure of the psychic 'wall' is a common and a powerful one – at this point it's barely a metaphor, such is its use. Perhaps one of the more interesting things about this album in general is that we get a vision of these lyrical ideas in their earliest form. Not so much unhewn but less vivid than they appear later on.

The image of the narrator 'wish[ing] them all away' is interesting insofar as it indicates a passivity that is less common with Swift's lyrics later on (as we'll see). At this point, we still have a younger person – no matter how sophisticated the psychic apparatus she's building, the narrators of these songs are still inclined towards self-doubt. It's perfectly reasonable – who as a teenager can confidently say they know themselves and is able to have fulfilling relationships as a result? – so this self-doubt is hugely compelling for an audience which is younger too – seeing themselves reflected back.

> *Every smile you fake is so condescending counting all the scars you made*

Pure emo, in a sense – and interesting once more to note that the 'faked smiles' theme appears in nascent (but not brutish) form here. Elsewhere: 'he can't see the smile I'm faking' ('The Way I Loved You', *Fearless*); 'Forcing laughter, faking smiles' ('Enchanted', *Speak Now*); 'And wonder about the only soul / Who can tell which smiles I'm fakin'' ('tis the damn season', *evermore*).

Authenticity – and its counterpart, faking – is huge in the teenage drama world. It's not a surprise to see it come up here; it's interesting that fake smiles appear a few times in Swift's lyrics – and more interesting still that it persists after the teenage works (*evermore*, released a couple of days before Swift's 31st birthday). It's probably unnecessary to read too much into it as a figure here – simply because it's *de rigeur* for teenagers to burn with anxiety over authenticity – but there's a precarity to using it later on, after a decade of being in the public eye and, presumably, not smiling authentically at all times. The idea of fake smiles is very Hollywood, very celebrity and for all the brand work the Swift machine has done, surely she's part of that machine of fake smiles?

But regardless – focusing on that too much would miss the gorgeous euphony of 'condescending counting ... scars' here, something that I could well imagine being etched into teenage notebooks.

'The Outside'
There's a sense in which there's a competition between this album and its follow-up, *Fearless*, as to which is most 'commercial'. It's difficult to attach commerciality as a quality to music but this album certainly stands as hitting a lot of the standards for pop country; *Fearless*, meanwhile, is perhaps larger sounding and more thoroughly produced. *Fearless* has a more consistent writer's voice in it – the voice that became 'Taylor Swift, global megastar'. Bigger drums, more dynamic-sounding tunes.

'The Outside' *sounds* very radio friendly – major key, slide guitar, upbeat. Everything about it is bright and friendly, such that the solipsist lyrics don't jump out on first listen. In a sense, this song is perhaps the most tragic of this record – it's a very standard production hiding some quite smart lyrics; were this part of the *Fearless* record, it'd be a lot more polished and stand out more. There is a lovely thick guitar line in here and the arrangement does extend for a few bars but there's not quite enough to make the whole thing jump out at a listener, which is a shame.

> *I tried to take the road less traveled by*
> *But nothing seems to work the first few times*
> *Am I right?*

By the time of Swift's later albums (*folklore, evermore, Midnights*) the notion of obliqueness is fully hemmed into the style. The line here 'the road less traveled by' has the slightly ungainly 'by' at the end; here it qualifies the rhyme with 'times'. In terms of conversational speech, the phrase is less likely to have the jutting 'by'; however, the reference is presumably to Robert Frost's 'The Road Not Taken':

> *I shall be telling this with a sigh*
> *Somewhere ages and ages hence:*
> *Two roads diverged in a wood, and I—*
> *I took the one less traveled by,*
> *And that has made all the difference.*

Frost is a mainstay of poetic education in the US so it's not outrageous that Swift be directly citing this; it's perhaps more peculiar that her reference should be so thorough – the same atypical (for modern English) use of 'by'. Her quotation brings with it an inversion – where Frost's tone is that that road less travelled is of paramount importance, Swift's inference is that that lesser-travelled road is of minor consequence.

> *Nobody ever lets me in*
> *I can still see you*
> *This ain't the best view*
> *On the outside looking in*
> ...
> *I've never been on the outside*

What *is* of consequence is the perspective. You might call it Schrödinger's loneliness – that the position of the observer affects who is feeling lonely. There's a play of paradoxes here – 'This ain't the best view / on the outside looking in' suggests that the narrator is outsided; immediately the switch is '...I've never been on the outside'. Assuming we don't read this as incoherent, it's an observation on 'outsidedness' – the narrator is outside of the antagonist, in the sense of emotional exclusion but very much on the inside of loneliness. Presumably these two states are mutually exclusive.

It's also contiguous with a way of using spaces as bodily-emotional metaphors that's common to Swift – where relationships are cities or towns, not merely walled buildings. It's a powerful metaphor that starts throwing connections out to notions of body politics, incorporation (in the sense of organs forming a body).

We can, additionally, read our contemporary ways of thinking into the difference between Swift and Frost. Frost's imperative was in the decision made by the individual – in 1916, the metaphysical quandaries of individualism were paramount. I'm not an expert on Frost so I don't know if satire or irony are at play but the poem leans on the imperative of decisions. Swift's context – early twenty-first century, and distinctly from the millennial generation – is much more inclined towards a kind of situationism, where the context of a given decision is as reflective as the motivations and actions of the agents within it. It's not outrageous to intimate that each reflects their time.

'Tied Together with a Smile'
This is one that's begging for a re-recording. It's a spare arrangement and oddly doesn't sound like other tracks on this record. It's *almost* like a demo version – there's only so many vocal takes and there's a few more synths than elsewhere on this record. There's a lovely guitar line but it's fairly low in the mix and there's a fadeout that feels somewhat abrupt.

And you're tied together with a smile

The smile here is the connective architecture of the antagonist's self. The 'tied together' is doing a two-part job – first to suggest a kind of presentation (we make presents nicer by tying them with a bow, for instance) and also to suggest a jerry-rigged (itself a sailorly and knot-related metaphor) and precarious construction.

The other oddity of this song is that Swift isn't using the first person – typically her songs are from an 'I' perspective – here it's still an 'I' speaking but the 'I' is not the addressee, subject of the song. It lends it a sympathetic, observational tone that's not most typical for Swift's lyrics. It's a song that's deftly more complex than it seems at first pass, and certainly one that deserves the re-recording, re-thinking treatment.

'Stay Beautiful'
By contrast with the previous track, this jumps out as very radio friendly – all slide guitars and bouncy vocals. One of the key music elements to Swift is her simplicity – and that also means a minimum of extemporisation. Here we have a final chorus where the lead vocal takes a different, higher path. It's a very typical thing to hear in a pop song – and almost expected for someone who's known for an expressive range, like Mariah Carey – but for Swift, it's practically unheard of. That's not to say that Swift can't sing, but rather than the key to the Swift musical brand is in her laser focus on the song – the arrangement, the lyrics, and not much else. That 'not much else' is deceptive – a huge amount of effort goes into eliding the work of that 'not much else' such that Swift's *very produced, very worked-over* music registers with the listener as simple and approachable.

As a side note – if you search for 'Taylor Swift cover' on YouTube, you can quickly see what approachable means; anyone who can pick up any instrument, and particularly an acoustic guitar, feels comfortable singing Swift's songs and the relatively simple melodies are only grease for that wheel (that greasy wheel is also promotion, of course).

> Cory's eyes are like a jungle
> He smiles, it's like the radio
> He whispers songs into my window
> In words that nobody knows

Writing about Swift's earlier music often remarked on the transparency, the teenage simplicity of writing songs with very specific characters. Using the name 'Cory' here doesn't scan any better than 'my boy's eyes' or 'my lover's eyes' but it's a semantic detail that invites the listener to associate with Swift on a personal level; ironically, the specificity is potentially more inviting than a more general signifier. Here we've got two quite peculiar similes – 'like a jungle' and 'smile … like the radio'. So the specificity is complemented by odd, if not unspecific, similes. 'Like a jungle' might be evocative of dark green and brown colouring but not enough to denote clearly. 'Like the radio' is more of a semantic association than invoking a particular quality of smile. The very next line, the 'radio' simile is elucidated – his radio-smile whispers songs into her window. Again, the window-view-body-self collocation of metaphors, with added pellucidity. The smile is transmitting into Swift in an opaque language.

It's an oddity for Swift at this point insofar as its unspecificity or broad evocations are closer to surreal associations than they are descriptive positions. It's a glimpse into the sort of part-opaque writing that Swift thrives on later.

> *I'm taking pictures in my mind*
> *So I can save them for a rainy day*

Here again the trope of Swift having a very vividly visual, filmic imagination. She never goes so far as to suggest that she has an eidetic memory but her lyrical imagination is consistently visual such that it's difficult not to imagine her memories as less filing cabinet, more film archive.

'Should've Said No'
One of the stronger songs on this record, such that it appears in a slightly sheared version on international versions of the next album, *Fearless*. The difference in the two versions possibly being dictated the markets they're aiming for – while *Fearless* is still lyrically close to country, the version on this album is much more heavily saturated in country effect – the banjo is well up in the mix, the violin line here much more central and wayward, and perhaps the pronunciation here is more peppered with rhotic 'r's.

> *You should've said 'No', you should've gone home*
> *You should've thought twice 'fore you let it all go*
> *You should've known that word*
> *'Bout what you did with her'd*
> *Get back to me*

Later on, we rarely see these contractions ('should've', ''fore', ''bout', 'her'd') so prominently; these small clues to the intended audience. Or less cynically, a Taylor Swift who was closer to her Pennsylvania roots before the onset of fame and all the moving that comes with it.

One of the more notable differences between this and the *Fearless* version is that after this chorus there's a fraction of a second of fiddle playing very loosely, somewhere between excessive vibrato and Indian style glissandi (meend). It's only very brief but it's the kind of musical effect that says 'real musicians' in a way that an assiduously tight and clipped production does not. These are both equally studio decisions – it would be fascinating to know *whose* decisions – while later Swift has her 'voice' all over production (see 'Business'), at this point it seems unlikely Swift herself would have that capacity, at least in terms of how big labels and studios would treat a minor.

There's a subtle lyrical effect here that I was oblivious to until I read the lyric sheet. The chorus dotes on the functions of binary 'yes' / 'no' – the *sine qua non* of binaries, perhaps. And the pinion, the pivoting joint of the chorus is 'should've known that *word*…' – that is word in two senses, one literally, another as a synecdoche for conversation, communication in general. Considering she was a minor at the time it's likely that she was already so immersed in lyrical form that this was intuitive, perhaps unconsciously so.

> *But do you honestly expect me to believe*
> *We could ever be the same?*

Something we see more of later on in Swift's form but fleetingly on this album – a contraction or expansion of lyrical rhythm which draws the lyrical focus in different directions. 'Hon-est-ly' and 'to bel-ieve' are split into triplets next to the longer syllabism of the earlier strophes in the line; this play of long and short generates a tension which is then released by the relatively prosaic 'we could ever be the same'; our attention is pushed towards the lynchpins 'honestly' and 'believe' but the terminal line in this stanza is an annunciatory question.

'Mary's Song (Oh My My My)'

The penultimate song on her first album, and it's once again very radio country – banjo-led and wistful.

> *Take me back when our world was one block wide*
> *I dared you to kiss me and ran when you tried*

The stories of country music are built around families and small towns and this is a piece of charming juvenilia. At this point, Swift hasn't quite formed a style – while all of the elements that would later constitute Swift's form are present on this album, there's also elements that end up marginal to her music. Mary's song is closer to the margins. The song reads a relationship from different generations – and critically, it does so from a generation to which Swift doesn't belong when it talks about later life, weddings, parenthood. For now, though, her sense of perspective and framing produces that lovely line about a world 'one block wide', characterising the perspective of infants.

Part of what makes this atypical is that the repeated motif is 'take me back' – typically Swift doesn't retrospect nostalgically; at the time of writing this it can only be a caprice, given that much of this was written when Swift was 15. It's a sign that her songwriting chops and storytelling imagination were well-formed early on. The shortcomings of this song aren't so much that this story rings inauthentic but rather that Swift from after this point builds her songwriting voice around a first-person authenticity – much of the appeal is in believing Swift to be the person who's narrating the stories.

> *Take me back to the time when we walked down the aisle*
> ...
> *You said 'I do' and I did too*

So here we get the leap of imagination where the theme of the song is a relationship that's persisted over several generations and stages in life. It's a cute song, but it's perhaps not the strongest from this era. It does show us what later appears as a rupture in Swift songwriting, though – her brand of personal, personable first-person songs about heartache and boys is difficult to reconcile with songwriting which is more general, and perhaps more generic. While this is a charming song, it's difficult to reconcile, as fantasy, that it's written by a teenager. It leans on some fairly generic experiences that Swift cannot possibly have experienced. And, again, that's fine, but it shows two dynamics in Swift as a writer.

Later on in her career, Swift used the pseudonym 'Nils Sjöberg' for 'This is What You Came For', Calvin Harris featuring Rihanna. While that tune is a piece of simple dance-leaning pop music, it still illustrates the potential breadth of Swift as a writer. We could say in this context that 'Mary's Song' is the first work we might recognise as one of Nils Sjöberg's.

'Our Song'
The closing song according to my rules on canonicity and it's a track that was revived and remixed for international versions of *Fearless*. And like 'Should've Said No' (above), this version has more prominent banjo, more erratic, sinuous violin melodies, and is a lot more country.

And it *should* be a country song; for the debate as to whether Swift's accent changed or is subject to affectation, this is resolutely country in tone and setting:

> *I was riding shotgun*
> ...
> *In the front seat of his car*

Again, the setting is the car; the social dynamics of where someone sits ('shotgun' means the passenger seat) are alluded to. The hair is undone – a distinction that's distinctly teenage, where school tends to dictate how young women keep their hair. The steering wheel grip is described as louchely one-handed. This detail is significant for that teenage world where cars connote so much. Cars and their importance, their layering of social semiotics, diminish once the car is no longer the primary scene for teenage sociality away from parents/adult-dominated spaces. This is all part of the scene which tells us we're in the realm of country music; the bluegrass-ish banjo and fiddle backing is just icing on that cake.

> *When we're on the phone and you talk real slow*
> *'Cause it's late and your mama don't know*

Edifying here the strong family-centricity of non-urban living. It's not just that younger people are under the cosh of parents, but also that the family is the currency of country living (or at least, that's the impression that's being projected here). Less formal language dotted around here – 'real slow' in the sense of 'really slow', a contracted form of that intensifier more common to informal language; ''cause' is presumably a distinct linguistic choice, as 'because' would just as easily fit here – assuming again that this is pointing towards a country audience; 'mama' for that down-home, filial familiarity. Finally, we also have 'don't know' – a more neutral, formal would suggest 'doesn't know' – the language becomes more inviting and familiar (also in the sense of familial) and the marginally shorter phrase allows for a nice punch double emphasis (in turn echoed with a big snare hit).

> *And when I got home, 'fore I said, 'Amen'*
> *Asking God if he could play it again*

Here again the domain is that very Christian, family-oriented world – and while a lot of this music is suffused with a *sense* of being Christian, here we have an explicit marker. The unduly contracted ''fore' is pushing the country vibes but it's certainly remarkable, and a marker of country music, that an explicitly Christian sentiment is here – it's very rare for English-language pop music to gesture towards its religious surroundings but it's not so uncommon in country music. As I say in 'This is country music', paraphrasing, you're not supposed to talk about God, but this is country music, and we do.

The other notable thing here is we have yet another early indicator of Swift's strongly filmic, visual descriptions – 'play it again' as if it were a film real and life were a cinema under God's direction. It might not sit neatly with the later, distinctly urbane (in several senses) Taylor Swift but it's a sentiment that is strongly compelling for those of us who were raised in the church (including those of us who've not been for decades).

Like 'Teardrops on My Guitar' (above), this song closes with a circular affectation – that the song we've just heard *is* the song that she's describing writing down. It's interesting that this device doesn't recur in later Swift – perhaps either because the songwriting is confident enough that it's not felt necessary, or because as her voice grew into a more particular style, this very writerly affectation no longer feels necessary. Later on, any self-referential gestures are made towards Swift's own canon – re-using her own lyrics – so it's most tempting to say that a young, 'developing' songwriter is much more likely to draw upon writing *itself* as a particular and remarkable act. Here it's certainly cutesy and charming – I'm glad the circular song-referencing-itself didn't become a trope further on as it could quickly become trite. That it isn't here is a real testament to Swift's astonishing precocity.

Fearless

If *Self-titled* is a nascent form of Swift, then *Fearless* is the teenage form. It's got all of the hallmarks of what ultimately forms her style – the sharp observations, the heartbreaking intimacy. Her writerly voice is consistent across the whole record and there's a lot less of a feeling that she's playing about with her style. While it's still decidedly a new country album, it's a very different proposition to *Self-titled*. There's not an ounce of fat on the arrangements and all instrumentation is decidedly in service of 'the song'.

What's distinct to the later Swift – besides the country vibes – is that Swift's narrators are less *confident* at this point. There's still a raft of love songs, a raft of break-up songs, but the narrators are a lot sweeter, and more simple, than later iterations. A songwriter reaching for adulthood and writing an absolute banger in the process and, arguably, much of Swift's best country material.

'Fearless'

A very big snare sound here; from the off it's a big country production – ample guitars, banjo, mandolin, fiddle… of all of Swift's productions this is perhaps the most transparently commercial, everything clear and big and designed to push through the radio waves.

> *You walk me to the car*
> *And you know I wanna ask you to dance right there*
> *In the middle of the parking lot*

Thematically, cars appear quite a lot in Swift's music; during this earlier phase, though, they are more often the *focus*. Later on, cars are incidental to the song – 'kissin' in my car again' ('Betty', *folklore*), a means of getting around. For *Fearless* and *Self-titled*, cars and car *places* are used more often. 'Picture to Burn' (*Self-titled*) with its focus on the truck's status in the relationship, and here where the whole song takes place in a car or a parking lot.

Part of the reason for this is country music culture – the non-urban parts of the US are typically navigated by car. Country music typically speaks to less urban living, more agricultural or small-town notions. Cars are indispensable. At the time of *Self-titled*, cars are status symbols; by the time of *Fearless*, the car is the medium for interaction. This is important to the setting of intimacy at a certain point of a teenager's life – typically not old enough to drink in public (21 is the most typical minimum drinking age) and often not yet living separately from the parents. Communal spaces for younger people are less popular if everyone lives a car ride away. So the setting of the car as the space where young people get to experience relationships is shot through with a very particular time-and-place sense. Hence the stage for teenager relationships looks like the front seats of a car: 'I wanna stay right here in this passenger's seat'.

While the lyrics here are more typically redolent of a stage, setting – which we'll later come to realise is part of Swift's capacity for filmic, strongly phantasic writing – there's still a glimpse of the intensive metaphors: 'You take my hand and drag me head first' – the 'drag me head first' is more about the state of intensity (one doesn't take a hand to drag a person head first); the less typical sense of dragging head first operates to intensify the metaphor of what is happening with the hand holding – intensifying with a kind of mixed metaphor.

'Fifteen'

Again, big production – lots of overlaid stringed instruments, a lightly feedbacking, heavily reverbed guitar.

Swift's writing in this period is shot through with precociousness; it's not so much a lyrical theme as it is its capacity, mode. While pop country is certainly built on pith and sociological observation, by dint of age Swift's observations intuitively feel at odds – observing *being 15* while being not so much older (the album was released when Swift was 18). The later re-recording of this is *uncanny* insofar as it retains the qualities of the earlier version – an astute observation on the mentality of a 15-year-old.

> *And when you're fifteen*
> *Feeling like there's nothing to figure out*
> *Well, count to ten, take it in*
> *This is life before you know who you're gonna be*
> *Fifteen*

It's a cute, and an acute, observation on the state of the 15-year-old – recognising two opposing notions as *true* for a teenager. Rather than rendering the teenage state as *false* – that is, saying that the 'nothing to figure out' is false – observing that the feeling is true whilst recognising the potential states to come at a time before 'you know who you're gonna be'. It's difficult to imagine these observations carrying weight in other songs – either because someone who's too old doesn't get to be convincing when talking about those feelings in a direct, present sense; and as such older people's observations on the teenage state struggle to convincingly *be* authoritative, in several senses.

Put another way – Swift is *sympathetic* to the teenager, the 15-year-old.

> *And then you're on your very first date and he's got a car*
> *And you're feeling like flying*

That observation is necessarily mundane – one doesn't typically invoke feelings of ecstasy for someone having a car. But it's important, imperative, to observe teenagers' capacity for over-subscribing, for reading everything into asinine detail. The problems of hormones and burgeoning identity lead to a certain lack of clarity such that mundane details are rendered ecstatic. Like a boy having a car.

'Love Story'

> *We were both young when I first saw you*
> *I close my eyes and the flashback starts:*

In some senses this is the song that's most paradigmatic of Swift in general: we open with this very filmic vision, explicitly so. Stating her reliance on filmic language to express visuality ('flashback'). And the collapsing of fantasy – 'close my eyes … I'm standing there' – it's not clear the extent to which this is an imagined or a 'real' event and, principally, it's more important to suspend any notion of ontological orthodoxy to enjoy the fantasy. Also, this is a 'love story' leaning heavily on the Shakespearian figures of Romeo and Juliet, arguably history's most emo couple – the narrator is described as standing on a balcony.

Given this is Swift's most direct literary citation in song, it's no surprise that the metaphor is extended, stretched, and overlapped to emphasise intensity:

> *"Cause you were Romeo. I was a scarlet letter*
> *And my daddy said, 'Stay away from Juliet.'*

The second literary allusion here is to *The Scarlet Letter*, a work by Nathaniel Hawthorne – in which the protagonist Hester Prynne is condemned to wear a scarlet 'A' for 'adulteress' following the birth of a child of unknown father. It's difficult (and perhaps undesirable) to pin what this means in the context of this song down too precisely, but we can say with some confidence that Prynne is a complex feminine figure – the woman carrying society's puritanism with quiet, stoic pride, the subject of extreme sexism.

Now the line itself is easy to miss in its rolling oddity – she was not *wearing* a scarlet letter but she *was* a scarlet letter – she was that mark of female shame. 'My daddy said stay away from Juliet' is curious insofar as in the rest of the song the 'Juliet' is presupposed to be Swift, or the narrator – here it's Swift qua scarlet letter who's told to stay away from Juliet – in which sense the scarlet letter is the mark of adultery (or, in its original puritanical context, sexually active women, in which the difference is near-immaterial).

It's a subtle line and one that bears unpicking because it seems less like Swift is occupying the Juliet character than that she represents the shame of women which is being attached to Juliet.

Later on in Swift's lyrics, especially on *Midnights*, we see Swift leaning into a kind of dream-laden hinterland – which is to say, while here there's a relatively formal relationship with fairytale fantasy, it's a theme that's leveraged numerous times in Swift's songs.

And again, to add more allusions into a heady mix: 'You'll be the prince and I'll be the princess'. Romeo and Juliet weren't prince and princess; those figures are common to a whole different sort of story, and typically one less tragic than Shakespeare. The affirmation 'it's a love story' is perhaps as if to assert – it doesn't matter if it makes sense. The listener is invited to join with the fantasy with scant disregard for the trammels of sense.

'Hey Stephen'

It might be the case that after *Fearless* there's a lack of *plain* songs. Not plain in the sense of boring but rather in the sense of drama, or lack thereof. Speculatively, the reason for that could be on account of Swift's age – during our teenage years the presence of a stable relationship is remarkable; the presence of relationships *in general* is remarkable. It's not to say that every teenager is some unhewn, credulous and wide-eyed dope but that a sense of stability is a unique state.

And this plain-ness should be separated from love songs – which typically describe the burning desire of a person for another. Here Swift isn't so much describing an overwhelming intensity as she is expressing that she quite strongly *fancies* someone (in the very British sense of that term).

> *Hey, Stephen, I've been holding back this feeling*
> *... But I never seen nobody shine the way you do*

This image of a person shining is common with *Speak Now*'s 'Innocent': 'Your string of lights is still bright to me'.

There's a marker here of the country vs pop phase – the double negative of 'never seen nobody' which is typically more informal, more homely US English. And also more aggravating to English teachers but nobody cares nothing for what they think. Also indicative of the first two albums is the use of specific personal names ('Stephen') – characteristic of the manner in which Swift invites the listener to read her personal narrative into a song, characteristic of the 'teenage diary' quality.

> *Hey, Stephen, why are people always leaving?*
> *I think you and I should stay the same*

To return to the plain-ness notion, here's the complementary notion of stasis. There's an opposition between *leaving* and staying the same – which is interesting in that leave/stay are oppositions but leave/stasis are of different orders. One is active, describing a continuous observed action, the other is passive, describing the potential absence of an action. Oppositions still, but more conceptual opposites than semantic ones (e.g. night/day describe different states of the same thing). And again, this is to intimate that in a life of relative tumult – 'people always leaving' – that the radical or contrary action is to 'stay the same' – it's to valorise stasis, perhaps not so much as a kind of proxy for burning desire but as an agreeable outcome.

It's a lovely song and it's underpinned by a lovely and exploratory church organ-like keyboard that's very much in the background but also atypically expansive for an album that's more commercial in focus, perhaps, than any other album. We also get some lovely handclicks which I don't think we've had front-and-centre in any other Swift song.

'White Horse'
Once again, we're in the realms of fairytales and magic but this time the end of the relationship is aligned with the shattering of the fantasy:

> *That I'm not a princess, this ain't a fairytale*
> ...
> *Now it's too late for you and your white horse*

There's a lot here that's almost mirroring the fantasy setting of 'Love Story' – where 'Love Story' doted on the blurred ontology of closed-eye fantasy, here princesshood is negated, dreaming is negated. And the white horse figure – the prince charming swooping in to save the day – is also negated. There's no fantasy which can un-puncture the rupture.

The details portray a fairly severe violation – it's not merely a (presumed) break-up but it's coloured by gaslighting dynamics:

> *My mistake, I didn't know to be in love*
> *You had to fight to have the upper hand*

This feigned-apologeticism is to snatch spite from the jaws of defeat – gallows-black humour about being condescended to, the riposte which ironically ('my mistake') valorises the antagonist's combative relationship dynamic.

> *I'm gonna find someone someday who might actually treat me well*

This line is nested in a chorus which is otherwise temperate stress-release, on/off flow – overloading the line with additional syllables that are not fulfilling much semantic content – 'someone someday', 'might actually'. The notion being that these over-designations work to draw attention to the subject of the line ('treat me well'). If the whole song was oversubscribed like this then the lyrics would become cluttered and messy; by and large, the lyrics here are clipped and measured, so the explosion of verbiage has the effect of drawing attention in like a large object's gravity, focusing to the centre of the song.

'You Belong With Me'
It's maybe Swift's most pop moment to date – still all the hallmarks of being a country song but a production that says 'no holds barred' – right down to the banjo-wah stereo percussion-like effect. For maximum radio impact, the verse is largely drum-less, and the chorus is a big heap of stuff. Wafting slide guitar haunts the second verse – it's a case study in how to make a crossover country hit.

The song is perfectly teenage – and so far as sentiment goes, it'd work as a straight-up pop song, or a straight-up indie song, or a straight-up emo song… maybe even a straight-up metal song – it's the classic 'you're with the wrong girl' idea. The protagonist likes the same music, wears the same clothes.

And so far as that goes, it's perfectly observed to hammer the bullseye of teenage preoccupation and anxiety:

> *I'm listening to the kind of music she doesn't like*
> *But she wears short skirts, I wear T-shirts*
> *She's Cheer Captain and I'm on the bleachers*

All these details which affirm the sorts of identities that are most strongly adopted by teenagers – as we get older, we less (explicitly) group around cohorts of clothes or music. The figure of cheerleader vs non-sporty girls is profoundly American (or at least profoundly not-British) but the teenage sectarianism is deeply familiar, surely, the world over.

The Swift songwriting brand isn't merely about observation of social commonplaces, though – it's all in the details. Swift is inclined to narrativise her stories, such that each song has its dramaturgy. So it makes sense that where Swift's songs so frequently have a filmic quality, that narrativisation is applied to the object of the narrator's desires – 'And she'll never know your story like I do'. The image, taken from a certain remove, is that each person has their own idiomatic story, to be read and understood; that story's teleology is:

> *All this time, how could you not know, baby?*
> *You belong with me...*

This observation keeps in line with a lot of the fairytale flavouring of the storytelling on *Fearless*; 'teleology' alludes to the idea a natural occurrence and its consequences are inevitable. Or put otherwise – within the romantic narratives there is an inexorable outcome, typically that of romance. While there's no direct fairytale intimations here, the star-crossed lovers/assertion of the 'correct' outcome is deeply coupled with the structures of fairytales.

As elsewhere with *Fearless*, and Swift's writing in general, it's the observations of intimate details that ironically are most inviting. There's a litany of ways to describe a sense of comfort with another person, from the verbose ('I feel very comfortable with this person, for reasons [X, Y, Z]') to the oblique ('this is chill'). Swift's observations in this song have the levity of the instantaneous, sudden and inspired; the spare observation, as if conversational, of 'hey isn't this easy'; it's off-handedness obliquely intuiting that the interactions' easy-ness doesn't *need* to be observed because it's just so *easy*. It needs to be off-hand to carry the sense of lightness; the apparently inessential 'hey' does a lot of work in connoting insouciance for the spare few words of a short phrase.

'Breathe'
Keeping with the romantic storytelling of *Fearless*, but also with a smidge of the over-extended metaphors common to Swift's writing in general, 'Breathe' is a gentle break-up song shot through with the tragic vim that only teenagers can muster (and brilliantly so).

Music starts playing like the end of a sad movie
It's the kind of ending you don't really wanna see
'Cause it's tragedy and it'll only bring you down
Now, I don't know what to be without you around

It's a stanza that escalates to a terrifying vertigo; from the plain observation of more filmic narratives ('sad movie'), to 'tragedy' to the verge of existential annihilation. It's a brilliant sentiment and deeply teenage; the break-up isn't 'merely' a tragedy but threatens to destabilise a whole being. I don't mean that in the sense of suicide ideation – though it's important to recognise that that's a potential reading here – but rather in the sense that 'I don't know what to *be*' rests on some substantially existential notions. Without going full Heidegger, the 'be' here is precarious – as if the narrator's whole existence is predicated upon the antagonist's presence. Note also that the line isn't '*who* to be without you around' but '*what*' – implying a state of object-ness rather than person-ness.

These are minor distinctions but they're important to note – Swift's work is one of intimate detail and often that intimate detail gives more diffuse readings than an 'obvious' line might – it's not 'I will struggle to define myself after our relationship' but 'I will struggle to *exist in the world* after our relationship'. Again, that needn't allude to suicide ideation – I don't believe Swift is interested in non-existence per se – but rather that the state is extended beyond 'sadness' and soaks up some of the ground from 'existential terror'.

And keeping with that confounded metaphor notion – the chorus's motif is about breathing, the narrator being unable to breathe without the antagonist, yet compelled to. The 'breathe' is doing a lot of work *simultaneously* – 'I can't breathe' in the sense that 'I am struggling emotionally such that my existence is damaged', but also 'I have to' in the sense that breathing is an autonomic process. That's all that's said in the chorus, all we have is an allusion to the collapsing, circular metonymy of 'breathe'.

Ensuring that we're still within a setting of teenage romances outside of urban settings – that is, keeping the song within the realms of country music – we've got intimations that the dialogue of the tragic scene of the song takes place in a car – 'Every little bump in the road, I tried to swerve'. A neat exposition on the frailty of being the losing partner in a failed relationship – typically a feminised role where one person desperately tries to avoid conflict.

Oddly as well the song closes with a repeated 'I'm sorry'. It's tempting to suggest this is a kind of volte-face – 'it was I who needed to break us up'; but I'm more inclined, given the passivity of avoiding conflict earlier, to suggest that it's an act of *bathos* – a low point of kneejerkedly apologising *despite not being the one at fault*. It's a state very familiar to the British.

'Tell Me Why'

Speaking from the British perspective, there's a sense in which US pop country is a lot more expansive than we might assume; while the hallmarks of non-urban living and stereotypes are rampant – trucks, Christian values, heartache – it being pop music, there's also a fair amount of ventures into novelty. Although Lil Nas X has traded on his country-hip-hop crossover, he's not the first to allude to hip-hop in country. Though importantly, there is certifiably a dearth of black folk and other people of colour in country music. It's not unprecedented to have a guest rapper, however clumsily – and if you're keen to define clumsy, Brad Paisley's 'Accidental Racist' featuring LL Cool J is groundbreakingly clumsy.

'Tell Me Why' starts with a mildly off-piste circular violin motif (suggesting earlier Appalachian styles) with a distinctly synthetic drum sound. It doesn't persist for long in the song – but it's enough to give the faint impression of a commercial hip-hop song. By the time of the chorus, it's a welter of 'acoustic' instruments – banjos, guitars, shakers, fiddles, slide… but the impression remains.

With many relationships – and typically in the breakdown – there's at least two stories of how it happened. Once again here there's the narrator who's belittled and the antagonist who's abrasive. It's tempting to characterise this as gaslighting – as it is elsewhere – but it's also important to reserve the storytelling element and not make that connection every time.

I say this if only to eke out one of the skills in Swift's songwriting; while there may be a typical or transparent narrative, part of the assiduous detail of her writing is that it's frequently still as close to indistinctness such that it can be read in multiple ways, but never so indistinct as to be devoid of emotions to be projected upon by the audience.

> *Here's to you and your temper*
> *Yes, I remember what you said last night*

The interesting thing here is that there's a sense in which this could be read as a cowering, fearful response; it could also be read as the withering, piss-take, weary rather than cowed. 'I remember what you said last night' implies its contrary, that the antagonist doesn't remember, and as such draws into a reading of a dreadful (ahem) antagonistic drunk.

Whether that's a satisfying interpretation to the listener is perhaps less important – the notion here is that popular song 'works' by appealing to the widest audience. It's not to say that a song with infinite interpretations concomitantly has infinite *appreciations* but this is a song which, at least potentially, has a strong and a weak interpretation of the nature of the antagonist. A strong (gaslighting) interpretation would say that this is contiguous with the gaslighting interpretation of 'White Horse'; a weaker interpretation gives us a different perspective – 'I take a step back, let you go / I told you I'm not bulletproof' is coloured by the finality of not putting up with bullshit, rather than escaping from terror.

> *Why do you have to put down my dreams*
> *So you're the only thing on my mind?*

It's a line of some simplicity but it is delightful – to figure the depression of dreams, a kind of synecdoche for full personal expression, as to diminish the psychic space such that the antagonist is the solitary focus of the narrator. Strong interpretation sees this as bullying; weak interpretation likewise but the bullying is more pathetic, arrogant. Either way the antagonist is an idiot but in the latter he's vestigially pitiable. Again, it's not imperative to align with that interpretation but it is remarkable that Swift can concurrently express multiple *cogent* readings.

'You're Not Sorry'

> *You used to shine so bright, but I watched all of it fade*

Once again this metaphor of dimmable lights. Potentially linking the 'string of lights' of 'Hey Stephen' here, or at least an expression of the mutability of a person's appeal.

> *And you can tell me that you're sorry*
> *But I don't believe you, baby, like I did before*
> *You're not sorry*

The key here is in the triplet feel (you-can-tell/that-you're-sorry) to the first two lines which is flattened out entirely for the final line. We get a sense of a lot of information being drilled towards us with a payoff of a plain 'you're not sorry'; no extemporisation and a line which ends with a rest such that the full weight of its sentiment can be felt. For all the decoration, the intention is simply to land the assertion that the antagonist is not sorry.

The verse is relatively simple; a few guitar arpeggios and a shuffly drum figure pull us towards the chorus; the chorus adds ostinato strings to keep the rhythm clear. Ultimately there's not a great deal *to* this song; it's not quite as taut and spare as some of the later material but it seemingly exists as a loose means of delivering the 'you're not sorry' assertion.

'The Way I Loved You'

One of the imperatives to this period of Swift is the honesty and lucidity in observing teenage relationships. For every sentiment of a 'fuck you, you make me insane' type, there's a counterpart reflection. This is songwriting and if songwriting is drawn from the self and experience, Swift was an exceptionally self-aware teenager. It may well be that the abstraction of songwriting offers a kind of therapeutic analysis.

That said, sometimes the lucidity looks like a reflection on the bloodrush intensity of one relationship in comparison to another, which is 'The Way I Loved You':

> *... I miss screaming and fighting and kissing in the rain*
> *It's 2AM and I'm cursing your name*

That escalating trio of gerunds – screaming/fighting/kissing – which leads from conflict to compassion. The usual escalation of that pattern is to ascend in a given hierarchy (think 'friends, Romans, countrymen...'); the irony here is that the zenith of conflict is 'kissing'. This isn't so much to impute some masochistic relationship so much as to indicate the complex, fiery passion of a complex relationship. The relationship to which it is counterposed in the song is pacific and stable, the model of non-conflict.

The current and previous relationship are implicitly compared in terms of intimacy. Intimacy, from this configuration, is a many-sided thing.

For the volatile previous relationship, we learn that, despite the conflict, there was an intimacy such that the other partner saw the narrator with a sense of honesty: 'He can't see the smile I'm faking'. For the current relationship, he 'talks business with my father' – if we infer that the volatile relationship *didn't* have those qualities, we also assume that the partner was less closely integrated into the narrator's social and family life. Somewhere in these outlines is a complex whole – that whole being the map of social relationships which form our place in society; obliquely we see part of the American family value system – not every community or society would regard knowing one's parents as in any way indicative of the intimacy of a relationship.

There's a list of qualities which are valorised for the non-volatile, current relationship: 'he respects my space'. The romantic narrative here is that a partner's 'being comfortable' is insufficient relative to an argumentative relationship that, nevertheless, was full of love.

This romantic notion is also perfectly teenage. I don't mean to say that having romantic notions is in any way juvenile; but rather that few teenagers desire anything so perfectly banal as *stability* in their relationships. But also past tense is used to describe the preferred relationship; the narrator stops short of ever saying that the volatile previous relationship was desirable; rather the 'that's the way I loved you' suggests a kind of distance which allows for a neutral description. We, the listeners, are inclined towards implicitly valorising the previous relationship but the narrator herself actually stops short.

'Forever & Always'
Typically, Swift's song structure is relative limited – verse, optional 'pre-chorus', chorus, bridge. It's a predictable pattern. 'Forever & Always' has an extra couple of parts to it – an extended bridge, a solo.

Now in terms of songwriting in general, this is not that complex; it's not using classical antistrophe or exploring contrapuntal exposition. It is, in the context of Swift though, peculiar. The nature of the pre-chorus/chorus is such that it does come across as one long chorus; the dividing marks for sections are not entirely clear. So you end up with a song that, until the bridge, carries the listener along with some aplomb. In that juggernaut there's a fair few lines that are sharp and striking:

> *Here's to silence that cuts me to the core*

The ironic 'here's to', as if raising a toast. The 'silence that cuts…', where silence has the capacity to shake and unsettle a person, physically maim them. 'Cut to the core' is necessary for the complementary rhyme 'I don't [know] anymore' and it's a subtle manipulation of the more typical 'cuts to the quick'. 'Quick' in this context refers to the bone underneath a deep cut; 'core' extends that further into the central, fundamental part of a person.

> *And it rains in your bedroom*
> *…*
> *It rains when you're here*
> *And it rains when you're gone*

Here we have Swift in some of her more poetic form. The charming figure of rain in atypical places. Rain which haunts the bedroom, presence, absence. Rain clearly a figure of depression or sadness but also liberally applied as a universal presence. It veers towards the absurd, having rain everywhere, which is unusual for a pop song – pop songs typically qualify metaphors less obliquely. The motif of 'forever and always' becomes increasingly pathetic, the only counterpart the narrator has for the indomitable (figure of) rain.

'The Best Day'

In the interest of full disclosure, this is probably my favourite Taylor Swift song. It's an unusual one in her oeuvre in some senses – the bulk of the song describes a young person's changing relationship with their mother and is largely conflict-free. There is a subtext suggesting the narrator has fallen out with friends at school ('don't know how my friends could be so mean') but it's never made explicit.

We are led to believe that the narrator's emotional state is not good, but we're given no details. Rather we're told of her relationship with her mother, and how the narrator had the best day. Later on, we see Swift developing a more oblique sense of the story that's being told in a song; I argue that it's one of the hallmarks of 'late Swift'. During this phase of her writing, the stories are more transparent, and more typically straight-up break-up or love songs. So 'the best day' is odd in that sense.

> *we talk and window shop 'til I've forgotten all their names*

That detail of a mother's response to a child's upset being to immediately take the child away from the norm, take them on some pointless errand. It's not so much that this is to distract the child but rather that these actions are those of *centring* the child. Conflict unsettles us in many ways, and one of the critical ways is in that it un-centres us, makes us aware of our frailties. The mother who re-centres that child may well be acting contra-ration but she is also working pro-ego – and teenage identities are so volatile and mutable that this re-centring is given as an act of compassion.

This song is also a really beautiful paean to her mother, a maternal figure who the narrator describes as fearless, perhaps circling to the album's title. Again, to provide and expose that sense of solidity and stability is critical for young minds in flux. Whether Swift herself would be aware of this at the time of writing is perhaps moot – what's more important is the delicate observation of a mother providing a decent and a solid role model.

There's also an important element to this song where the fantasy-fairytale aspect is smoothly blended with reality itself.

> *Don't know if Snow White's house is near or far away*

At the risk of being entirely Freudian (mea culpa), one of the functions of fantasy for children (and adults) is to provide a realm in which desirable notions can be played out. It's not so much to indulge in fiction as to recognise that our desires are narrativised and can be re-narrativised. Elsewhere on this record –

especially 'Love Story' and 'White Horse' – there have been strong if not explicit allusions to canonical fantasy figures; for this song, 'Snow White's house' takes on a secondary role, next to the fact that she 'had the best day with you'.

So when I say it's a *charming* song I perhaps mean it in several senses – it's cute and some might say cutesy but it's also a song which sets out to express gratitude for her mother's actions. Rather than a song which affirms whatever it is that's caused the sadness, it's a song that asserts the imperative of her relationship with her mother.

'Change'

The oddity of this closing song is that it's bombastic; coming after the subdued affirmation of 'the best day', it's quite a contrast. Later on – and particularly in the album *Red* – this stadium-friendly sound with big drums and crashing guitars becomes much more de rigeur. It's not quite that it's at odds with the album as a whole, and it's still within the realms of country music, but it's perhaps odd that they didn't choose this song to have a big dramatic guest guitar solo from someone like Keith Urban (something of a ubiquitous guitar player in the realms of country music in the 2000/2010s).

It's also one of the rare instances where Swift sings in terms of a collective 'we' – and not a 'we' which is describing a romantic relationship – 'Tonight, we stand, get off our knees'. It's an ambiguous and perhaps disingenuous use of 'we' – bearing in mind that this was a time when Swift had less control over her career. And given that we're still in country music, and therefore Christian sentiment, 'we'll sing hallelujah' might put a specific spin on the collectivism of the pronoun 'we'.

Once more we're in the realm of the cinematic, visual: 'And it's a sad picture, the final blow hits you'.

> *'Cause these things will change*
> *Can you feel it now?*
> *These walls that they put up to hold us back will fall down*

Finally here, perhaps the key is one of the abiding themes, and contexts, of the whole record – teenage volatility dictates that 'things will change' and teenage desires are most typically revolutionary. Breaking down walls (mental, physical) is a constant theme, especially in punk and heavy metal. While this song doesn't directly 'tell a story', it's not outrageous to assume that what a teenager sometimes needs is a big heap of affirmative 'fuck it, we're great!' and this song is certainly that.

Speak Now

Speak Now is the last of the definitely-country albums. It's by no means Swift's swansong to country, as her writing never veers too far from that realm. We see the emergence of Swift's castigation mode, which forms one of the key threads to her style. Break-up songs, love songs, and perhaps the last time we can describe her as 'precocious'. She's peeling more layers off her narrator's innocence and revealing a sophisticated thinker and writer of impressive and cohesive tunes.

If this is the swansong to country, then there's no better way to say goodbye than with a song called 'Dear John' – the song which is our first intimation of her capacity to steal the higher ground from powerful, usually older, bastard men.

'Mine'

> *You were in college working part time waitin' tables*
> *Left a small town, never looked back*

Those piquant, country observations back again. As soon as you speak about small towns, you're clearly in country territory. Shortly after the above, we get 'I was a flight risk with a fear of falling' – jammed with alliteration; the 'falling' here is amphibolous insofar as it could be falling … in love or the more typical fear of falling down. It speaks, in itself, of the narrator observing her own precarity in matters of the heart.

> *You made a rebel of a careless man's careful daughter*
> *You are the best thing that's ever been mine*

'Rebel of a careless man's careful daughter' is a beaut – on/off stresses, alliteration, hard plosive assonances backed up with semi-plosives to keep the line ticking along. And of course it's still pushing at those country narratives – the rebels, the strong family lines. The implicit narrative of families, where the foibles of one generation (carelessness) become the inverted foibles of the next (carefulness).

> *Flash forward and we're takin' on the world together*
> *And there's a drawer of my things at your place*

The 'flash forward' that's resolutely part of the Swift brand by this point – a deliberate self-conscious reference to the filmic setting that frames the storytelling. The domestic touch of 'drawer of my things' – vague enough to be nondescript, specific enough to be redolent. It's a trope that appears elsewhere in her songs – the personal effects which are like talismans of a person's being, that abstract cement for a kind of intimacy. See also 'my old scarf from that very first week' of 'All Too Well' (*Red*, 2012).

We're also still in the familial realm of country. The couple's parents and their mistakes are mentioned. That sort of intimacy, where two families know each other well, is the kind of thing that only comes from profoundly intertwined couples and people getting together in the same hometown. It's an appeal again to that very Christian, normative small-town vision that's very 'early Swift' – and the later invocations of cities, starting with *Red*, that mark the transition from town to city, young to old Swift.

The other characteristic that marks this as 'early Taylor Swift' is the self-doubt; while earlier narratives are more definitive, that narrators are more likely to express the nerves and self-effacement of being a young woman:

> *Braced myself for the goodbye*
> *'Cause that's all I've ever known*

The frailty of the established character who struggles to expose herself is self-conscious enough to recognise that; but happily she's taken by surprise in the next line, where the antagonist expresses his love. It's a denouement, of sorts, but it's not a shocker. Swift may have a reputation, already, as a songwriter of heartbreak and heartache but here she's projected her own failure only to have it thwarted.

'Sparks Fly'
Opening with a brilliantly OTT metaphor: 'The way you move is like a full on rainstorm and I'm a house of cards'. There's something to be said for Swift occupying a kind of cultural space also occupied by emo and some TV (*Dawson's Creek*, *One Tree Hill*) – all emotions overloaded, all metaphors taken to extremes. It's not so much that she *is* emo in a musical sense (certainly here we're still in new country territory) but the sense of being *extra* (a very terminally-online-millennial term) marks it as belonging to a time and a place. It's not enough for the antagonist to be a 'full on rainstorm' (that's rainstorm + *intensifier*) and Swift to be something delicate and small; she is, in this metaphor, something dramatically fragile even under the best conditions.

The arrangement here is, on the one hand, fairly slight – a standard band setup of guitars, drums, bass and an infrequent fiddle. But the *sound* is pretty massive in the mid-range – Swift's vocals double tracked and processed into a big thick band that's almost overwhelming on headphones but punctuates car radios and imperfect listening conditions. The chorus loses a little diction (especially relative to later Swift) to that processing; the chorus line 'get me with those green eyes' is not entirely clear. Again, great for blasting on the radio, less directed towards home listening.

Despite the strongly OTT nature of the lyrics, there's also a sense that some carefully extended metaphors are at play here -the chorus motif of 'I see sparks fly whenever you smile' is subtly referenced with the bridge's 'I run my fingers through your hair and watch the lights go wild' – it's striking that a fairly common figure of 'sparks flying' – electricity in overload as a metaphor for strong affection (or lust) is repeated here in a minor form. 'Watch the lights go wild' – Swift is not deriving pleasure from the physical affection directly but rather in terms of amusing herself with the overloaded electricity metaphor; it does a lot of the work of reifying the combustible state.

'Back to December'

One of country music's greatest conceits is the 'Dear John' song. There's a Hank Williams song called 'Dear John', there's a song on this record called 'Dear John'. There's a strong tradition of the 'this song is the listener intruding on a letter'. One of my favourites in this mode is 'whiskey lullaby' – (Brad Paisley ft Alison Krauss) about two star-crossed lovers drinking themselves to death (seriously, it's a banger, go check it out).

This isn't quite a 'Dear John' but it has the same sense of 'intruding on an intimate moment'.

> *How's life? Tell me, how's your family?*

The verse this is from moves from reportage – plain descriptions of asinine descriptions of family and work – to a reflection on the conversation to a more abstracted detail, the antagonist's guard being up (that is, being reserved in the conversation); it's a rapid acceleration from asinine detail to observing mild hostility. Suddenly, in the ellipses between the words, we've constructed a whole narrative. This is important because, as Swift's career progresses, there's more of the song-story details are elided.

A few wee effects here – 'how's life? Tell me...' has a trochee-iamb inversion, a bit of alliteration. This is building tension sonically around ostensibly asinine detail; and if one thing's true of country as a form, and Swift's writing, it's that small details are leveraged to build intimate detail – with the art being in building enough detail to be evocative but not so much as to be specific.

> *So, this is me swallowing my pride*
> *Standing in front of you saying, 'I'm sorry for that night'*

The big stringy chorus sits on a stuttering, tribrachal stress – 'This is me / Swa-lo-wing', 'Stan-ding in / front of you'; later, more alliterative short-long ('TURNS out FREEDOM ain't NOTHING but MISSING you'); each line subtly pulling at a different rhythmic, poetic effect to press the dramatic tension; the terminal line about making it all right is pacific by comparison; all the volatility and drama in the description contrasted with the comparatively banal restitution, the return.

The switching perspectives of the verse are allayed temporarily in favour of the conversational-confessional mode – it's directed to the interlocuter but really it's a confession for the listener; no direct admission of guilt but the ghost-outline of a night for which the narrator must apologise.

We also get the slightest hint of generational form as well – there's a 'very millennial' conjunction 'so' at the beginning; a particular function that's very particular to that generation, where it acquires a kind of ironic use. Where typical usage is asinine, phatic – think 'so, how are you?' – the millennial usage is more alluding to a banal statement but subverting that with a follow-up that's profoundly personal. It's an effect that's moderately humorous, as if to protect or misdirect. 'So…' is connoting a moderate embarrassment at the heavy statement to follow; that kind of padding or subversive effect misdirecting from direct speech.

Later on in the song, we get some fully dramatic vim – the bridge is one-line-too-many, extended with:

> *So, if the chain is on your door, I understand*

It's a magical effect, something like a 'one more thing' but that isn't so much a denouement as it is self-abasement; the final prod at self-doubt before the last confession of 'I go back to December all the time'.

'Speak Now'

One of the imperatives of writing songs as a teenager is that you're allowed to be snotty and petty. By and large, Swift is somewhere between teenage and wistful; sometimes occupying both axes (in her earlier period, at least). Occasionally her storytelling eye turns towards something more traditionally teenage, unhewn.

'Speak Now' is a lovely daydream about the kind of dramatic things that teenagers are into – big romantic and hugely disruptive gestures. Lines here like '…her snotty little family all dressed in pastel' – those long double syllable words that can be spat and hissed out (snot-ty, dressed, pas-tel). Elsewhere the kind of absurd similes that might strike a teenager as profoundly uncool:

> *'she is yelling at a bridesmaid*
> *...*
> */ Wearing a gown shaped like a pastry*

Who wants to look like a pastry, am I right?

The fantasy here is of telling the man that he's marrying the wrong girl, in the church, during the ceremony. It's the stuff of countless teen dramas and it's also very much the stuff of Swift songs. Speaking broadly, one of the oddities of reading Swift in *purely* autobiographical terms misses the fact that there's a lot of her work which is absolutely fantastical storytelling.

'Dear John'
'Dear John' being the perfect title for a country song, this might well be Swift's country period high point. There's a notion that follows this that Swift may well be moderating her diction with a view to appealing to country audiences. There's a notion in linguistics of the 'flap t' in words like 'water' where the 't' sounds more like a 'd' sound; in International Phonetic Alphabet (IPA) terms, a word like 'water' is pronounced like /ˈwɑːdɚ/. In this song, we have the word 'traitor' pronounced like 'trader' – where standard US English says /ˈtɹeɪtɚ/, many accents pronounce it like /ˈtɹeɪdɚ/; if the IPA is difficult to read, just know that the flap t that's on show here tends to be associated with more Southern US accents – that is, the main demographic of country music.

That pronunciation is not typical for Swift – I'm not able to mark another song where a flap t is used. This isn't to say it should be regarded as suspect or an affectation – Swift was born and bred in West Reading, Pennsylvania, I was born in North Somerset, England, so she's got a lot more claim to that accent or expertise thereon than I do. But it is to say that it strongly connotes this as *appealing* to those accent groups that use a flap t.

Pronunciation aside, the song is a masterpiece of what you might call country inversions – couplets which contradict each other by extending metaphors, witty aphorisms that verge on malapropisms but never so far as to be gaudy (depending on taste, of course).

> *Long were the nights when*
> *My days once revolved around you*

Enjambment here to denote the volta night:day. A mess of conversational syntax – typically such a sentence would go 'when my days revolved around you, the nights were long'; despite being ostensibly a simple line we've got three diversions from standard clausal structure – 'long ... nights (1) / days (2), once (3), (2) revolved…'. It's the kind of poetic profundity that's alluded to in pop music but rarely met; that it's done so effortlessly as to be easily missed as merely an opening couplet is remarkable.

> *… I lived in your chess game*
> *But you changed the rules everyday*

This is still in the realm of metaphors but the rough idea with the volta 'chess game: changed … rules' is that of gaslighting; changing the dynamics so as to bully a person into not trusting the commonplace sureties that we rely on for our sanity. Chess here is quite a *particular* metaphor – so highly associated with intellectualism and freighted with such connotations. The metaphor here is again eking out an outline of gaslighting – chess is a game of (more or less) fixed and immutable rules, it's also notorious for the non-homogenous nature of its operational schema. Or in simpler terms – each piece moves in a different way. It is not the archetype of a 'complex' game (one might look to something like Mao for that) but it suffices to insinuate it; and principally, the game would be made substantially harder if the rules were to change every day. It's something of a *tortured* metaphor.

These are potentially what we might call Swift being *extra*; but it suffices to say that the overloaded metaphors here are less indicative of dramatic overdetermination and more of the state of extreme anxiety and tumult.

'Mean'

More in the line of Swift's precociousness, 'Mean' is a meditation on an intergenerational relationship.

One of the common tropes to Swift's music is a sense of *place*. More on this in the tropology (in the section 'Love's architecture') but at this point in her writing there's a sense of tension between 'hometown' living and city living; by the time of *1989*, with its opener 'welcome to New York', the emphasis has shifted almost entirely to city-based. For *Speak Now*, the city is seen from a distance – in 'Mine', earlier on in the album, it was viewing the '…city lights on the water'; here it's a promise that 'Someday I'll be living in a big 'ole city / and all you're ever gonna be is mean'.

'Mean' is another track that dotes on precocity; the younger woman talking to the manipulative, presumably older man – while the story is primarily of the gaslighting man – 'You, picking on the weaker man' there's a precocious abstraction from the situation with into psychoanalytical terms:

> *Somebody made you cold*
> *But the cycle ends right now*

Which is alluding to the kinds of abstractions familiar to anyone who's read psychology from Freud onwards – abusive cycles of maladaptive behaviour. This in itself isn't remarkable but given that Swift was 21 when this was released – and therefore only just 'not-a-teenager' when writing it – there's a sense that those acute reflections on an abusive relationship aren't typically expressed by younger women. That isn't by any means to suggest that young women are *incapable* of those reflections – far from it – but rather that it's atypical for them to express it in song, in pop music.

Further in this preciousness – typically in break-up songs, songs of anger, there isn't anything as explicit as 'Someday, I'll be big enough so you can't hit me' – usually the hurt is euphemous or wrapped in metaphors. It may well be in this case that 'hit' is a metaphor for hurtful behaviours; but it's also apparent that this could be a simple confession of physical abuse. The kind of candour and honesty that's rare, not least to pop music for teenagers (ish).

Elsewhere this violence is wrapped in more euphemistic, nursery rhyme allusions: 'Well, you can take me down / With just one single blow' (as in three little pigs). It's far more discrete and far more typical of pop songs, no matter the inspiration for the lyrics.

While the tune carries itself with a cheerful self-affirmation, there's also a sense of Swift's self-deprecation. Later on in her lyrics she's substantially less likely to be self-deprecating (until perhaps *Midnights*) but for this time we still have the signs of a less mature woman (albeit a very mature lyricist), talking about having flaws pointed out in a paternalistic way.

In terms of 'hell hath no fury', this might be one of Swift's finer takedowns. With the self-affirmative chorus, and the exposition of abuse, there's a bridge which is perfectly acidic in its promise of future revenge.

This is the sort of reputation that Swift has in the public eye, frequently – that of the take-down song. I'm not convinced that the songs *purely* function as takedowns but 'Mean' is probably the most pure form of that; a song dedicated exclusively to telling someone that his solitary remarkable characteristic is being mean.

'The Story of Us'
The consistent tension in talking about Swift's writing is that there's so much which invites comment on Swift's life in itself. That 'inviting' potentially obscures that many of the themes and patterns in her writing are not so much confessions as they are a writerly voice – or put another way, just telling the story of one's life is less compelling than being an effective songwriter.

Earlier on in this album, we had 'Sparks Fly'; it's not outrageous therefore to draw a line between that song and 'The Story of Us' saying: '…we met and the sparks flew instantly'. It's not so much that they both may describe the same IRL relationship but that they are built around similar stories.

The stronger theme here is a kind of meta-narrative about relationships following romantic narratives (in the literary sense): '...the story of us looks a lot like a tragedy now'. Also, in keeping with the excessive, full-blooded and near-overwrought metaphors of teenage romance: 'The battle's in your hands now'. We also get 'next chapter' between verses and an annunciatory 'the end' at the end.

These excessive metaphors have a counterpoint in the tautly bound but impotent exchanges:

> *Now, I'm standing alone in a crowded room*

This figure is self-repeating and oxymoronic, the perfect counter to the very teenage, very emo 'I'm dying to know / is it killing you'. Elsewhere a piquant and delicate description of the kind of failed distractions a young woman would do when caught in an awkward situation – 'See me nervously pulling at my clothes'. As ever it is shot through with Swift's capacity for evocative imagery to carefully but loosely outline a situation without creating so much context as to lose its capacity to be evocative.

> *This is looking like a contest*
> *Of who can act like they care less*

We get the sense that the narrator is caught in a tense impasse with someone whose principles are at odds with their desire. This is close to a very typical evocation of heterosexual (or more inclusively, heteronormative) relationships where one party is more cerebral than the other, which plays out as an odd war of attrition, heart (which is body, blood, physicality) versus mind (the abstract, unembodied).

'Never Grow Up'
And once more in the category of 'precocious', which may well be the overriding theme of this album. 'Never Grow Up' is a song from the perspective of someone offering advice to a younger person, as written by someone who was 19/20 when they wrote it.

While that might sound like condescension, I mean it more in the sense that it's a very *particular* generation gap that's being broached here – if Swift is 19/20 at the time of writing, the subject of the address is described as being 14. Typically an older person addressing a younger person in a song will do so from a more severe vantage. Here the age gap is only a few years *but* they're a tumultuous few years, filled with hormones and puberty and all the mess that entails. So the sense is that of a late teenager advising on all the *raw* stuff of the preceding years.

> *You're in the car on the way to the movies*
> *And you're mortified your mom's dropping you off*

It's more of the quaint and insightful observations of small interpersonal details that Swift excels at. And key here is how those memories are still red-hot when a person's 19 – as an older adult, my memories of being 14 are of being awkward and weird and not having found myself – all abstract qualities. Swift's exposition here is one of those memories that would tend to be plastered over in our own memories later – that of being deeply embarrassed by our parents. The stultifying state of being largely powerless: needing to be driven everywhere by parents, not having individual space, a burgeoning personality which is independent of school/family… Its rawness is palpable and recent for Swift.

The chorus dwells on the line 'don't you ever grow up' but it later becomes clear that Swift is addressing herself. 'Never Grow Up' has a really peculiar turn in it – during the bridge, just after an assertion about memorising details there's the sudden mood switch to 'I just realized everything I have is someday gonna be gone'. The whole song to this point has been whimsical observations directed to a younger person, but the tone dramatically switched with the existential crisis. That extravagant volte-face is inviting insofar as it's atypical, charming insofar as it's excessive.

> *So here I am in my new apartment*
> *In a big city, they just dropped me off*
> *…*
> *I wish I'd never grown up*

And that volte-face also paints the preceding in a very different light; it's a dramatic switch into existential mode to illustrate that the song is self-directed, the impossibility of talking to oneself. We (once again) get the 'new city' narrative and the anxiety of 'I wish I'd never grown up' – the juvenile warnings now revealed less to be precocious advice and more a sense of relativising anxieties from two sides of teenhood. The 'don't you ever grow up' is rendered less cutesy affectionate and more wishing away current anxieties.

'Enchanted'

An atypical structure to this tune – two verses in a row before the chorus proper, and a rare guitar solo. There's a slight acceleration in syllabic form as well – where the first verse is straight one-syllable-per-beat – 'there I was again to-night' – the second compresses more syllables into the same space – 'your eyes whisp-ered 'have we met?'' – 'whispered' sounding more like 'whisperd'. This is all delivered in a lower, calmer tone; by the time of the third verse, the second half of the stanza is in a higher tone, more agitated to meet the line 'Now I'm pacing back and forth' – music rising to meet the agitation of the lyrics.

By the third verse, the key line 'it was enchanting to meet you' is now shot through with desperation. The chorus circles around 'this night is flawless / don't you let it go' and it's never clear whether Swift does hook up with the guy from the sparkling night.

The broad narrative in Swift's career at this point is that she's breaking away from country, little by little – this is more apparent on this album's successor, *Red*. But here we still have a wee touch of less 'formal' US English – 'Please don't have somebody waiting on you' rather than 'waiting *for* you'.

The story here is a crystalline moment – the narrator doting on meeting someone and having a perfect night but she will 'spend forever wondering if you knew' (that she fell in love with him). The compelling part here, by comparison to something like 'Love Story' (*Fearless*) is that it's not a (ahem) love story, it's a precise occupation of the running thoughts after meeting someone and having a romantic connection. Storytelling as emotional occupation rather than conclusive narratives.

'Better Than Revenge'

One of the primary issues with country music, for those of us more inclined towards leftist perspectives, is that it's a broad church which is accommodating of conservative perspectives. Perhaps doubly so from the British perspective, where guns and (say) libertarian fiscal policies are substantially less popular. That isn't to say that Toby Keith is singing explicitly about the dynamics of Laffer curves (just imagine, though...) but just that one stumbling block for British people is that there's a popular music that is frequently conservative (or, more equitably, is conservative in a specifically American way).

'Better Than Revenge' is anomalous for Swift insofar as it's expressing a perspective that falls short of being *feminist*. Swift is rarely expressly political (perhaps until 'you need to calm down' in 2019); Swift isn't the most hardcore feminist of writers but it's atypical for her to express anti-woman perspectives.

> *She's better known for the things that she does*
> *On the mattress*

It's not the most grievous of anti-woman crimes but it's also not that cool; the idea that a woman should be judged according to her sexual proclivities (or even the assumption of her sexual proclivities) is pretty poorly regarded in feminist thought. As a sidenote, there's a song by Lana Del Rey on *Ultraviolence* (2014) called 'Fucked My Way Up to the Top' – taking ownership of precisely that slut-shaming narrative, and audaciously so.

It's a shame that this is the chorus to this song because otherwise it's more on the acceptable side; a simple story of the woman who stole the man and how there's nothing Swift does 'better than revenge'. While Swift has expressed dismay at relationships elsewhere in lyric, it's not typically blamed on an individual. But also, by way of clemency, it's again worth noting that Swift is still only just an adult at this point and it's gratifying that she is able to express the anxieties of late teenhood in song, even when those anxieties are more conservatively expressed.

It's a shame in another sense because it's otherwise a witty and whippy song – 'I think her ever-present frown is a little troubling / And she thinks I'm psycho 'cause I like to rhyme her name with things', intimating that kind of state of being which is deeply unsettling to some people, a kind of irreverent playfulness which disregards social norms (and also very common to neurodivergent people).

> *Oh, they didn't teach you that in prep school so it's up to me*
> *But no amount of vintage dresses gives you dignity*

Here we get another of Swift's more acutely acidic put-downs – plus the euphony in the near rhyming pair vin-tage: dign-ity rings the insult through perfectly. There's a degree of – perhaps self-deprecating – irony here. The dig about 'prep school' is complicated by the fact that Swift went to a Montessori school (a kind of specialist private school) and Wyndcroft private school in her early education; given her relative wealth, the 'prep school' dig is perhaps to be read in the context of exaggerated storytelling rather than direct autobiography.

'Innocent'

Another song with the dialogue between a narrator and older person and a degree of precociousness on Swift's part. The second chorus tells us the antagonist is 32; the rest of the song strikes a pacific, conciliatory tone: 'Who you are is not where you've been'.

In keeping with country's idea of subverted idiom, we have a lovely update on the old 'salad days' to become 'lunchbox days'. The original idiom of 'salad days', typically cited to Shakespeare's *Antony and Cleopatra* – '…my salad days

/ when I was green in judgment…' – the salad:green pairing is what invests the idiom with 'youthfulness' (green typically meaning youthful or immature, based on some plants being green before being ripe). The lunchbox days replaces the colour-time pairing with a social context indicator – 'lunchbox', an item most associated with school. It's a timely update to an idiom that, in losing its complement, 'when I was green', also loses the intuitive *sense* of what it means.

> *Lost your balance on a tightrope*
> *Lost your mind trying to get it back*

There's a kind of intensive amphiboly here – if the two lines are read as separate clauses, then the object of the second is 'mind' (i.e. 'lost your mind trying to get your mind back'); if they are contiguous then the object of the second is 'balance'. Interpreting doesn't require that either be 'correct' and both interpretations suffice to indicate the metaphor is of dissociation, infelicitous mental states.

The chorus uses the evergreen 'it's alright', a pop standard of louche reassurance. Most charming, though, we describe 'your string of lights is still bright to me' – conjuring images of dimmed fairy lights or streetlamps. It's also reminiscent of a lyric by Manchester stalwart punk band the Fall: 'The mad kid had 4 lights, the average is 2.5 lights / The mediocre has 2 lights, the sign of genius is three lights' in which we learn of a lighting-intelligence correspondence. I'd be surprised if Swift is alluding to Mark E. Smith here.

This song pivots around a sense of sympathy for a 32-year-old 'still growing up now'. It's perhaps odd for a 19-year-old to sympathise over such an age gap – certainly at the age of 19 I wouldn't have written a song to reassure someone. And perhaps it also speaks to gender roles – men are typically less emotionally stable for longer than women. Asserting that a person is still growing up may come across as prodigiously arrogant from someone substantially younger, but it's also *intuitively correct* and placatory for the anxieties that follow the early 30s.

The phrase 'old soul' can carry connotations of pre-maturity – younger people who've spent time around adults such that they miss out on the innocence of their (ahem) salad days. That may well apply to Swift here as author – it's a kind of precocious wistfulness to sympathise, or emotionally support, someone substantially older.

'Haunted'

> *You and I walk a fragile line*

Lines are a relatively common image for Swift. Lines are crossed (as in contravention of rules), lines are read between (as in relationship subtext) –

but this image of walking fragile lines only appears once more that I'm aware of, in 'exile' (*folklore*): 'We always walked a very thin line'. It's interesting to me insofar as the use in 'exile' is far more story-led, given that two protagonists are walking that line, inclined to comment on its precarity; here it's more indicative of self-doubt on the narrator's part.

Here the figure is less focused on the precarity per se so much as the observations of the end of a relationship: 'Something's made your eyes go cold'. Ultimately another break-up song but rather than observing the after effects, it's another instance of being haunted (see 'The monsters turned out to just be truths', in tropology).

> *Can't breathe whenever you're gone*
> *I can't go back, I'm haunted*

'Haunted' here describes the moment of one person signing out of a relationship, emotionally, before the other – rather than a presence/non-presence (personal effects carrying a person's presence, eerily familiar places, etc.) it's a haunting invested with being in limbo; between lives and paralysed at the moment of collapse.

This song's bridge, in turn:

> *I know, I know*
> *I just know*
> *You're not gone*
> *You can't be gone, no*

Is a sense of denial but also an uncharacteristic repetition; repeating phrases, especially thrice in two lines, is atypical. The repetition invests the line with a degree of desperation, each repetition more pathetic – it's not a technique Swift uses frequently and it's more effective for being rare.

'Last Kiss'
And again in 'Last Kiss' we see the early-Swift notion of self-doubt and lack of confidence – the plainly deflative 'I don't know / how to be something you miss'. It's at once struck with the simplicity and frustration of a younger person as much as it is the songwriter's flair for the pithy and unsettling line. We've also got the haunting in the sense of clothes bearing a person's presence, as if studying the clothes will reveal the secrets of how to be missed by a person.

Sly shot of Swift with her pals in HAIM taken by my pal Helen. Don't they all look lovely? (*Photo by Helen Boobis*)

Isabelle Crisp's portrait bringing out the personality in glam Swift – the colours and contrast and the glimmering spark in Swift's eye. (*Artwork by Isabelle Crisp*)

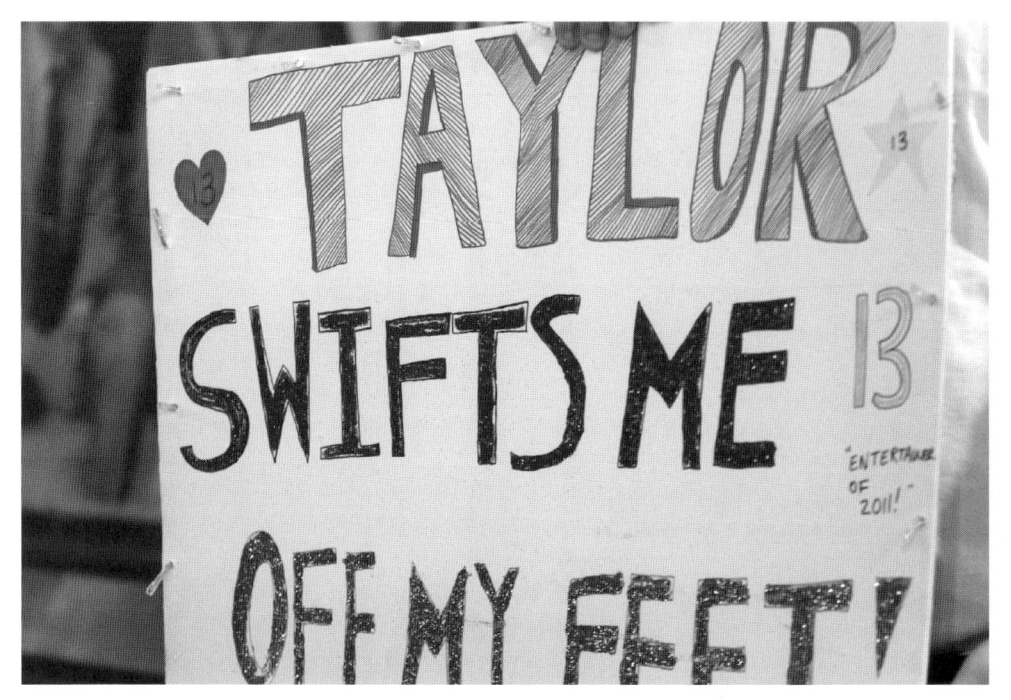

The devotion of Swift's fans is adorable – there's at least another book this size to be written about the fandom and how that community organises and talks about itself. (*Wikimedia Commons*)

Thirteen is a lucky number for Swift and her fandom – Swifties have single-handedly revived the friendship bracelet industry. (*Wikimedia Commons*)

Early Swift – note the very country personalised guitar, the very country perfect blonde hair and the very country flashy-but-modest outfit. (*Wikimedia Commons*)

Surf's up, for some reason – while Swift is very much in control over the narrative of her career now, there's plenty of faintly ridiculous photoshoots in the archives. (*Wikimedia Commons*)

Attention to performance-detail in full force – Swift's mic and guitar with matching designs. (*Wikimedia Commons*)

Swift in motion – a magical shot where the outfit and hair seems in motion but Swift's face captured as if in stasis. A great example of live photography. (*Wikimedia Commons*)

Nothing says fabulous like lamé, darling. Making the whole place shimmer (*Wikimedia Commons*)

The Swift brand in action – make-up emphasising lips and complementing the dress; subtle and decorous, photogenically sitting plum in the offhand shot. (*Wikimedia Commons*)

The RED tour and its production values – personalised gear, big shiny signs and a consistent branded typeface for all Swift-related text. (*Wikimedia Commons*)

The rock look, with the Jonny Marr signature guitar. Note the guitar hung low enough that the high-waisted belt is visible. In another context, that'd be a punk rock strap height. (*Wikimedia Commons*)

Swift bobbing atop a sea of press – only 22 and already swamped by press and entourage. (*Wikimedia Commons*)

Swift's 2023/4 tour breaking box office records for sales and scale, a million blinking mobiles capturing the moment. (*Wikimedia Commons*)

The arthouse shot – capturing the blurred hair of Swift in motion, recognisable even so. (*Wikimedia Commons*)

There's another book to be written about Swift's outfits – this watery, flowing beauty from the Eras tour, set against the blinking wash of audience mobiles. (*Wikimedia Commons*)

Possibly all of Swift's style over the years in one picture – asymmetrically sexy and modest, glimmering yet sheer. (*Wikimedia Commons*)

The extent of Swift's recognition by the music industry is enormous – here we see her overwhelmed by MTV Music Video Awards. (*Wikimedia Commons*)

There's something really fun about the unfortunately-timed shots – here Swift looking faintly silly but eminently fun. (*Wikimedia Commons*)

> *How you'd kiss me when I was in the middle of saying something*
> *There's not a day I don't miss those rude interruptions*
> ...
> *And I'll keep up with our old friends just to ask them how you are*

Two lines that are alternative sides of the end-of-relationship pathos: the first in the sense of missing faintly obnoxious behaviour; the second in terms of exhibiting pitiable behaviour to cling to the dying remnants of the social structures which inform and define intimate relationships. Ultimately the song is occupying the inescapable *absences* which define the aftermath of an intimate relationship.

'Long Live'

A euphoric song of self-affirmation – and given the general sense of juvenile self-doubt from this record, it's a welcome close to the record. It's also run through with mythic allusions – the fairy tale-ing of its own narrative:

> *You held your head like a hero on a history book page*
> *We are the kings and the queens*
> *You traded your baseball cap for a crown*

Worth noting, of course, that kings and queens are a particular imago for people in the US – unlike Europeans, monarchism is the stuff of ancient history and faraway lands. Sometimes a matter of satire and ridicule – understandable, given the actions of 1776 and its subsequent celebration every 4 July. The 'hero [of the] history book page' and the 'kingdom lights' are straight out of mythicism, and of course all the 'magic we made' likewise. The image is still that of normal (ahem) Janes and Joes who are magically transformed – with the exotic shift from baseball cap to crown.

It's an exaggeration of a moment, and one that is pushing towards the work of commemoration:

> *If you have children some day*
> *When they point to the pictures*
> *Please tell 'em my name*

Ultimately this is a song of using the excess of mythicisation and the realm of magic to embody the commemoration of a specific time of the life; and while it's excessive, it's also shot through with a degree of modesty – 'please tell 'em my name', a polite and simple request that belies the self-aggrandisement of the 'kings and queens'. If it is a close on Swift's juvenile work, it's a charming one.

Red

Red is still strongly informed by country but it's also the point at which more regular listeners start getting on board. The vibe is closer to bratty, brash, pop for teenagers but there's the mature (if not measured) writing of someone who's well-immersed in her own form. By now she's gotten to know the radio banger intimately and is writing the textbook songs for younger women to shout on girls' nights out.

For all the bangers, there's still a sense of her being a serious writer, especially of break-up tunes. It's steadily becoming clear that regardless of the arrangement, Swift's lyrical voice can work in multiple modes. What perhaps the public at large couldn't have known at this point was how tenacious she is in her capacity to write songs for the top of the charts – she's not just the country-girl-gone-pop.

'State of Grace'

Big epic drums, drawn out guitar notes; by contrast to *Speak Now* this is a very U2 opening. It's an arrangement that's a lot less country, a lot more stadium.

> *We fall in love 'til it hurts or bleeds*

This is the first instance of Swift using 'bleeds' – prior to this point the dramaticism has been less vivid, visceral; not to say that bodily metaphors are indicative of maturity but there's a distinct sense, with *Red* in general, that the *import* of the heartbreak is greater, and the imperatives get more severe.

> *We are alone, just you and me*
> *Up in your room and our slates are clean*
> *Just twin fire signs, four blue eyes*

Two things to note here – this is an odd instance in the Swift corpus of extending a syllable to fit a rhyme – the you of 'just you' is subtly extended to meet the metre of the line. Elsewhere in pop it's not atypical – there's a whole history of melisma in song form – but it's atypical for Swift, who is usually taut and clean as possible.

Second thing is that this 'twin fire signs' motif appears twice on this record (kind of) – it's also on the long version of 'All Too Well', though that wasn't released until the time of the re-recorded version. It's in keeping with a general approach in Swift's music of inviting interpretation of how the songs relate to Swift's personal life (which the Swifties diligently and obsessively do) by means of repetition of thematic material. At this point, Swift is still often drawing heavily from her personal life – or put another way, is hiding specific details less keenly.

The lyric sheet states the line as '...twin fire signs, four blue eyes' but there's an amphibolous reading of 'twin first signs FOR blue eyes' – less a passive description of astrological identity, more a kind of fire-as-warning 'for blue eyes' (assumed to be the protagonist).

> *We learn to live with the pain*
> *Mosaic broken hearts*
> *But this love is brave and wild*

Mosaic here is a lovely extension to the 'broken' heart metaphor (so commonplace it's probably not even a metaphor by this point) – putting detail and materiality to that broken-ness such that the integrity of the heart is formed by its restitution as mosaic; it makes sense that the erratic constitution of mosaic is paired with '...this love is brave and wild'.

The final chorus is perhaps Swift's most ecstatic to date – open-mouth near-shouting at the top of the song's register, big open notes for 'never / be the same'.

'Red'

While the opening features a banjo arpeggio, this is still listing closer to rock territory; the driving bass drum articulating the pulse is indicative – typically country drums are more discreet, incidental.

In which we learn through a series of 'loving him is like...' lines of a relationship which is abruptly ended; there's extensive alliteration in the line: '...flying through the free fall'.

It's worth noting these two types of 'f' sound – the strong 'f' of 'flying' and the weaker 'f' of 'through'. In IPA terms, this is transcribed as /flaɪ.ɪŋ/ (flying) and /θɹuː/ (through) – the two sounds produced in a neighbouring part of the mouth: f is a labio-dental fricative (that is, friction created by vibrating air through the bottom lip through the teeth), θ is a dental fricative (vibrated from the teeth). Analysing Swift through IPA would also be exhausting but here it's useful to emphasise the weak/strong 'f' sound which allows the alliteration to fall cleanly without being a struggle to say; the weaker /θ/ sound also allows the sonic rhythm to shift the line from a staccato, stabbing sound to a more emphatic strong-weak-strong-strong pattern which, nevertheless, maintains the 'f-' sound-shape.

The chorus is fascinating in terms of the development we're witnessing in Swift's songwriting:

> *Losing him was blue ...*
> *Missing him was dark gray*
> *Forgetting him was like trying to know somebody you've never met*
> *But loving him was red*

Colours threading through each line. First, blue – a pop lyric standard to intimate sadness. Grey, strongly associated with 'dull'. So far, so standard. But it's the next two lines that really jump out. It's difficult to mentally parse how *forgetting* – the process of losing information – can be like 'trying to know somebody you've never met' – the *absence* of information. Not so much that the metaphor is unclear but rather than an unclear metaphor is used with a degree of irony to explain the un-explainable. Parsed another way – forgetting him was impossible (later we get 'moving on from him is impossible'). The three negatives (losing him – blue; missing him – dark grey; forgetting him – impossible) are implicitly contradicted by the 'but...' however, there's no detail given to what this contradiction is – we merely get 'red'. Red isn't strongly associated with a particular mood; sometimes 'red' is associated with 'red mist', i.e. anger, but the 'but' implies it's *not* a negative association.

Put in other terms, the transition of the chorus is: well-known metaphors around colours, an impossible metaphor for an impossible task, and a highly abstracted and almost obstructively simple 'red'. I've argued in 'Taylor and colour' about the function colours have in her lyrics – but for now I'll just say that it's an astonishing lyric, and one that refuses to cleanly submit to interpretation without quite evoking obstinacy on the part of the songwriter.

It's worth saying as well that the arrangement for 'Red' gets very fulsome – there's a raft of strings, background synths, driving guitars, banjos – later Swift tends towards a less massive arrangement – less 'all the instruments' and more 'accentuated carefully'. So in some senses the way in which Red might be considered Swift's first 'pop' record are that its arrangement is very stadium; as her confidence grows with writing for a non-country audience, so too do her arrangements shrink.

'Treacherous'
There's a lot in mix that's focusing on one note, not quite a drone but certainly there.

> *Put your lips close to mine*
> *As long as they don't touch*
> *Out of focus, eye to eye*
> *'Til the gravity's too much*

It's a piece about romantic tensions; implicitly an illicit affair wrought with the should-we, shouldn't-we. Swift's isolation isn't so much the state as the kind of ephemeral arrangements that dictate behaviour – lips close to each other that don't touch... until gravity takes over. Lips of course don't tend to respond to gravity so the 'gravity' is a metaphor for love, or lust, drawing the people together.

The next line has what may be the first sighting of Swift's more obtuse lyrics:

> *And I'll do anything you say*
> *If you say it with your hands*

It's interesting in that it's unlikely to be about talking in sign language. How do we 'speak' with our hands otherwise? Body language; so the things said with the hands are likely a fidgety effect from a state of nervousness, or the touching of a person's body. This is ambiguous also insofar as there's a potential reading where 'say it with your hands' is a metaphor for mutual masturbation. It feels unlikely because Swift at this point is much more typically non-sexual – but with my adult ears on, I struggle to ignore that interpretation. More broadly it's an instance of sudden ambiguity nested within otherwise transparent metonymy, a disconcerting indistinct evocation among the sharp clarity. From the concrete to the abstracted.

It's a song that occupies those intimate and particular moments of confusion.

'I Knew You Were Trouble'
And here's one of the two songs that occupied radio and TV for much of late 2012; this is one of the triumvirate of songs – the others being 'We Are Never Ever Getting Back Together' and '22' – that cemented Swift within a popular consciousness that was less concerned about country music. There is, naturally, an imprecision in dictating what is 'Taylor Swift's country music' and what is 'Taylor Swift's pop music'; nevertheless, in terms of the kind of media that pushed Swift's music, these three are the ones that first most strongly reached outside of country music in general.

Uniquely for Swift, it also features elements of dubstep – an originally British underground dance music synthesising elements of British (or Jamaican-British) dance music such as grime, dub, drum 'n' bass (etc.). Dubstep, by 2012, had largely shifted from being the underground phenomenon of its early 2000s origins to being something the pop charts were aware of; this song's use of a dubstep wub (an onomatopoeic word to describe the bass sounds) is a fairly ersatz use of dubstep effects.

Whether or not this song is 'authentically' dubstep, though (and it's clearly not), the chorus's use of a dubstep wub also operates as a wedge between Swift and her reputation as being a country singer; it's a palpable decision within the arrangement to dissociate Swift from country music. There are plenty of moments in Swift's subsequent output which are strongly informed by country music, but no more will she be considered by the listening public to be 'purely' a country-pop singer.

And for all this talk of breaking with country norms, a lot of this is more about the arrangement; certainly the verse is only so far from being a country song – remove a few keyboards, put the acoustic guitar higher in the mix and it'd do fine in the country charts. The principal difference in terms of the song itself is that the chorus is relatively spare – a few emphatic 'oohs' and the word 'trouble' repeated. As with elsewhere in Swift's canon (e.g. 'Ready For It?', *reputation*), the spare chorus is bolstered by exciting production.

It's an interesting development in pop music in the last generation or so that the dense verse → spare chorus has become a significant trope. It has also allowed for choruses that are very international in reach – K-pop (Korean pop) act BLACKPINK have found a substantial international fanbase using it – it makes sense that a chorus that is simple and understandable is appealing. For my money the best example of this trope is in their 뚜두뚜두 which translates to 'ddu-du ddu-du du' – a simple nonsense sound emulating loud drums (or similar). And similarly for Swift, her international reach is afforded by shearing off some of the layers most associated with the US, and country music – as I argued in 'This is country music' – is surely one of the US's most insular and inward-looking cultures.

To return for a moment to the 'bolstered by exciting production' – it's important to emphasise that this isn't a country song with a spraytan pop production. There's lots of chopped and looped rhythmic parts that are mirror in the lyrics (e.g. 'You're drowning-ing-ing-ing-ing'). There's a very different notion of harmony to country music – the line 'And I heard you moved on from whispers on the street / a new notch in your belt is all I'll ever be' is punctuated in backing vocals on the fourth beat. This is a small effect but it's not common in country music, where backing vocal harmonies tend to be rhythmically similar to the lead vocal, typically in a consonant harmonic interval. If this is 'radically' different to the country period, it's due to a different but distinctly *integrated* arrangement.

For all that, though, the lyrics are very new country; a boy who was trouble on first sight. Critically 'And I heard you moved on from whispers on the street

/ A new notch in your belt is all I'll ever be' evokes the kind of small-town, everyone-knows-each-other's-business sentiment, as well as the pervasively moral ('So shame on me now') opprobrium which reflects the broadly conservative, broadly Christian genre of new country.

'All Too Well'

In 2021, Swift released a re-recorded version of *Red*: *Red (Taylor's Version)*, released by Republic Records. By and large, it's not substantially different to the earlier Big Machine version. It does feature different songs to the original release but I've decided not to review the re-recorded albums as if they were substantially distinct – treating them more as deluxe versions of the canonical albums rather than new material. However, there's one song where that is a problem – for *Red (Taylor's Version)* there's a new (or as-new, given that it's the version of the lyrics that were cut from the original album), longer version called 'All Too Well (10 minute version)'. It nearly doubles the length of the original, which was already long at around five minutes.

So here I'm going to draw on *both* versions of the song. It seems that the new longer version has been a real hit with fans – at the time of writing there are a load of versions of it on YouTube – '...from the vault (lyric video)' (74 million views); '...live on Saturday Night Live' (19 m views); '...from the vault' (19 m views); '...(Sad Girl Autumn version)' (10 m views). There's also *All Too Well: The Short Film*, directed by Swift, with 83 m views. That is, different versions of the same song, which is a new (or as-new) song, have accrued some 205 million views in a year. That's a substantial amount for a re-recorded song from an album that's nearly a decade old.

Perhaps most striking about the two songs is the breadth of difference. There's only so much new content to the longer version but it entirely changes the tone of the piece. Let's quickly describe the shorter version.

'All Too Well (short version)'

The shorter version is a break-up song, detailing the sadness of a split. It's mostly one-sided and dealing with the narrator's side of things – 'And I might be okay, but I'm not fine at all'.

There's a lot of quaint relationship details that seem to suggest an equality between the two – or rather, there's nothing to suggest any age difference. Details about seeing old pictures, meeting the family and so on.

The apex of the song has Swift singing fully, open-throated, the music in full drama. The implication in the shorter version is that the antagonist is 'merely' intransigent and cruel. I say 'merely' because this intransigence is shitty enough but there's worse to come.

By the final verse, there's a kind of mollifying equivocation – the antagonist shares in the burden of the relationship's fallout. There's mention of how he keeps hold of the narrator's scarf as a kind of affectionate keepsake. And so the shape of the song is something like 'articulate protagonist's anger; antagonist's sorrow is equivocated'. At least, says the audience, he's also suffering a little.

This is a great song and notoriously one of Swift's fanbase's favourites. And in the spirit of shoddy Internet listicles by feckless linkfarm churn, what happened next will shock you…

'All Too Well (10 minute version)'
So the critical difference between the two versions, in short, is that in the first the antagonist is a bastard and it's just a bad break-up. In the longer version, the antagonist is fully a *total* bastard.

The two songs are fundamentally identical up until the end of the first stanza of verse three. So the cute details – leaving affects in each other's houses are equivalent. The picture of the antagonist is of someone who's marked equally by the relationship, who uses clothes of the narrator's to commemorate her.

And then the divergence kicks in.

First the scene is of a drive in which the narrator anticipates the antagonist will call it love, which he never does. The image then is that of a dissymmetry – a partner who is unwilling to admit that he loves his partner. It's not the most outrageous thing committed to song, but it is indicative of what's later shown to be an emotionally abusive, neglectful relationship.

With the next chorus we get an extreme dissymmetry – the narrator is kept 'like a secret' but the narrator keeps the antagonist 'like an oath'. The antagonist is keeping the narrator secret, which carries implications of shame and pity. Meanwhile the narrator is more strongly invested and more equitably invested in the relationship. In terms of commitment, one side is sorely lacking.

Within verse four, we get the picture of being in a 'new hell / every time you double-cross my mind'. The pun on double-cross neatly imbricates a typical usage, and marks that the relationship is not thought of kindly by the narrator. The real dirt follows:

> You said if we had been closer in age, maybe it would've been fine
> And that made me want to die

Age differences in relationships are murky territory when both parties are adults (and let's assume they are here) if only because it's very easy for someone who's early 20s or younger to still feel complimented by a substantially older man. No shade whatsoever on a younger person who falls into this but all shade in the world to exploitative older men. And even if that power dynamic is removed, it's beyond shitty to attribute the failing of a relationship on a property that neither party has any control over, i.e. their age.

Where by this point in the shorter 'All Too Well' we had a picture of a bad break-up, by this point we've got an image that's much closer to abusive, with a power dynamic that's profoundly unsavoury.

> *But then [my dad] watched me watch the front door all night, willin' you to come*
> *And he said, 'It's supposed to be fun turning twenty-one'*

And once again there's another nail in the 'antagonist is a total bastard' coffin here – what kind of a shit doesn't turn up to their partner's 21st birthday? It's not elaborated on but the image of an anxious just-21-year-old fidgeting and looking at the door, and the dad quietly and plainly expressing fury, is a powerful one.

Verse five then returns to the earlier version – the relationship now terminated. In verse six, the narrator refers to herself as a soldier who's 'returning half her weight'. It's a dual sense – on the one hand, it's someone returning from battle half the person they were, defeated and belittled. But also it carries the boxing sense, someone punching above their weight class, someone able to fight well with someone substantially heavier than them (or, in this metaphor, substantially older).

> *But all I felt was shame and you held my lifeless frame*

This line pushes, at least potentially, to an even darker territory – that image, of shame and a lifeless frame, suggest a person who's paralysed (lifeless) and afraid and shamed by what has happened. It's difficult *not* to think of this as describing the aftermath of being raped.

I don't want to pursue that because it's grisly enough without that interpretation but just to say that the options for interpreting the longer version of this song then range from 'absolute bastard' to worst bastard imaginable.

That this has become a fan favourite song is ultimately no surprise – despite its (in pop terms) extreme length (10 minutes, 13 seconds) it's a gorgeously told story and one that bears multiple listens. And it is, in another sense, a proper country song. It doesn't sound like it but you can sure as hell have a good old cry to it.

'22'

The second in the declaratively pop triumvirate of singles on *Red*. It might be the last time a Swift song could be described as 'precocious' – insofar as the narrator occupies a position of talking from the perspective of a 22-year-old.

As well as observing the existential state of the 22-year-old: 'We're happy, free, confused and lonely at the same time / It's miserable and magical oh yeah'. It's relatively atypical for a song that is ostensibly celebratory in that it occupies different perspectives at once – 'happy, free, confused and lonely' … 'miserable and magical…', positive alongside the negative. In that sense it matches a lot of millennial perspectives – a generation (at that time) who were young adults with all the liberation and exploration that entails but also with a broad fear of climate apocalypse and housing/job markets that are distinctly unfavourable for them. So any happiness is necessarily tinged with melancholy.

It's tempting to describe Swift as the troubadour of millennial contradictions but I think that would be unfair – Swift's subject matter rarely directly confronts existential conditions. Nevertheless, there's a lot to be said for her being *the* songwriter for that generation – their age, grew up in public.

There's a small irony in this song in that there's a passing allusion to Swift's cultural status in 2012; the second verse:

> *This place is too crowded*
> *Too many cool kids*

In the background a voice is saying 'Who is Taylor Swift anyway?' after the 'cool kids' line – Swift's music doesn't appeal to cool kids. This self-referentiality appears elsewhere on *Red* – 'We Are Never Ever Getting Back Together' has a reference to 'some indie record that's much cooler than mine'. It's ironic insofar as later on, perhaps starting with 2020's *folklore*, Swift's albums very much appeal to a more 'adult', more 'indie' fanbase (though those terms are mutable and porous in terms of who those fans are in reality). If those lines reflect an anxiety about Swift's self-perception then it's an anxiety that's resolved by the other side of her 20s.

It's a song that's made for girls' nights in (or out), a proper shout-out-loud chorus which states (as many pop songs have before) how to create the proper conditions for 'alright'-ness:

> *Everything will be alright if*
> *We just keep dancing like we're*
> *Twenty-two*

That 'like' does enough lifting to appeal outside of folk in their early 20s – a subtle sleight-of-lyric which allows for older people to feel included. Who doesn't want to dance like they're 22? I guess the same people who don't want to party like it's 1999.

'I Almost Do'

Giving the lie to the '*Red* is a pop record', here is a song that could easily fit on any of the first four. A kind of apology:

> *I bet you think I either moved on or hate you*
> *'Cause each time you reach out, there's no reply*
> *I bet it never, ever occurred to you*
> *That I can't say hello to you and risk another goodbye*

Hello… goodbye bookending each other in a phrase as antonyms but of course the 'goodbye' is invested with a lot more weight and import than is the 'hello' – this goodbye isn't the counterpart to a greeting but the goodbye of ending relationships. Neatly the counterpart to 'hello' is exploded, pregnant with very different romantic interpretations.

This song is a fun caprice insofar as *if* the letter-song ever arrives to its intended recipient then the principle of its construction – to describe the problems of being in touch – are moot. We are presumed to be privy to part of a relationship but this is really the private thoughts of one side, making it a very different observation. Perhaps not entirely dissimilar to the impossible descriptions in 'Red' earlier, it's the ironic presentation of the auteur, not the confession of the lover. And if that sounds too much like postmodern theory – it's a smart tune that's telling a one-sided story as if it were two-sided.

'We Are Never Ever Getting Back Together'

It's a song that starts off with an acoustic guitar but immediately switches to pop production, reversing the opening motif to form a loop that is the backbone of the verses. The verses are carefully constructed to dictate a memorable rhythm:

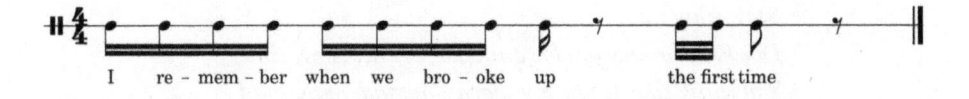

If you don't read music, then hopefully it's clear enough that the rhythm jumps along quickly and has a little gap. This rhythm is a juddering thing, ramming a lot of syllables into the first half and then stuttering a few more at the end. It's almost as if the rhythm is mimicking the speaking styles of an over-excited teenager – which is in line with the song in general.

The chorus repeats the motif 'We are never, ever, ever getting back together', which is very much encapsulating the sort of emphatic language used by younger people, especially younger people all hepped up on rampaging hormones. It's on the verge of mimicry – in the heat of the moment, younger people are less likely to reach for complex vocabulary (e.g. 'our reconstitution is inexorably damnéd') but are more likely to repeat a simple word for emphasis. A lot more people can sympathise with repeating 'ever, ever, ever' than my example. And conveniently for a song, repeating the same word does a good job of accentuating the rhythm, committing the song to people's memories.

A lot about this song is wickedly combative, sarcastic, and petty – 'I'm really gonna miss you picking fights'; 'And you would hide away and find your peace of mind / With some indie record that's much cooler than mine'. The last line ends up prophetic for the style that defines Swift's later work (especially *folklore*, *evermore*, *Midnights*). It's delivered in full-on sarcasm akimbo mode – far from Swift's usual cool delivery.

For a lot of people outside of country, this song, or 'I Knew You Were Trouble' from this record, were their first encounters with Swift. So it has all the trappings of pop music – highly produced, lots of oohs, a dynamic and memorable arrangement. It's got little ad libs after a few lines, just to ensure that the pop audience is not left without information for more than a second or two. And it's rightly a big pop hit – it's fun and silly and teenage. And it's very much a song that hits to the heart of teenage relationships, the strongly felt and committed things we say as teenagers that look like hyperbole or exaggeration when we look back as adults.

'Stay Stay Stay'
Ukuleles and jangly guitars abound here for a song that's distinctly cutesy. There's very little else in Swift's catalogue that's like it – it maintains Swift's general pattern of acute observations and paralysed moments in time, but they're rarely *cute*.

> *Stay, stay, stay*
> *I've been loving you for quite some time, time, time*
> *You think that it's funny when I'm mad, mad, mad*
> *But I think that it's best if we both stay, stay, stay, stay*

It's interesting that there's an instance of what seems like affectation here – the line 'Before you, I'd only dated self-indulgent takers / Who took all of their problems out on me' sits oddly relative to later Swift annunciation – 'on me' sounds more like 'awn me', that is, closer to a southern pronunciation. It's difficult to pin this down – while it may be that this is the last instance where Swift 'countryed up' her vocals, it's also the case that people's accents change as they get older and it's fairly predictable that woman in her early 20s who travels around a lot is likely to lose her Pennsylvania accent. Nevertheless, from hereon in Swift's songs, her diction and pronunciation are consistent and closer to pop pronunciations than the southern inflections of country.

'The Last Time' featuring Gary Lightbody

This is the first instance of a hocket-like piece – hocket being a kind of dialogical, call and response form; it's a duet with Gary Lightbody of Snow Patrol. Later on, we see the idea of the dialogical duet return in 'exile' (*folklore*) with Justin Vernon of Bon Iver.

This one, like 'exile', occupies the confusion of an indistinct relationship – two characters, two takes on the same event, the 'find myself at your door'. That door is the setting and metaphor of state – romantic predestiny: 'All roads, they lead me here' (Lightbody) and the repeated paradox of making oneself available to an ex:

> *And all the times I let you in*
> *Just for you to go again*
> *Disappear when you come back*
> *Everything is better*
>
> (Swift)

The renewed relationship comes with the patently false statement that 'everything is better'; that lavender haze (see *Midnights* review) that closes off rationality.

Unusually for a Swift song, there's a guitar solo featured; it's probably more Carpenters than Van Halen and certainly doesn't take up too much space. It's notable that it appears here, on a song with a guest singer from the indie world – again signifying Swift's pushing away from country-pop and into something 'cooler'.

It's a shame, in one sense, that the string section is so far down in the mix – it's a lovely accentuation of the main chords rather than the more typical approach of aping the lead melody/chords in string form.

> *This is the last time I'm asking you this*
> *Put my name at the top of your list*

And of course, in order to make sure that this is rendered with all the drama it demands, most of the song takes place in imperatives. 'The last time I'm asking you this' – this is in common with soap operas. Rarely do matters slide for a length of time, it's important that everything be given the sense that it's do or die, now or never. It's interesting that it does suddenly seem more *dramatic* when it's dialogical – at that point, both parties are (roughly) equally invested. Most of Swift's songs are more like monologues or dreams or diary entries – modes in which imperative forms, dramatic over-telling are a lot easier to get away with.

This is a lovely song – Swift's guest vocalists aren't always so well enmeshed in the song (see 'End Game', *reputation*) and as a caprice the hocket-like form genuinely elevates the tension to the level of high drama.

'Holy Ground'
There's a lot of jangly acoustics here; some big rock drums.

There's two lines here where a form of conversational citation takes the place of a more typical noun phrase:

> *Took off faster than a 'green light, go'*
> *…*
> *We blocked the noise with the sound of 'I need you'*

It's a really personable effect; rather than appealing to metonymy, the typical work of metonymy is done by the implied conversation – 'green light, go' is an imperative device to suggest moving ASAP; 'faster than a "green light go"' is to connote faster than the imperative. 'I need you' operates slightly different, in that 'I need you' has no inherent qualities that suggest noise-blocking properties; nevertheless, the assumed conversational circumstance is that 'I need you' operates with a force of attention such as to drown out the 'big wide city'.

> *It was good*
> *Never looking down*
> *And right there where we stood*
> *Was holy ground*

Two things worth noting in the chorus – the 'never looking down' doubles as connoting held eye contact, as you'd expect from a strong affection, and also implying a kind of vertiginous state, as in flying. The 'holy ground' element is an exaggerated statement – it's not to say that narrator and partner are religious figures but it is to say that it this setting the relationship's import is consecrated in the place where they stand.

'Sad Beautiful Tragic'
More of the delayed Edge/U2-esque guitars for the intro.

The instrumental parts between verse and chorus are atypical and emphasise the slow delay of this song.

It's a real pivot piece of a track – on the one hand, it's a kind of mopey sad heartbreak song that'd sit easily on any of the preceding albums; on the other hand, there's a parity and an ellipticality to the lyrics that reappears more frequently in later Swift – a kind of writerly confidence such that a very few heavy words are less to carry the narrative and more to pin it down like a deadweight.

For the chorus we have a fairly plain, static 'What a sad, beautiful, tragic love affair'. Not much accentuation, just an over-described 'sad, beautiful, tragic', bittersweet collocations.

> *Distance, timing*
> *Breakdown, fighting*
> *Silence, the train runs off its tracks*

In the bridge there's a set of pairs, minimal cases to invoke the collapsed relationship. Syntax abandoned except for 'the train…' returning to metaphors.

'The Lucky One'

This is the pop music trope of 'poor little rich girl' (a term, incidentally, from Eleanor Gates, a rare instance of a successful female playwright in the early twentieth century). It's difficult not to read Swift's life into the narrative – the child star who's told she's the 'lucky one' but whose status is precarious and based on her youthful good looks.

> *And they tell you that you're lucky …*
> *'Cause you don't feel pretty, you just feel used*

This is distinctly 'storytelling mode' Swift – by and large the narration is second person, describing the protagonist with a series of 'you' assertions. It's returned, with the denouement, to the more Swift-like first person:

> *And they still tell the legend of how you disappeared*
> *How you took the money and your dignity and got the hell out*
> *…*
> *And it took some time, but I understand it now*

There's a tendency with 'poor little rich girl' stories where the poor little rich girl is in the midst of some tragedy – see Noël Coward's 'poor little rich girl':

> *You're only a baby*
> *You're lonely, and maybe*
> *Someday soon you'll know*
> *The tears you are tasting*
> *Are years you are wasting*
> *Life's a bitter foe*

That is, the youthful *joie de vivre* is a bulwark against the coming tragedy. Swift's version of this story inserts a denouement about 'took the money and your dignity and got the hell out'. It's refreshing to have a version of this story where the pretty young thing is also credited with the self-assertion and intelligence to escape; it's a subtly feminist gesture from Swift to insist that these tragic young pretty women are also blessed with agency and self-awareness. Patriarchal narratives, even in the twenty-first century, still hold that women can't be pretty and smart, or that their being is predicated on their looks. Inverting that in a songwriting trope, however fleetingly, is an important and noteworthy event for Swift.

'Everything Has Changed' featuring Ed Sheeran

Everyone's favourite ever-present troubadour Ed Sheeran guests on this but it's a much less dialogical song than the other duet on this record.

While most of this record has been notably production-heavy, this opens with Sheeran saying 'we good to go?' as if we've intruded on a rehearsal tape. It's worth noting that records like this don't get made by accident so we should consider that the idea of an 'off mic' part is to set the scene – gentle, acoustic, spare.

By the time of the chorus, the idea of it being some home tape has largely been exploded, albeit none too obviously – guitars are double tracked, drums are recorded with mics on each of the parts, vocals are highly treated, studio silence surrounds the drop in the instruments. Later there's closely recorded cellos, volatile basslines and big chorus vocals.

It's a fairly standard song – it's not a bad one but so far as the lyrics go, it's a simple 'I saw you and I fell in love', very romantic, very pop. Very Ed Sheeran for that matter, which would explain his guest spot.

> *And all my walls stood tall, painted blue*
> *And I'll take 'em down, take 'em down*
> *And open up the door for you*

We get two of the established tropes here: the house-as-body metaphor ('all my walls stood tall') and colour-coding. It's also got the door-house/romantic love metaphor from 'The Last Time'.

'Starlight'

This has a driving drumbeat, a highly articulated $\frac{4}{4}$. It's maybe a preamble to the sorts of more explicitly dance-oriented vibes of *1989*. The chorus dotes around a night out, shout out 'woo' kind of thing '…dancing / Like we're made of starlight'. It's certainly ecstatic and fun.

The storytelling element of Swift is manifest here – 'The night we snuck into a yacht club party / Pretending to be a duchess and a prince'. The fantastic way of thinking that's very appealing to teenagers – all risk-taking and play-acting. And that's an important aspect of *how* things like this appeal to teenagers – at a point when a person's personality is unformed, they have more malleability, so the idea of play-acting as a duchess and a prince is more appealing.

> *You'll spend your whole life singing the blues if you keep thinking that way*
> *…*
> *Don't you see the starlight, starlight?*

The notion of a partner who tells you all the nice things, who sees the world in epiphanic terms, is hugely alluring. We can be swept up by these people – seeing the world through their eyes. But it's also interesting that the counterpoint to this, the discrete narrative, is that the narrator is, at least potentially, quite depressed. 'Singing the blues' is marked by a certain sadness and it could be read that the antagonist, the love interest, is manifesting a desire – 'don't you see the starlight?' because the narrator is too sad. It's not a strong subtext, granted, but it's not uncommon for younger people to be a bit mardy from time to time and boys who are enthusiastic about starlight can really lift you out of that funk.

'Begin Again'

Another track that's distinctly 'early Swift' – no reason it couldn't have been on any of the previous. Not least *Self-titled*, on account of the narrator boasting about the number of James Taylor records she has.

James Taylor isn't quite country gold but he's certainly the sort of songwriter who's less well revered outside of the US – certainly for someone Swift's age. It's the kind of down-home, simple hometown life (or at least 'songwriting geek') that's more common to *Self-titled* than *Red*. It's also got banjo and slide guitar padding out the arrangement so strongly has the 'feel' of *Self-titled* more than *Red*.

It's also got the demure teenager, innocent and inexperienced insinuations that suggest earlier incarnations – assertions of 'comin' off a little shy'. By this point in Swift's writing the assertions of self-doubt are fewer; it's the first juvenile qualification on this record.

> *...you start to talk about the movies*
> *That your family watches every single Christmas*

Here there's more of Swift's cute and piquant observations that do the work of creating a dramaturgy – a slightly goofy but disarming anecdote about the crap films the family watches 'every single Christmas'; it's a disarming gesture of fidelity and closeness that allows Swift to note that '…what's past is past' – mapping to the ways in which a lot of important emotional conversations and states don't happen in explicit terms; we seal over and move on from the past by allowing someone into our intimate, silly details.

1989

1989 represents another shift in style for Swift, the second in as many albums. It's also cementing that she's not in country anymore, Toto. If it's an adult pop album then it's still got plenty of the drama and headstrong tenacity to appeal to teenagers. The electro-pop vibes of *1989* end up being a mainstay for Swift – if not her core MO then one of the more pronounced strings to her bow.

She's still a resident of banger-town but she's also making albums that have enough of a mix of styles that her name is growing as a writer of *albums*. *1989* may well be the point at which her fanbase came to realise that her albums were worth shouting about consistently and the point at which she switched from 'ex-country' to electro-pop purveyor par excellence.

'Welcome to New York'
If *Red* is Swift's first pop album then this *1989* is certifying her pop credentials. The transition from the country era is complete – gone are any of the instrumental signifiers, and gone too are acoustic instruments. Kind of – there are acoustic instruments on the record but most of the album is driven by synths. Lovely warm round synths.

The sense with this album at the time was that it was a strong break with previous tradition; thematically, there's a really strong push for Swift to bring in dancing as a theme – 'I could dance to this beat'.

The song is uptempo (relative to previous works) and distinctly electro-pop – and lyrically it's fairly spare. Nevertheless, in amongst the gaudy celebration of New York ('The lights are so bright, but they never blind me, me') there's still space to insinuate heartache: 'When we first dropped our bags on apartment floors / Took our broken hearts, put them in a drawer'.

This being pop music, Swift's also lopped off a lot of detail from the vocals. Most often one-syllable-per-note, keyboards sharply articulating the rhythm –

the rare melisma comes to accentuate the end of lines (be-e-eat/me-e-ee) but otherwise lyrics are staccato, as if the whole song is pointing towards its rhythm.

> *Everybody here wanted something more*
> *Searching for a sound we hadn't heard before*

This being the opening track, it's setting the stage for the whole album – and while this song is lyrically not much more than a succession of choruses, there's still a sense that this is a big, forthright transition. Where previous themes were typically alluding to either a kind of non-denominational sense of space, or small towns (for the country albums), this song declares that the transition also means that we're now speaking for and to an urban, and in fact urbane, audience. It's also worth noting that this is a really good example of Swift's capacity for arrangement – there's *very* little melody in this; the lead vocal is predominantly one note, which is accentuated by echoing harmonies to form chords. It's only in the second half of the chorus that the lead vocal deviates from that one note. Nevertheless, the song is flush with lush synths and it's not a song lacking in harmony; but what harmony is there is simple and effusive.

'Blank Space'

The arrangement of this tune is *explosively* pop – each section bringing in more thick layers of synths, drums, *sounds*. Again, it's very clearly demarcating itself from *Red* – this isn't 'live band in the studio' style music, it's very much in line with pop – and further, the kind of 'classic' pop that could've been made any time since the golden era of Madonna.

One of the key differences between the lyrical personalities of country music and pop music is that country personalities tend to tell stories, while in pop music the singer *is* the story. Whether that assertion stands up or not, *1989* is clearly the point where the public perception of Swift shifts from 'nice girl singing country (kind of)' to 'Taylor Swift, global pop star'. So the lyrics here are much more self-directed and the separation between the narrator's voice and Swift's own voice is less clear. We haven't completely abandoned the lyrical world of manipulating aphorisms and witty one-liners – 'You look like my next mistake' but it's much more about 'the public perception of Swift' than the story and the protagonist.

> *Boys only want love if it's torture*
> *don't say I didn't, say I didn't warn ya*

This is possibly one of Swift's more lasting aphorisms (and there's a book's worth of them). It's nestled in a lot of twisted puns and extended witticisms but it's here as plain as day. The latest description of the problems that men frequently have in handling emotional relationships.

'Blank Space' is maybe one of Swift's *lighter* songs – while it's nominally about breakups and short romances, it's self-deprecating and funny, exaggeratedly dramatic ('…it's gonna go down in flames?') but there's nothing in the way of grievous attacks or impossible heartache.

'Style'

This is the first appearance of a musical figure that becomes quite common in Swift's work – what I've termed the helicopter synth. It typically pulses away in her synth arrangements, adding semiquavers to the regular crotchets. In fact, the pulse isn't precisely on every downbeat on this song but the presence of the fast pulse is felt – it creates a sense of urgency for the arrangement while allowing the song itself to be unhurried.

The rhythm on the chorus of this is hugely compelling – a triplet that rolls into an offbeat stab, a really effective contraction and expansion of relationship to the pulse. The words in the middle of the chorus lines are cleanly split, clearly enunciated or syllables splitting naturally with the offbeat (James Dean/daydream) but the terminal word falls on the last beat of the bar. It's not hugely complicated in rhythmic or poetic terms but it is satisfying; nothing in the chorus is forced or stretched but it swoops down and lifts up like these words fell naturally out of the song.

Probably one of the hardest things about writing pop lyrics is that they shouldn't feel forced. And if they don't feel forced, no one notices. Swift's eight or so years into her career at this point but she's only 24, possibly 23 when she's writing this; nevertheless, she's doing the kind of effortless, rhythmically variegated and simple lyrics that take a lifetime for most songwriters to arrive at.

Sticking with the owning-sexuality, feminist theme, this is another instance where Swift carefully outlines the narrator's sexuality:

> *You got that long hair, slicked back, white t-shirt*
> *And I got that good girl faith and a tight little skirt*

It's a neat and missable contrast between 'good girl faith' and 'tight little skirt'. It's clearly not explicit in the sense that a lot of pop music can be but it's also a narrator who is not a passive wallflower in terms of her own sexual identity.

'Out of the Woods'

Pop music lives and dies on the effectiveness of its chorus and, consequently, you get arrangements like this – verse is initially spare, then slightly less spare, then the chorus piles in everything. It's a very powerful effect. Vocals seem singular in the verse and then by the chorus there's a mountain of Swift's to climb over. The synths are all lush sounding, and by the chorus the voice has joined with the synths, both sounding *chunky*.

Most Swift songs follow a predictable form – verse, chorus, verse, chorus, bridge, chorus. Instruments are typically harmonic or rhythmic – lead melody is typically Swift. By the time of *1989*, Swift's arrangements almost never deviate from this form. Later on, her choruses are more lyrical – in the sense of quite literally having more words. This being Swift's definitive pop turn record, the chorus is minimal – it's a battering ram of Swift's repeating the 'are we out of the woods yet?'

There's an odd effect for this chorus insofar as the hardest sound for the repetition is the 'w' sound in 'are *we* out of the *woods*'; it's phonetically an 'approximant' which is less clearly articulated than a harder sound like a plosive (b, p, etc.) – so it stands out less. The production, then, is super sharp insofar as the vocals step back, ever so slightly, relative to the keyboards so the whole thing is like a juddering synth. It's not merely that the semantic content ('are we out of the woods yet' – which we might parse as 'is this relationship stable/ going to last') is passive but that the voice steps back from being declarative in the mix – the whole musical arrangement is reiterating the sentiment, just to make sure that the audience gets it.

'All You Had to Do Was Stay'

Swift's lyrics are most typically very well-balanced. That is, it's unusual for her to stretch or extend lyrics excessively and most of the stanzas have an equal number of syllables. There's plenty of intelligent devices but the delivery is most usually predictable. So one of the uncharacteristic things on this track is that there's a consistent pause which is somewhat unsettling. It looks a bit like this:

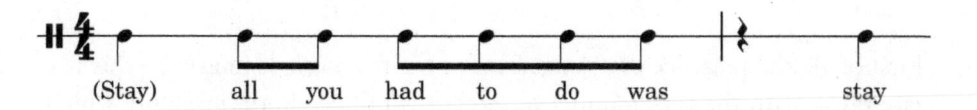

(Stay)   all   you   had   to   do   was   stay

That is to say, there's a kind of rhythmic enjambment where the syntactic termination of the line over-reaches the bar; further, there's a rest on the first beat of the bar, where the listener intuitively expects content. Many of the lyrics throughout the song mirror this awkward stop.

That awkwardness is deliberate, though – it's an intentional device, a dramatic rest which adds dynamic tension; almost as if the musical and rhythmic pattern are mimicking the sense of awkwardness from the semantic content, where the narrator is saying that all that was needed of the relationship was that the antagonist stay. As one does at the end of the relationship, the lyrics stutter like a person would.

And that stuttering is persistent throughout the track *except* at the moment of revelation:

> *You were all I wanted*
> *But not like this*

This is in the bridge – typically the moment that gives the final detail for the song before the final chorus. Rather than following the pattern of stuttering and disjointed, this is plain, on-beat. It's a very sharp instance of lyrics marrying arrangement; the denouement of the story in the song is also the moment where the synchrony between lyric and music occurs.

'Shake It Off'

Arguably the moment at which Swift moved quite firmly into the realms of 'proper pop'. It's a dancey number with a big snarey drumbeat and a chorus that stays in your head for a week. The lyrics are something of a departure, insofar as they're fun and light, something to sing along to in the car but not necessarily imputing too much.

It's also a moment of Swift commenting on her own public persona – at the time that she was spoken of in various quarters as someone whose songs are all about boys who have besmirched her, she pulls out this line in the breakdown:

> *Just think, while you've been gettin' down and out about the liars*
> *And the dirty, dirty cheats of the world*
> *You could've been gettin' down*
> *To this sick beat*

First of all, the presence of a *breakdown* in Swift's music is unusual – this is a rare break with the verse/chorus verse/chorus/bridge/chorus structure which dominates Swift's songs. Secondly… it's kind of ridiculous. Despite my push not to render the songs as autobiographical, it's very difficult not to read this as about Taylor Swift – but not the person, so much as the brand represented by the person. That is, this line is talking about dancing as an antidote to the problems of heartache; it's like if the song was addressing Swift's detractors in a fanciful and archly self-knowing way.

This song has all the good things that a dancey pop number needs; the drumbeat is hard and steady but carefully varied. There's handclaps. Probably my favourite detail is that there was no shortage of money available (one assumes) but still the synth sax sound is quite deliberately inauthentic, perhaps even goofy.

It's dealt with in more depth in the Internet Culture section of tropology but there's a wee reference to the very 'Internet speak' phrase 'haters gonna hate'. Something to locate the song with a time and a place and for an audience.

The song as a whole is somewhat outrageous and off-brand for Swift; it perhaps wasn't repeated, in terms of her having a single which is fun, brash, danceable and without much need for lyrical depth. It's of a piece with *1989* as a whole and is quite boldly like Swift saying 'I get to decide what my music is like and if that means fun pop numbers, so be it'.

'I Wish You Would'

Back to more typical lyrical content here – it's a song about looking back with regrets at those moments at the end of a relationship ('Wish I never hung up the phone like I did'). It's a song that works strongly on a sense of sonic intensity. The first instance of the chorus seems all the more massive for widening the EQ of the track, making the space of sound it's occupying suddenly more open.

It's another track with that helicopter synth I mentioned earlier – a pulsating, throbbing, propulsive heart in the middle of the tune.

> *Wish you knew that*
> *I miss you too much to be mad anymore...*

Plenty of this song dotes on that idea of propulsion – here those constant repetitious plosive '*m*iss you too *m*uch to be *mad*...', each m sound falling heavily on the stress of the rhythm. It's quite an overwhelming effect, one that makes it feel like a shorter song than it is (it's in the perfect pop range of 3 minutes 30 seconds).

It's also a song where most of the action is a consequence of the setup – the first verse closes with 'You're thinking that I hate you now / 'Cause you still don't know what I never said' and the remainder of the song – the constantly affirmed 'wish you...' motif occurs in the possibility of that 'don't know what I never said'.

'Bad Blood'

Another song which breaks the typical Swiftian form, but only insofar as there's a chorus before the first verse. In keeping with the notion that this whole album is a lot more pop than the preceding records, this is a song which is almost pop hip-hop in form – the verses are one or two notes, the chorus likewise and it creates an effect where the more noticeable melodic element in the bridge/pre-chorus are striking.

Swift is largely enunciating lyrics – it's not rap in form but it's not a million miles away from it. The single version – featuring Kendrick Lamar – opens with a rap from Lamar rather than Swift's chorus and it's not entirely incongruous. It's difficult to imagine any other song in Swift's catalogue where a rapper could drop in (or drop out) with minimal disruption.

Speaking of minimal disruption, the video for the single is absolutely outrageous – it's an overwhelmingly shiny noir-ish futuristic action-fighting broken glass mess of incredibly famous and attractive thin people, like Selena Gomez and Gigi Hadid. While I've avoided videos in this book for fear of overkill, it merits comment because it's another indication that Swift has moved decisively from 'singer-songwriter' to 'big pop star'.

Overall, the pattern is expand and contract – spare verses and huge chorus; a near-acapella bridge, a drop in the chorus. Really it's got 'big pop production' all over it, stomping drums to drill the rhythm into your head, a melody base enough that it's nearly monotonic. Every trick to give the impression of dynamic and a density in the chorus that's only possible with huge studios but all with a kind of self-effacing sense of simplicity. I say that it's almost like hip-hop, and that's a comparison borne of specific drum samples, but it equally sits next to something like Queen's 'We Will Rock You' where the drums are nearly as repeatable as the chorus.

'Wildest Dreams'

If *1989* is an album where Swift is experimenting with what her sound *is*, then this is the most traditionally Swiftian song on here. While it's still in the realm of largely electronic instruments, there's a snifter of acoustic strings articulating the chorus, decorating this as 'a classic pop song'.

It's a wistful forget-me-not, sentimental post-relationship memorial – 'Say you'll see me again / Even if it's just in your / Wildest dreams...' Swift is, at this point, relatively circumspect about being 'the other woman' but there's an insinuation here that the subtext is an intense, sexual, and probably clandestine relationship – 'I said, "No one has to know what we do"', 'Red lips and rosy cheeks' – as in the rush of blood to the face of sexual arousal – 'Say you'll see me again'. At this point, Swift is not overtly sexual but it's interesting to note the contrast between this and the outright call-it-what-it-is of 'illicit affairs' (*folklore*). In those six years between *1989* (released 2014) and *folklore* (released 2020), Swift (or Swift's narrators) are more candid, forthright. It's indicative of how *1989* is still resting on a kind of perspective on Swift as 'juvenile' – still emerging from the conservative country world. It's worth saying as well that outside of country and this more conservative pop, hypersexualised late teenagers are the norm (which is a nest of complexity all of its own…).

This is very *sophisticated* pop, though – the subdued bassline on this is like a heartbeat, very adult and demure; soft sonic edges that raise the pulse but don't jump in your lap.

> *Some day when you leave me*
> *I'll bet these memories*
> *follow you around*

At this juncture in Swift's writing there's a definitely theme of 'hell hath no fury like a woman scorned' – a large part of her appeal to teenage and young women is her assertiveness in the face of an emerging womanhood, sexuality; her broader appeal to the millennial generation is predicated on growing up with her. Memories following you around is sharply bittersweet, brilliantly contrasted; on the one hand it's a soft and forlorn farewell; on the other it looks like a hex, a curse from the scorned woman. Swift's skill as a songwriter here is operating on that amphiboly, letting audiences develop their own Swiftian interpretation. Vague enough to be imprecise but clear enough to be barbed, at least potentially.

'How You Get the Girl'

A truism of musicology is that the borders between certain genres are not always clear. Popular music tends to rely on a limited number of harmonic ideas. There's still an infinite number of combinations but the difference between 'a pop song' and 'a country song' can be as little as matter of production or the instruments used. 'How You Get the Girl' has a strong new country feel; while there's some careful cutting of reverberation on the acoustic guitars and the drums are synthetic, this is principally an uptempo new country song; swap out of some of the instruments and you've got a song about boys and girls and their relationships – specifically heteronormative for the country crowd, specifically traditional.

I don't, unfortunately, have recourse to an annotated chronology of when Swift wrote songs. But it feels most like a song from before *1989*; for all the shine and pizzazz of the production, the thick and lush synths, it's a well-decorated song written on an acoustic guitar. There's a lot of very produced vocal harmonies that play out well on the radio but this is absolutely continuity-country.

> *I want you for worse or for better*
> *I would wait forever and ever*

This is a relatively innocuous couplet, but it's worth noting the ways in which traditional values are evoked – 'worse or for better' is very obviously a reference to (specifically) Christian wedding vows. Pledges of chastity ('I would wait forever') are very much part of Christian cultures; non-denominational but nevertheless saturated with Christianity. It's very difficult to separate a lot of US culture from its Christian surroundings – especially if the person singing is a white, cis-gender, heterosexual person (or at least passes as such) – but in contrast with the distantly alluded to sexuality of the immediately preceding 'Wildest Dreams', there's a Swift who isn't yet fully comfortable, or fully forthright, with expressing sexuality directly. And that is, of course, fine – it's certainly not the place of a guy in his forties to prescribe the lot of a singer in her early twenties.

'This Love'
And speaking of the Swiftian crossroads – this is a song that's dreamy and blissful and softly drifting; it's very similar in vibe to *Midnights*, all soft hues, soft focus.

> *Lantern, burning*
> *Flickered in my mind, only you*

Later Swift frequently uses elliptical storytelling – letting the story happen between pauses and allusions. It's frequently taut and spare lyrically – more than a few songs with use this kind of minimal description to set a scene – for example 'Half-moon eyes, bad surprise' ('Question…?', *Midnights*). *1989* shares a lot of sonic territory with *Midnights* and there's an amount of it that sets the store for later Swift – confident electro-pop, highly emotional, clear and articulate but also not lacking for bangers.

This song's chorus is odd-shaped, distended, and quite magic. It's got a similar feel to the 'Lavender Haze' of *Midnights* too. There's a nursery rhyme articulation – repeating what this love *is*. It's described as 'unlike back from the dead', which is a quandary of a line. It's a sentence fragment so there's a syntactical oddity to it. How is love 'unlike' 'back from the dead'; the elision which marks it as a sentence fragment could be filled with 'being' or 'coming'; as it is it has a tender awkwardness. Despite the plangent delivery, there's almost the impression of a skip, a rushed phrase. It has to be *deliberate* – if Swift had wanted to match the metre of the line, she could easily have slipped in a contraction, e.g. – 'this love's unlike [coming?] back from the dead'.

It's possibly more louche than it is poetic – a very Internet-savvy syntax where 'back from the dead' is made into a noun phrase. If it was 'this love's unlike hard old cheese' it'd maybe make more sense, though in the process would lose several thousand 'sounds poetic' points. My inclination is to read it as indicating a renewed, or failing-to-die romance and that the narrator is saying that it's not like getting back with an ex but is rather a slippery, contracting/expanding thing or has the gravity of tides.

Perhaps most of all it's an *effective* chorus – if the sentiment is 'this love is confusing, in that it exhibits multiple properties' then it would make sense also that its syntax is oblique.

'I Know Places'
Elsewhere in this book I've written about tropology – that is, the themes and ideas that thread between songs. There are a few instances in her work which aren't quite threads so much as they are different perspectives on an idea; like a workshop with multiple outcomes. Here the story is about a couple who are being hunted; the metaphor being that a beleaguered couple are like prey for certain people. 'They are the hunters, we are the foxes and we run'.

This is strikingly similar to the theme of 'The Archer' (*Lover*) – 'I've been the archer, I've been the prey'. On that song, Swift's narrator muses on having occupied both sides of the hunted/hunter. Lover is characterised by being more self-reflective, and frequently self-critical. *1989* being Swift's first proper pop album, her place in 'I Know Places' is determinedly as the 'prey': "Cause they got the cages, they got the boxes and guns'. If this is read as a metaphor of a couple who are beleaguered by the public eye, then that's in keeping with the sense that *1989* is a record 'about' Swift as a public figure, celebrity. The subject of her own songs rather than the observer or storyteller.

Those sorts of themes – the Swift-as-celebrity – are more common on *reputation*; so once again the oddity with *1989* is that it's got the green shoots of the themes and styles that come to dominate her later albums. The preceding 'This Love' is very *Midnights*-y; 'How You Get the Girl' is very country-era. It's not so much that *1989* is an incoherent album – by no means – but rather that it's *diffusely* different to the preceding albums, and lays the foundation for the themes that later define Swift's writing entirely.

The song itself is entirely charming; it's also in keeping with the general fantastic approach Swift has to romance – the binding of two people securing a private place amongst the terrors and barbs of the world around them; it's an entirely compelling narrative and one of innumerable teenage romances, from *Romeo and Juliet* to *One Tree Hill*.

'Clean'
To speak once more of contrast – 'Clean' stands out on this album, and indeed in Swift's whole canon, as one of her most *hallucinatory* pieces. That isn't in a trite sense of psychedelic music and fatuous mystical cliché (mercifully) but in a sense that what's described is hypnagogic, dream-like; a coherent logic but a described world that's impossible.

> *When the butterflies turned to*
> *Dust that covered my whole room*

This kind of thing. A very embodied sense of metaphor, a sense that the settings described are not abstractions – as in, imaginative figures used to aid comprehension. Rather they appear as quite literal descriptions of a psychic state, like the idea of our internal, mental houses. Deeply intensive.

Butterflies are typically a kind of rebirth, or springtime growth; their traces leaving a patina of decay.

The theme of the whole song is to do with water; if I was an English teacher, I'd use this as a clear example of how many turns you can get out of a metaphor. Because the water is variegated – it's rain, it's drowning, it's cleansing, it's the liquidity of alcohol, it's nourishing, it's the staining wine, it's the airborne storm.

> *Rain came pouring down*
> *When I was drowning, that's when I could finally breathe*
> *And by morning*
> *Gone was any trace of you, I think I am finally clean*

And back again to the hallucinatory, hypnagogic notion. The drowning is clearly a metaphor for being overwhelmed; there's a clarity that comes (it's surprising there isn't an 'eye of the storm: clarity' metaphor here) in its midst. And of course the directly contrary 'that's when I could finally breathe' is deliberately jarring, impossible. The real sense of is that the drowning, the confusion of a break-up, of emotional turmoil, is *contaminative* – and hence the revelation of feeling clean.

> *You're still all over me*
> *Like a wine-stained dress I can't wear anymore*

This sense of contamination persists elsewhere – not merely that we are contaminated by unsavoury relationships in a sense that marks us way more deeply than a stain, but also that we model ourselves, we become a person who is defined by the other.

These are all very powerful metaphors and, quite strikingly, uncommon for *1989*; it's the kind of deeply entrenched and intricate working of a metaphor that's been largely absent from *1989*. It's much more *writerly* than the rest of the album has been. It's not atypical for Swift in general but it's the most strident instance of her songwriting lyrically.

It's difficult to say that it's necessarily at odds with *1989* too much – there's so many instances on this album of Swift pointing in different directions, forward and back and sideways... but it is, as a closing song, a gorgeous and touching renewal; perhaps even therefore a comment on the role the album itself plays in moving Swift from 'singer-songwriter in a country vein' to 'pop star proper' who's also an astonishing songwriter.

reputation

If Swift is following the Prince trajectory then this is the *Controversy* album – Swift positioning herself in the centre of her songs and doting on the public eye and the press. It's the album with some of the most spare writing – fully optimised for peak pop performance. And it's also the album that pushes the studio-as-instrument notion. Max Martin's involvement on production is very noticeable.

Despite its bombast and dance-influenced pop arrangements, it's still an album with enough honest-to-goodness proper songwriting on it to register Swift's songwriting as substantial and impressive. It's not a side of Swift she shows again, and it's maybe her most BIG sounding record.

'Ready For It'

1989 took shots in plenty of different directions as to what Swift's music could be like. By the time of *reputation*, Swift is established as much more on the pop side of things; the transition looks something like country singer-songwriter (*Self-titled, Fearless, Speak Now*) to the pop-country hybrid singer-songwriter (*Red*) to song-based pop singer (*1989*). One of the key pop moments in *1989* was the line about 'you could've been gettin' down to this sick beat' on 'Shake It Off'. 'Ready For It', the opener for *reputation*, is very definitely inclined towards sick beats. Where *1989* was firmly electro-pop, songs with synth arrangements, 'Ready For It' opens with the kind of high-production, heavy bass and skippy hi-hats that's very much influenced by a lot of dance musics, especially dubstep.

This isn't a dubstep record (by any means) but it's certainly informed by the simple, bass-focused, drop-heavy style.

'Ready For It' is also uncharacteristic in terms of the construction of the chorus; where Swift's choruses are more typically well-balanced and wordy, this chorus is a relatively verbose build-up to 'are you ready for it', where the music drops out almost entirely, and the whole thing builds up again. It's effective insofar as the name of the song is front-and-centre, and it's been a technique which has meant that non-Korean-speaking audiences enjoy K-pop – the chorus is emphatically simple.

'Ready For It' isn't quite Swift rapping but it's not a million miles away. There's a weird African American Vernacular English (AAVE) inflection on a couple of lines, for instance: 'Younger than my exes, but he act like such a man' – where non-AAVE English would say 'he acts like such a man'; here Swift quite awkwardly uses what I think is technically the *intensive continuative aspect* proper to AAVE. It's not atypical for white performers to drop into AAVE registers as a way of signalling 'coolness'. It's a well-heeled and well-known phenomenon in music – think blues, jazz, etc. – but suffice it to say the fact that it's typical and predictable doesn't make it okay. Mercifully these affectations are fleetingly rare in Swift and I suspect their rarity is reflective of Swift's capacity to absorb some legitimate criticism.

Less controversially the rap influence takes the form of mutating semantics between terminals and newlines – e.g. 'Holdin' him for ransom / Some boys are tryin' too hard' where the 'som' of ransom is re-used in the next line – a strongly phonetic device which ensures that the beat is articulated and clear to the listener. Same technique later on – 'We'll move to an island / And he can be my jailer' – and/and. In poetic terms, the repetition of the last word of a preceding clause as the first of the next is known as anadiplosis. Here Swift is also beginning a sentence with a conjunction, the sort of thing that people whose notions of grammar calcified in the Victorian era get upset about. And while it's perfectly fine to start a sentence with a conjunction (did you notice I did it there?) it's still indicative of the sort of 'low grammar' that connotes 'cool' in pop music.

'Ready For It' is a fairly common story of narrator getting the bad boy. Perhaps the most significantly peculiar thing about the song is that, for all its signalling of cool and urbane arrangement – the quasi-dubstep parts, the AAVE allusions – there's still a pun on Richard Burton and Elizabeth Taylor: 'And he can be my jailer, Burton to this Taylor'. For younger readers – Burton and Taylor were the hip and happening 'it' couple of the early 1960s.

'End Game' featuring Future and Ed Sheeran

And just to cement the allusions to hip-hop, here's a big hip-hop beat, a drum sound strikingly similar to that of Rihanna's 'Umbrella' (2007), and a guest rap from Future. While Swift has had rappers on her songs before – Kendrick Lamar's guest on 'Bad Blood' (*1989*) – this is the first time a rapper has appeared on an album proper. The song also features Ed Sheeran, who may or may not be considered a rapper – he definitely raps on his songs, in a kind of half-sung way – but his primary thing is arguably nice boy singing.

The song is a yearning-for-commitment number – 'I wanna be your end game / first string / A-Team'. Swift's verses are marked by her usual tricks such as extended aphorisms ('And I bury hatchets, but I keep maps of where I put 'em'). Parts of Swift's vocals on this track are autotuned – or a similar vocoder-alike effect. This is putting her vocals closer to Future's register, keeping a consistent vocal feel through the track.

Now the problem with this track really is that there isn't enough time to explore the themes – by the time Future and Sheeran have had a go at a verse, there's not really much time for development; three slices on the theme of 'end game' is more like the first result of a workshop than it is a coherent whole. It's not that individually anyone's part is bad, so much as it's an excess of voices. This method works incredibly well in some formats – the terrifying array of ideas that occur in a single song on something like Wu-Tang Clan's *36 Chambers* dotes on a profusion of ideas; a pop song about commitment is not necessarily the best forum. It's probably worth considering this song as an experiment on Swift's part. There are later songs with additional voices – like the duets with Justin Vernon of Bon Iver on *folklore* and *evermore* – but the predominant voice and structure is Swift's there. So perhaps this is an experiment that she declined to follow up.

'I Did Something Bad'

Here then is a watershed in Swift's albums – the first use of a swearword. Sadly, the first swear is fairly mild – just an innocuous 'shit' ('If a man talks shit, then I owe him nothing'). Nevertheless, it's significant in terms of Swift's turn towards 'adult' writing; there's parity between Swift's age and that of her audience such that we're now in the realm of 'shit'. Later in her career we get the odd 'fuck' or 'fucking', which is a real delight.

The production on this track – this album in general – is very shiny; there's a lot of detail, there's a lot of carefully engineered, timbrally varied synth sounds. Acoustic instruments are frequently chopped and cut and looped and reversed. Rhythms are tightly articulated but variegated – handclaps, bass drums all pushing different parts of the pulse. 'I Did Something Bad' is maybe the track with most production tricks, including some more autotuned vocals. The contrast with *1989* is substantial – while there timbres were electronic but plain, here we have a production which is massive sounding. It's emblematic of commercial pop music in the 2010s.

One of the problems with pop music, though, is that the more commercial it is, the more lightweight its content becomes. This isn't always true and it's certainly not true for Swift in general but the problem with paring something down to its more base form is that it replaces nuance with bombast.

Nevertheless, Swift still manages to get in a feminism reference – 'They're burning all the witches even if you aren't one'. A commonplace association whereby the persecution of witches in history is associated with the persecution of women, especially those in the public eye. This is an important sentiment to hammer home and the track is *really* nice sounding. It's just that Swift's lyricism runs dangerously thin here.

'Don't Blame Me'
And by immediate contrast, 'Don't Blame Me' is a simpler song in terms of production and arrangement, but also more lyrically dense.

> *My name is whatever you decide*
> *And I'm just gonna call you mine*

This line isn't quite delivered as written – there's a pause after 'my name', the 'and' of the second line actually comes as part of the second line. So the verse has a kind of skippy flow, a set of pauses and rushes that keep the lines popping out. The pre-chorus switches the stresses to longer notes, so you get a variegated transition between different parts of the song.

Part of the process of growing up for Swift means a kind of candour about sexuality for her narrators – 'I've been breakin' hearts a long time'. Where earlier Swift lyrics were circumspect about partners, here it's strongly implied that her narrators are comfortable with their sexuality. It's not outrageous in a broader context of English-language pop music but relative to the Swift of *Self-titled* this is pretty ribald.

The song rests on a chorus which is a metaphor of love-as-drugs – it's a trope of Swift's (see tropology – 'Love/drugs') that pops up from time to time. Where earlier there were distinctively AAVE inflections to connote 'coolness', here another trope of black American music is used, in the form of a gospel chorus of Swift singing 'Lord save me'. It's one of those effects that's alarmingly commonplace in pop music in general but it's still uncomfortable here, to my ears at least. Nothing in Swift's previous has suggested that she's from a Baptist

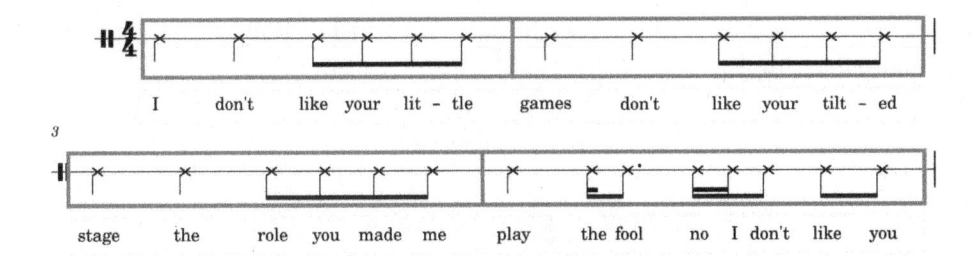

```
♩ 4/4  x   x    x x x x  |  x    x    x x x x  ||
        I   don't  like your lit-tle  games don't like your tilt-ed
```
3
```
        x   x    x x x x  |  x    x·   x x x x  ||
       stage  the  role you made me  play  the fool  no  I don't like you
```

That is – the musical phrase has four beats throughout, while the lyrical phrase has an extra beat for the first line, pushing all the subsequent, four-beat lines onto the next phrase. It's an interesting technique – because the music doesn't quite match the lyrics (in terms of rhythm) it means there's a constant air of disjointedness. Similarly in the chorus there's a (faster) pattern of disjointed lyrics. Words in the chorus are quavers (8th notes) except the 'ooh' and 'do' which are crotchet (4th note). If you don't follow the music theory, don't worry – the upshot is that the lyrics of the chorus end one beat after the musical end – it's an unsettling feeling, perhaps in line with the air of malevolence and control Swift is expressing.

In the context of Taylor Swift's career at this point, this deliberate musical sore-thumbing is atypical. The arrangement is almost lacking in melody – not so much a rap as an incantation. It's certainly *audacious*.

> *I'm sorry, the old Taylor can't come to the phone right now*
> *Why? Oh, 'cause she's dead!*

If the rest of *reputation* wasn't a clear enough wedge between itself and the preceding, there's this fourth-wall breaking line to make it explicit. This whole song is a posture to insist that Swift's changing the way she perceives and expresses herself. Per se, then, the subject of the song is less a story and more Swift herself – and while I've been loath to recognise that elsewhere, it's important to this song. And, of course, this is again a shift to the thematic material where Swift herself is the subject.

'So It Goes'
And speaking of fourth-wall breaking, there's a moment in 'So It Goes' where a background whisper counts in the rhythm; as if the music was suddenly conscious of itself.

This is again another tune that has a less definitive narrative; the 'So It Goes' motif is a kind of attempt to be off-hand about being within a complex relationship. Or rather, the dynamics of the relationship outside of moments of intimacy are dicey – "Cause we break down a little / But when I get you alone, it's so simple'.

> *All eyes on you, my magician*
> *…*
> *Gold cage, hostage to my feelings*

This magician theme reappears in this song, it underpins the verses. This verse in full is an example of a used/re-used metaphor, contorting and twisting multiple ways. 'Gold cage, hostage to my feelings' is possibly the most impressive – gold cage in a sense of being prestigious, yet restrictive; hostage to (the narrator's) feelings working for both agents (as in, the narrator and the antagonist are both hostage). As a metaphor it does some impressive whorling around its own subject and possibilities.

> *And all the pieces fall right into place*
> *Getting caught up in a moment*
> *Lipstick on your face*

This is more common to the kind of writing Swift does later on in her career – the kind of plain, simple statements in terse, simple lines. Here a declining word-count leading to a kind of syllabic diminuendo – slowing down the pace to go with the glacial rhythm, opiated and sprawling synth chords. Besides being more expressly sexual than previous Swift ('scratches down your back now'), this is also more confident writing – by the time of *Midnights*, these are the sorts of songs that are Swift's mainstay.

'Gorgeous'
This is more in the box marked 'very produced'. There's a reverb tail at the end of each line of the verse that's almost dub-like – it's just used to accentuate the end of the line but it also goes on for a very long time.

Despite (or perhaps because of) this album being Swift's foray into 'adult pop', this is a brilliantly bratty, over the top tune. One of the abiding themes for Swift as a writer is her being very *extra* and that's true here: 'You're so cool, it makes me hate you so much'; 'You've ruined my life by not being mine'. It's an expression of the intensity of emotion, a kind of overspilling of affection into resentment.

It's also nice to have a revisit of articulating the kind of dopey way teenagers act – 'You're so gorgeous / I can't say anything to your face'. The way that teenagers are absolute idiots with regards to their potential paramours, having mutated the behaviour of punching someone's arm into the behaviour of ignoring.

By the time of the chorus, this is subtly drenched in reverb; if Swift's music is at its best when its hypnagogic then 'Gorgeous' certainly has the slurring and washy *vibe* of a dream.

And it's worth brokering a separation between what Swift writes and who she is. The character in this song is kind of bratty and a bit of a dick – if that's to reflect on Swift as a person then it's presumably in a self-deprecating way. Certainly we have a very archly delivered line about being the mad single cat lady – 'Guess I'll just stumble on home to my cats [pause] alone'. It's an exaggerated tale of how petulant and bratty we can be when someone's affected us significantly but it's not model behaviour. Songs are often wish fulfilment, expressing the stuff we wouldn't express about ourselves, and it's worth keeping that in mind even if we're inclined to interpret this material as autobiographical.

'Getaway Car'

Some citations dissolve into common parlance, divorced from their origin. 'It was the best of times, the worst of crimes' is probably such a reference – the line 'it was the best of times, it was the worst of times' is from Charles Dickens's *A Tale of Two Cities*. Alternately, 'it was the best of times, it was the blurst of times' if you're more inclined towards *The Simpsons* (season 4, episode 17). It's significant insofar as we haven't (so far as I'm aware) had a literary citation since Robert Frost was used in 'The Outside' (on *Self-titled*).

This notion of citational thinking is not entirely unusual to Swift – here we have a grammatically peculiar (but by no means incoherent) in-sentence citation, 'the first old fashioned "we were cursed"' where the sentence fragment 'we were cursed' is cited, incidental to its parent sentence. If that's unclear – 'we were cursed' is referring to something outside of its parent sentence. It's similar to 'This Love' (*1989* – see *1989* review), where Swift contorts typical grammar for artistic effect. Besides this, this couplet has a lush sibilance with the s/sh sounds (fa*sh*ioned/cur*s*ed /*sh*otgun/*sh*ot), the stresses dancing around the beat.

Swift's production MO around this time is very detailed; while the drums sound like a drum machine there's lots of careful timbral thinking – by and large they're backgrounded but still deployed carefully; the juddering helicopter synth on this one is tripletting away to give a kind of impeded motion effect, like moving a car with the brakes on.

And Swift's vocals are carefully detailed too: 'Don't pretend it's such a mystery / Think about the place where you first met me'. Here, the 'think' is held just a little bit longer, accentuated just a little bit more. It's not quite an affectation but it's distinctly dramatic, and sung, rather than emulating typical speech patterns.

Similarly the line 'No, nothing good starts in a getaway car' has a slightly peculiar short 'no' and a stressed 'thing' of 'nothing'. It's just enough to pull the vocals into the tightly regimented rhythms.

'King of My Heart'

Swift's voice here is slathered in effects – mostly a vocoder-like effect that blurs the lines between human sounds and machines. It's by no means unheard of in pop music but it's notable that *reputation* is followed by *Lover*, *folklore*, *evermore* – all albums where Swift's voice is more 'authentic'. That's not a descriptive 'authentic' but indicating that, while her vocals are certainly less transparently processed electronically, there's still a high degree of production applied (because that's true of pretty much any vocal in any pop song).

'King of My Heart' is once again a 'very pop' song – the structure is verse/chorus/verse/chorus/bridge/chorus but the chorus is elongated with a pre-chorus and a post-chorus. That is to say there's not much in the way of relief from the chorus – the verses end up somewhat perfunctory in the face of the great expansive vista of chorus.

In tropology I talk about the trope of Swift's relationship with Britain (see 'Bri'ish') and that's first exposed here – 'Salute to me, I'm your American queen' insinuates that the antagonist is not American; 'Say you fancy me, not fancy stuff' is using a British sense of 'fancy' meaning 'to be attracted to'. It's not quite as obvious as 'London Boy' (*Lover*) but it's the beginnings of those signallings.

There's an infrequent pattern in Swift's songs where there's more chorus than song – that is, the majority of lyrics are taken up with the repetition of the chorus. This chorus also has a lot of oohs and whoahs so it ends up being lyrically quite thin. Not a criticism but it explains why the production is so explosive and dynamic – plenty of dips and drops, crescendos and diminuendos. It's maybe Swift's song with the most prominent handclaps and I can't help but wonder if they're there because of the line 'And you move to me like I'm a Motown beat'.

> *'Cause all the boys and their expensive cars*
> ...
> *Never took me quite where you do*

Again, to speak of this as an 'adult pop' album – it's worth contrasting this mention of cars relative to the more truck-based *Self-titled*. There's a sociological element insofar as the cars mentioned are up-market. That's in keeping with the regal theme (*king* of my heart) but it's also to say that the subtext here points more to an urban world than a rural or suburban.

'Dancing With Our Hands Tied'

The beat to this is somewhere between two-step and drum and bass. It's not quite a full-on, ratchet club song but it's only a remix away from that. And it's pretty indicative of the way that Swift's label are very keen to sanitise Swift's presence on the Internet, in that I couldn't find any remixes with five minutes of searching. Keeping with the idea that Swift starts taking in British influences around this time (see above and the 'Bri'ish' section of tropology) it could be the case that Swift's alluding to British dance music traditions; however, those traditions are so well known by this point that it's not really possible to say decisively. Everyone and their dog has heard drum 'n' bass by this point in time.

It's also closer to the kind of dance music that Swift was alluding to with the 'this sick beat' line in 'Shake It Off' (*1989*). That is, this is distinctly dance music – as in generically, with a highly complex, very produced beat. As opposed to 'Shake It Off', which was more of a pop song with a prominent beat. That's not to say that the difference between pop music and dance music is in live drums versus produced beats but rather that there's a level of detail, a higher tempo and a more rhythm-focused arrangement here that pushes it a lot closer to the dancefloor.

> *But we were dancing*
> *Dancing with our hands tied, hands tied*

The chorus of the song is also a single sentiment about dancing; where many of Swift's choruses (away from this album) are verbose and varied, here the chorus is in service of the lead musical motif, all instruments punching away at a bass drum triplet. This isn't quite a hands-in-the-air, 'can I have a sip of your water mate?' ecstatic number but it's certainly a warm-up to poppers o'clock.

'Dress'

Panting is a vocal effect that's rarely used in pop, but is always welcome when it does appear. Think 1980s Prince, or the bridge of 'I'm a Slave 4 U' by Britney Spears (2001). 'Dress' is Swift's entry into the canon of 'songs featuring panting', where the pre-chorus line 'My hands are shaking from all this' is followed by panting sounds. It's a great music effect – a kind of sonic periphrasis that is less euphemism for sex, and more dysphemistic – that is, rather than hiding a connotation behind a more polite term (as in euphemism), a dysphemism is being more impolite than just saying 'sex we're having'.

Again, this is indicative of an adult turn for Swift; short of directly saying 'I'm doing a bunch of sexings', this is about as explicit as Swift's lyrics get. 'Only bought this dress so you could take it off'. And it's worth noting the way in which this sexuality is expressed – this is still relatively demure. There's a whole heap of bullshit that follows women being openly sexual and it's understandable that many are circumspect; conversely, there's a rampant over-sexualisation of black women that goes on too. In that context, women taking ownership of their sexuality is to be celebrated, whether it's the milquetoast allusions of Swift, or Cardi B and Megan Thee Stallion's 'WAP'.

> *All of this silence and patience, pining and anticipation*
> *My hands are shaking from holding back from you*

Where earlier the hip-hop borrowings were less well-integrated, here we have the kind of 'multis' (as in multisyllabic rhymes) that are hugely popular in hip-hop and typically considered a sign of a good rapper. Swift never goes fully into rapping, and that's as well, but there's a great many instances where it's clear that her lyrical form is strongly influenced by it; it's easy enough to imagine 'silence and patience / pining and anticipation', with its effulgent rhymes and sounds, appearing in a hip-hop song proper. The effect here (as with rapping in general) is to shift focus onto different parts of the beat, creating a lyrical extemporisation on a clearly defined beat.

Another idea from hip-hop is 'flow', that is how the lyrical rhythm interacts with the musical rhythm. Rappers are said to have characteristic flows – patterns that are like a signature – and many people in hip-hop fandoms get irate if someone is considered to be stealing someone else's flow... unless it's telegraphed as an homage. Swift is smarter than to borrow a flow from a legend like 2Pac or Ol' Dirty Bastard (funny as that would be) but with the line 'I'm spilling wine in the bathtub / You kiss my face and we're both drunk' she's seemingly referencing the flow of Barenaked Ladies' 'One Week' (1998).

'Dress' then is perhaps Swift's closest track to hip-hop and, unlike her slightly careless AAVE on 'Ready For It', it's a cautious but respectful development of her technique. Appropriate too that it should be on this album, in which she's gone closest to dance music rather than a kind of danceable pop music of her electro-pop albums (*1989* and *Midnights*).

'This Is Why We Can't Have Nice Things'

> *Here's a toast to my real friends*

Once more Swift is in referential lyrical territory. The original quote is 'champagne for my real friends, real pain for my sham friends' – the origin of which is attributed to various people but never quite convincingly, so it's become a kind of folk aphorism. The thread that's being tugged at here is along the lines of Swift as subject – back-stabbing friends and interpersonal conflict.

While six singles were released from *reputation*, 'This Is Why We Can't Have Nice Things' was not one of them. There's probably a good reason for it – radio doesn't tend to take too kindly to a wide dynamic range. This starts with handclicks, distance bass sounds but would likely come across as acapella on the radio. By the time of the final chorus, there's a chorus of Swifts, another chorus of ad libs, toy piano, big throaty synths, strobe-like flickering upper register synths, and big synth drumfills. It's not as long a chorus as 'King of My Heart' but it's just as massive.

The theme 'this is why we can't have nice things' is very Internet (see the tropology chapter) but the sentiment here is used to insinuate that Swift *herself* (or at least, the narrator of this song) is the nice thing that her antagonist has besmirched: 'But I'm not the only friend you've lost lately' in the verse and then 'This is why we can't have nice things, darling'. It's again worth driving a wedge between the sense in which this is exaggerative for dramatic effect and the sense in which this has a bearing on Swift as a person. Swift's writing is very inviting in terms of apparently dissolving the lines between theatrical gesture and autobiography but it's worth re-instating, and re-stating, that theatrical gesture in order that we don't come away from a song like 'This Is Why We Can't Have Nice Things' thinking that Swift is a self-obsessed narcissist. If we are inclined to think that these are autobiographical songs then we might want to temper that by saying that one of the finer and more discreet arts of Swift's writing are her powers of exaggeration to make a compelling song.

'Call It What You Want'

It's possible to divide pop songs into two principal types: ones where the writer wants the audience to pay attention, and ones where they do not. It's still eminently possible to produce a banger where the lyrics are of minimal importance – the history of dance music is full of it. While the lyrics to (say) 'I Feel Love' by Donna Summer are not bad in any sense, they are few and less imperative than the arrangement, beat, and so on.

Swift's capacity for subtly drawing the attention and pointing at different parts of a song are phenomenal; frequently this is done without resorting to jarring surprises. 'Call It What You Want' is a rare case where the lyrics stick out because of their odd grammatical features.

All the liars are calling me one

Here's an instance where the grammar is perfectly understandable, but it sticks out as atypical – in songform it's more typical that the listener not pause to assess what the sentence is saying. 'All the liars [subject] are calling [verb] me [object] one [repeated discrete subject, i.e. liar]'. It's a crisp and short line so the pause afterwards is enough to get a sense of what the narrator is saying. It's leveraging a grammatical oddity – correct, but less usual in songform – to draw the listener into the lyrics.

My baby's fly like a jet stream

To parse this out – 'My baby [subject] [is] fly [adjective] like [verb] a jet stream [object being compared]'. It's a directly ambiguous sentence – if it's not written down it's not clear (except from context) that it means 'my baby is fly [attractive] like a jet stream' or 'my babies fly like a jet stream'. And to further confuse matters, 'babies fly like a jet stream' makes a lot more sense as a simile. It's another hip-hop-alike lyrical form – many similes in rap are abstractly disjunctive, as a means of drawing attention to the lyric and drawing the listener's attention in.

My baby's fit like a daydream

This follows a similar pattern to the preceding; here the additional confusion is that 'fit' is not so well known as meaning 'attractive' in US English (it's much more common to British English). And again, the simile is less supportive, more attention-seeking.

Not because he owns me
But 'cause he really knows me

This might be one of Swift's oddest lyrics, insofar as the pun here is purely typographical – owns and knows look like anagrams of each other, so the balancing of the couplet takes place in writing. And of course the lyric is made to be delivered and heard.

It's interesting that these effects are buried solely in this song, towards the end of the album – the remainder of *reputation* has been relatively spare, lyrically and poetically, in service of big pop effect. It's tempting to infer that Swift insisted on having something more densely lyrical just to keep her nails sharp, as it were.

'New Year's Day'
This is perhaps the sorest thumb of *reputation*. It's not glaring or large or poppy or featuring a near-drum'n'bass beat, it's just… a plain and simple song. There's

a piano part that accentuates the first beat, and decays on the subsequent beats. It's not a noticeably effected piano (which isn't to say it's under-produced). It's fairly indicative of how *reputation* is anomalous in Swift's albums that 'New Year's Day' is probably the most typically Swiftian song on *reputation* yet the song that sounds least like any others on the same album.

The song is detailing a particular state of a relationship – cleaning up after a successful New Year's party and wanting to share intimate moments outside of extraordinary times – 'I want your midnights / But I'll be cleaning up bottles with you on New Year's Day'. It's a slight and a gorgeous number and it belongs for all the world on the *folklore* or *evermore* albums – there's even a line 'You and me forevermore'.

There's a degree of opacity here too – while the rest of *reputation* has been largely lyrically simple, there's something of a confusing line at the beginning of the chorus, 'Don't read the last page'. Confusing because none of the surrounding lines afford it any extra context. It's easy enough to intimate that it's a command about a text – maybe a diary or a long letter – where the narrator has divested details that she doesn't want to fully disclose, or perhaps wrote in a state of anger. But none of the surrounding text qualifies it. It's a cute little device, the sort of thing that draws a listener in and leaves them mildly unsatisfied. Exactly the sort of thing that Swifties love.

It's probably reasonable to say that this uses the sort of semi-opaque, elliptical devices that Swift hones for *folklore*/*evermore* and especially *Midnights*:

> *Hold on to the memories, they will hold on to you*
> *And I will hold on to you*

It's never clear if the relationship being sung to or from by this song is ongoing or in its dying embers – here it seems that 'I will hold on to you' is saying 'I will hold onto you like the memories do' – as in, I'm off, hope you remember me well. It's appropriate that it's set on New Year's Day then – an odd kind of in between, liminal time of hangovers from a whole year and the rebirth which is a new year. Given the soft and wistful tone, it's perhaps not important if this is from a live relationship or not but it's a delightful, delicate piece and a striking contrast to the high-pop, high-production of the preceding album.

Lover

In contrast with the chutzpah-to-the-wall of *reputation*, *Lover* is a demure and careful exposition of Swift as a songwriter. In parts, it has some of Swift's most delicate and thoughtful lyrics. If Swift has written an album that was a 'grower', it was this one. A range of songs, from the opaquely beguiling to the lightweight and winsome.

By now cemented as a permanent feature of the English-speaking pop landscape, Swift again explores the structures of her songs, finding new ways to wrest and mould her lyrics into global earworms.

'I Forgot That You Existed'

Straight off the bat, we're not in the same musical world of *reputation*. It's a much more organic and light sound. Handclicks on the 2 and 4 of the beat and a lighter production. This isn't quite in the realm of the wooded indie shed sounds of *folklore* and *evermore* but it's certainly not shiny 'very studio' like *reputation*.

The lyrical tone is also lighter immediately – in the pre-chorus/first line of the chorus, the narrator explains the process of getting over someone. Just forget them. It's delivered with levity and the music around it is a lovely, unhurried loop of spare piano chords.

Where Swift's narrators on *reputation* were more acerbic in their tone, the narrator here is more self-deprecating. Chill, in the common parlance.

> *Got out some popcorn*
> *As soon as my rep started going down*

This is a reference to a gif/meme (see 'Internet Culture' in tropology) but it's also a humorous approach to the antagonist; rather than regarding that antagonist's actions in a negative light, here they're rather rendered in an insouciant, carefree way. If one side of Swift's being *the* millennial songwriter is her *extra*ness, then the other side is the Internet-informed 'whatever' vibe here.

That whatever vibe in action: a line about what was learnt from a relationship, followed by 'I just forget what they [the lessons] were'; one of the characteristics of a lot of Internet humour, especially directed at millennials, is the nonchalance (or at least feigned nonchalance). In a sense, that's always been what 'being cool' meant. But just to drive a wedge between *Lover* and *reputation*, this song is very vibes, totes chill, yeah?

Just to refer to the production for a second – while *Lover* certainly sounds less obviously like there's a lot of vocal production – by comparison to the long reverb tails of *reputation* – there's still a lot here, operating quietly – if you listen closely to the 'sent me a clear message' on the bridge of this tune you can hear that the vocals are almost too clear, perfect. It may not be autotuned but it's certainly had a lot of production applied to sound *that* perfect. Similarly, the backing vocals with the reverb on the chorus do a good job of jumping in, all heavy production, to punctuate the terminal words of the chorus.

'Cruel Summer'
Here once again those helicopter synths that characterised *1989* and Swift's electro-pop numbers more generally. While *Lover* is less high-production pop, it's not quite in the realms of the highly acoustic-leaning *folklore/evermore* albums that succeeded it.

If *reputation* was one of Swift's least lyrical albums, *Lover* overcompensates; there's a lot of lyrical ideas come to fruition or begin here. Swift's confidence as a writer manifests as being more comfortable with odd and unusual phrases.

> *Killing me slow, out the window*
> *I'm always waiting for you to be waiting below*
> *Devils roll the dice, angels roll their eyes*
> *What doesn't kill me makes me want you more*

That is, killing the narrator by not being outside of the window; predicated on that very Hollywood, very *Romeo and Juliet* idea of the paramour who lies in wait outside the window, below the veranda. It's a well-known figure, a commonplace of romantic scenes but there's a few jumps to get the listener to that point – that is, Swift is confident that her listenership are able to make those jumps to understanding the lines, and confident in her writing that she can eke out a narrative by what is *absent* from it.

The second part couple in the stanza is a nicely mythical – there's nothing like working with the cast of eternity. 'What doesn't kill me...' is a reference to 'What does not kill me makes me stronger', an aphorism from nineteenth-century German philosopher Friedrich Nietzsche. Whether Swift is aware of Nietzsche or not (it's a phrase so common as to elide its own roots) it's definitely citational, aphoristic, and witty – in common with Swift's writing in general.

> *It's cool, that's what I tell 'em*
> *No rules in breakable heaven*
> *But...*
> *It's a cruel summer*

This is a gorgeously opaque line; the 'no rules in breakable heaven' doesn't clearly cede any obvious interpretation and the lines around it offer little in the way of elucidation. The line 'It's cool...' is simple enough; 'cruel summer' presumably referring to a less than auspicious period. 'No rules in heaven' would make sense – it's that modifier 'breakable'. It starts giving rise to positively Thomistic thoughts – if heaven is fragile, fallible, is it really heaven? Let's assume so. So what is 'heaven' here? Breakable is adding a modifier to perfection; a conditional perfection. A rule-less, conditional perfection. Are rules not another form of condition? Etc.

Somewhere in this whorling confusion it ends up like the kōan of Zen Buddhism – the contradictory or baffling short poem used to challenge a student's understanding. It's accepted that a breakable heaven makes sense, that there's a fragile perfection which is rule-less, navigated by itself and nothing more.

In a sense this may well be overwrought interpretation on my part – for which I'll have to shoulder the blame – but my point here is that the line is indicative of Swift's confidence – by including an enigmatic and potentially self-contradictory line, we see her maturing as a writer.

The other side of that confusion is that it potentially exposes Swift to criticism that's never been the case before – she has, up until now, been overwhelmingly coherent and clear, and where she is hypnagogic, or dream-influenced, it's been telegraphed clearly. This line is *exposing*, in a way.

Some cursory research suggests that it *could* be a reference to a stanza in 'Love Poem' by US poet John Frederick Nims (1913–1999):

> *Forgetting your coffee spreading on our flannel,*
> *Your lipstick grinning on our coat,*
> *So gaily in love's* unbreakable heaven
> *Our souls on glory of spilt bourbon float.*

…but it's a struggle to see how that does anything to aid interpretation besides saying 'it's a reference to this poem' and 'breakable heaven' is still peculiar and oxymoronic.

'Lover'

Some threads in pop music dangle around for decades but never get tugged at. This song is markedly similar to Mazzy Star's 'Fade Into You' – a song well known to people who were of age in the early 1990s but unlikely to be on Swift's radar as she was, in 1994, four years old. It's not so much that it sounds the same – although the reverby drums, minimal acoustic guitar, leading bassline are certainly similar – so much as it's the *vibe* which is 'woman in oversized jumper bittersweetly melts into paramour'. That's quite an exacting vibe but I'm sure you'll agree it's the correct description.

Lover is a good example of how production detail is all over Swift's music. While *reputation* had a definite aura of being highly produced, *Lover* (the album) and 'Lover' (the song) still have plenty of recording details that suggest some assiduous ears have been listening. During the line 'I take this magnetic force of a man' there's a small sound, a fraction of a second, that sounds like shaking un-trimmed guitar strings behind the guitar's neck. It's a very specific sound, and its use would typically indicate that it's an 'as live' recording – one of those incidental noises that happens and are blocked out by most listeners. Except it's not incidental, it reappears on the next phrase, in the same part of the rhythm. If it was just 'surface noise', recording artefacts, it'd more likely appear in random places.

We might want to refer to this kind of effect as 'authenticity signalling' – that is, effects which connote to listeners that this is an 'authentic' recording. If we hold *Lover* in contrast to *reputation*, there's a lot more that's 'organic' about it; however, each record will have gone through a comparable amount of work. For small indie records, it's likely the band haven't pored over every detail (although there's still an enormous about of sound-obsessives in that world too) but for a big pop production, its rarely the case that the whole thing hasn't been fine-toothed to the hilt. That isn't to say that authenticity signalling is detrimental; rather that it should be considered as no more or less authentic than your favourite made-on-a-computer techno or happy hardcore.

Similarly to the errant rattling string, there's a great hammered piano – in the final repeating build-ups of 'you're my, my my, my' (repeated thrice), there's a background piano, just within the threshold of hearing, which is wildly dissonant. It's not invasively so but it's still forming the musical build-up to the ultimate, solo voice 'lover' which decisively ends the song.

The lyrics dote on the compelling forces of love – first in their capacity to collapse experience – '…there's a dazzling haze … about you, dear / Have I known you twenty seconds or twenty years?', next on the polar attraction felt by the narrator 'I take this magnetic force of a man'.

There's an insinuation still that love exists within fairly normative, Christian dynamics – compare 'I take this magnetic force of a man to be my lover' to item 1627 of the Catechism of the Catholic Church: 'The consent consists in a "human act by which the partners mutually give themselves to each other": "I take you to be my wife" – "I take you to be my husband".' While Swift may have drifted into a more sexualised being, there's still enough conservative values here to appease the old country fans that are still on board at this point.

'The Man'

The musical tone here is very much in the electro-pop vein that Swift's had in her repertoire since the album *1989*. Synth basses and drum machines. The significance of this song though is primarily political. Swift is often framed as peak white feminism – that is, the kind of feminist whose commitment is minimal and superficial. The kind of people who regard Hillary Clinton as a girlboss rather than an awful product of the US political class (who was, to be clear, still legions better than Donald 'grab 'em by the pussy' Trump).

It's difficult to pin down Swift's politics too directly – it's possible to make inferences insofar as she's explicitly support queer rights: she cited the Gay & Lesbian Alliance Against Defamation (GLAAD) in 'You Need to Calm Down' and markedly chose a trans male lead – Laith Ashley – in the video for 'Lavender Haze' (*Midnights*). There's always room for a person to be more radical – she hasn't advocated unilaterally free PrEP for all those who need it, for instance – but the actions she has taken are actions that, from one the biggest pop star of the moment, do have lasting and far-reaching positive influence. I personally have queer friends who regard Swift with suspicion – for the exploitation of black dancers in the 'Shake It Off' video, for the cosying up to 'the pink pound'.

Pop music is typically conservative politically, though. Politics is treated as verboten such that it typically appears as a subtext – until relatively recently, singers like George Michael or Michael Stipe were very circumspect about their sexuality. And there's a long history of queering music – that is reading something as more queer than the author intended. The scene in *South Pacific* where the sailors all bemoan the lack of dames is a good example – superficially the notion is that the singers are all straight men, but the song has another life as a queer choir classic. Your local gay choir are probably practising it for a performance as we speak.

So there's typically a limit to how forward a musician can be with their politics. In turn, gestures like having a (really hot) trans man in her video is substantial and to be celebrated – trans folk are under attack from large swathes of the press and in the UK we've recently (early 2023) seen trans teenager Brianna Ghey murdered in a transphobic attack. That is to say, representation matters.

This is all to say that while Swift can be criticised for her politics, she isn't entirely politically vacuous, insipidly quiet. 'The Man', finally, is a song about the ways in which there's still a substantial difference between the way men are treated and how women are treated. In terms of sexuality, men are allowed to explore it with impunity, while women typically are criticised. If Swift were a man, 'They'd say I played the field before I found someone to commit to'.

Men tend to be listened to more than women: 'When everyone believes ya / What's that like?' Men's achievements are put under less scrutiny: 'They wouldn't shake their heads and question how much of this I deserve', and their outfits or attitudes are not criticised as a matter of course: 'What I was wearing ... / Could all be separated from my good ideas and power moves'. If any readers are looking for a citation for this: women, everywhere.

To put this into a political context – in terms of how radical this is, Swift isn't advocating expropriation – it's not *that* radical. However, it is substantial to be speaking these commonplace, well-known feminist truths to a huge international fanbase and further media. These are well-known ideas but the fact that they're not universally acknowledged means that it's still important to present them to the world in general.

'The Archer'
If Swift's *reputation* was the moment of her really pushing for a hard and bombastic style, then *Lover* is almost the complete opposite – subtle and demure, wistful and cautious. 'The Archer' is a relatively typical, if not predictable, in terms of its musical structure (C/G/Am/F: I-V-vi-IV). What's strongly atypical is that there's a drone note in C which persists through most of it. Drone notes are absolutely bread-and-butter in South Asian (especially Indian) music but they're far rarer in Western pop music. It's a note which persists continuously, ensuring that there's a constant root note which is audible, keeping the key of the piece in constantly present. The Archer has a C drone which only shifts for the beginning of the pre-chorus, persisting throughout the song otherwise. It's the kind of effect which is more common to a certain thread of indie music – Velvet Underground or Spacemen 3. Quite why drones aren't used in Western pop music is an essay unto itself – but suffice it to say that it introduces specific challenges with regards harmonic and rhythmic development.

What the drone introduces here is the thread around which the whole song spins – the melody contracts and expands around it. The whole piece rises to a sort of crescendo, acquiring rhythmic parts and density, but it's a crescendo which is subtle and driving rather than striking and invasive.

The lyrics are less deterministic than earlier Swift but the style is still typically Swiftian – a series of contradictions and paradoxes. 'I never grew up, it's getting so old', punning on the contrary of 'never grow up'.

Dark side, I search for your dark side

This is a darkly enigmatic line which shows a fascinating side to the protagonist – in the search for intimacy with the antagonist, and as a consequence of her (undisclosed) mis-deeds, she yearns for the antagonist to be darker than they have so far presented. The whole song has a confessional tone and this is hugely compelling – in seeking our 'others' we want them to be just as flawed as we are, which in turn speaks to the alienated-narcissist mentioned earlier.

'I Think He Knows'
From the delicate and self-effacing to the simple, classic pop song. 'I Think He Knows' isn't one of Swift's most profound lyrics but it is a cute little pop

song; lightweight squeeing about hot boys because that is kind of what pop is meant to be about.

> *It's like I'm 17, nobody understands*

While we've long since affirmed that Swift's lyrical base is adult now, it's nice to have the counterpoint thrust forwards again – it's only really as an adult that we get to reflect on teenage petulance and stubbornness. And of course it's a different feeling when you're actually 17 to when you're reflecting on it. Teenhood reflected on from adulthood is a state of excess and, as we can see here, a state of irrationality; a cute mini-exegesis on being in love as a (younger) adult.

> *Got that, ah, I mean*
> *Wanna see what's under that attitude like*

And as with 'Dress' (see *reputation* review), we have a sexy sound that's standing in for sexual attraction. And brilliantly – considering this is a cute pop song about hot boys – we have a wonderfully cheap euphemism in 'wanna see what's under that attitude'.

> *I think he knows*
> *When we get all alone*
> *I'll make myself at home*
> *And he'll want me to stay*

It's fairly well known from Swift's online persona that she is a big fan of cats. She has three of them, named Meredith Grey, Olivia Benson, and Benjamin Button. This is wild speculation but as a cat person myself I can't help but feel that this stanza is the narrator suggesting that she'll just do what cats do in order to inveigle herself into her paramour's life. Just kind of turn up and look cute until he forgets that she doesn't belong there. Cats are great like that.

'Miss Americana & the Heartbreak Prince'
To speak of Swift being the songwriter of millennials *par excellence* – there are a number of books that are widely read by millennials, but there are few as well read as the *Harry Potter* series. The song title 'Miss Americana & the Heartbreak Prince' is easily parsed as mimicking the names of the *Harry Potter* books – the sixth in the series is *Harry Potter and the Half-Blood Prince*. Mercifully Swift's perspective on trans folk is substantially more progressive than Potter author J. K. Rowling.

The links to *Harry Potter* are thin – besides the title, the song is set in a school. And the theme of the song might well be described as classic high school drama (think *Beverly Hills 90210/One Tree Hill*) – the couple who are denigrated by their peers.

Swift does picture this as a specifically American narrative – while we certainly have schools in the UK, the school described here, unified around sports, pageants, proms, and cliques, feels specifically US-centric.

> *And I don't want you to (Go), I don't really wanna (Fight)*
> *'Cause nobody's gonna (Win), I think you should come home*

This is an oddity in that the terms in brackets are shouted; while it's reminiscent of the kinds of cheerleading we see on teen TV dramas, it's also not so far from the kind of crew shouts that define a lot of hip-hop or hardcore culture – think Beastie Boys. Perhaps that's the wrong way around – it may well be that the Beastie Boys' most abiding influence is, in fact, with cheerleaders.

'Paper Rings'

This is a song of reminiscence, comparing the beginnings of a relationship to its current state. The song is called 'Paper Rings', so it's safe to assume that the relationship is about a year old – paper being the traditional gift for the first wedding anniversary.

Paper rings has the honour of being the first time there's been a key change in a Swift album track. It's an odd thing to think about, insofar as up to the late 1990s key changes were very much *de rigueur* – as the 2000s unfolded, pop became more streamlined and key changes typically disappeared. It's possible to speculate on why – perhaps it's easier for the average radio listener to sing along without key changes, perhaps there was a dearth of singers who could handle key changes (unlikely, not least with the advent of autotune) – but it's interesting to note that their inclusion now *feels* peculiar.

There's a lot of sounds in this song that are not strictly semantic – ohs and uhs and huhs – which lends it a celebratory, effusive atmosphere. Pop music is built on groans and *mouthsounds*, nonsensical sounds that carry a meaning without having any semantic content. The problem here is that there's not much lyrical content around it. There's a few witticisms – 'I hate accidents except when we went from friends to this' but by and large it's another simple pop song about being in love.

> *Went home and tried to stalk you on the internet*
> *Now I've read all of the books beside your bed*

This though is a lovely observation – two takes on the desire for intimacy; first, from afar, when we find out about a person online. 'Stalk' is used with a high degree of irony and hyperbole to describe finding out information about someone. And next when we've read the same books as our partner – the other side of the same coin, where rather than consuming the information about the person, we consume the same information that they have.

It's a song that's very similar to the kind of thing that Kesha writes when she's doing uptempo, trashy love songs. And no bad thing, Kesha is banging.

'Cornelia Street'
There's a real *throb* to this song. The beat is regular but the keyboard figure (maybe a Fender Rhodes keyboard?) just wafts in on the beat. It's not quite propulsive in the way that a drumbeat is but it just slickly lounges over the song like a model or a particularly elegant cat.

> *Windows flung right open, autumn air*
> *Jacket 'round my shoulders is yours*
> *We bless the rains on Cornelia Street*
> *Memorize the creaks in the floor*

The country-era Swift had frequent touches of strikingly well-observed intimacy, and this is a great example of that theme re-appearing; just enough information to evoke specific details, just vague enough to connect with a broad audience. We make ourselves cold for the people we love; we sing songs together on specific streets – in this case, 'Africa' by Toto (see 'Internet Culture' in tropology). We end up knowing the stairs of our houses well enough to recognise people walking up to bed by the pattern of the creaks. Small details that feel specific but are a lot broader.

> *'I rent a place on Cornelia Street'*
> *I say casually in the car*

There's a sense that Swift has a good capacity for the directorial – she's directed her own videos and her songs are filled with filmic narrative. Here we've got an instance of using two apparent off-hand statements – one a citation, one a description – neither of which directly speak of the relationship. But the audience is invited to empathise with the situation – knowing that in heightened romantic situations, nothing is casual, that the antagonist coming back to the place is freighted with romantic allure and invite. It's a case of telling a story by letting the audience fill in the gaps – a technique that pops up again and again with later Swift.

'Cornelia Street' is a great example of the way in which Swift has a lot of very *writerly* habits – while this album has a few lightweight pop songs, there's still a lot of storytelling here and much of it is in an increasingly sophisticated voice, growing differently to the country voice that preceded it.

'Death By a Thousand Cuts'
Swift has been playing live about fifteen years by this point; *Self-titled* was released in 2006, thirteen years prior. One of the interesting things about Swift as a musician is that, despite her being competent on a range of instruments, she rarely explores complex musical ideas. Her lyrics are often discreetly more sophisticated and while the music is *timbrally* complex, the structures around it are simple. It is pop music and, to an extent, pop music is often a simple form (but not always – ask your local musicologist to explain Britney Spears's 'Toxic' to you).

In the background of the chorus of 'Death By a Thousand Cuts' is a figure that sounds like a toy piano – or perhaps a cimbalom or celesta – that bisects the time signature with a triplet feel. That is, the time that would normally be divided into four beats is divided into three – one beat for every one-and-a-bit of the main rhythm. That sort of explanation makes it a lot more complex than it really is – it's something that's easily *felt* by a musician (and especially a jazz musician) and it doesn't involve internal maths. Here it's a background effect – something that's accentuating the main chorus and perhaps adding a sense of musical chaos to proceedings. It's a slight and not massively noticeable effect – it's not used to be expressly jarring. But the oddity is that it's a kind of musical spread that Swift doesn't typically reach for.

This song also leans on a metaphor of the now-defunct relationship being a house into which the narrator looks. I've gone into some detail on that in tropology but suffice it to say it's a really strong metaphor for the way our foundations and *being* can be strongly shaken by bad relationships.

'London Boy'
There's a real difficulty with a song like this insofar as all the novelty of the song is lost on me, as a British person who lived in London for a few years. Most of the slang that is atypically Swiftian is entirely pedestrian for most British people – 'darling, I fancy you' or 'Babes, don't threaten me with a good time'.

This isn't an ethnographic study on the UK – it's a fun pop song about someone from the US dating a Londoner. So we get some of the classic US takes on the UK – 'Show me a gray sky, a rainy cab ride', just to be sure to embody the idea that the weather in the UK is terrible (and don't get me wrong, it is primarily terrible).

In a sense this is a novelty song which is doubtless exciting and exotic for the majority of Swift's audience – it's just difficult for me personally to get excited about her singing about Highgate or Hackney.

'Soon You'll Get Better'

For the song 'Lover' I mentioned the idea of 'authenticity signalling' and there's a great instance of it on 'Soon You'll Get Better' – the last chorus has an extraneous close-miked breath of Swift's. The effect is to emphasise the intimacy of the recording – that we're listening close up to Swift's voice as if we were 'in the room' with her. This doesn't occur elsewhere in the song. And the thing to note is that this is very much a production decision – it's easy enough to remove and the reason to keep it in is to give the listener the impression of intimacy, 'real' singing.

Also on this song are The Chicks, who older readers may remember for being heavily criticised for their (sagacious, well-considered) criticisms of the second Iraq war. Whether the choice to record with them was deliberately provocative or no, it's interesting that this is the most obvious connection between post-country Swift and the country music industry that gave her her first break(s).

The Chicks are never quite front-and-centre of this track but their presence is still writ large – their three-part harmonies adding a really gorgeous body to Swift's voice which is has double tracking to bulk out a harmony.

This is a terribly sad song around the paralysing, overwhelming world of visiting loved ones in hospital. And as ever, Swift has acutely homed in on the details, the faff and confusion which makes it such a tribulation.

> *In doctor's office lighting, I didn't tell you I was scared*

That acuity – to remember the harshly agonising glare of hospital lighting and the panicked idiocy of sticking your coat on in a rush, described as hair tangled in buttons – another instance of details inferred from absent context.

> *You like the nicer nurses, you make the best of a bad deal*
> *I just pretend it isn't real*

One of the ways in which there's a failing of describing these intensely emotional situations is that, after the fact, there's a tendency to rationalise what's happening. Rather than saying 'I was emotionally overwhelmed' Swift picks at little details;

rather than rushing to narrativise the whole hospital experience, there's a plain and simple statement of naïvety – 'I just pretend it isn't real'.

For most of the song Swift is at pains to ensure that we're witnessing the moment *in itself*, in all its striplit terror. The denouement is that 'It's been years of hoping, and I keep saying it because / 'Cause I have to' – they won't get better and this song is like a tattoo of the moments that led to the repetition.

It's a very personal song (whether the story is fiction or no) and it's notable in terms of Swift opening up the storytelling to other kinds of sadness. Diversifying her sadnesses, if you will.

'False God'

At some point in Swift's career, it'll be possible to compile whole albums of different threads in her songwriting. For instance, the songs that sound like they belong on *folklore* but belong to another album. And here, a song that belongs on *Midnights* but pre-dates it – a soulful, blurred edges, downtempo, sexy number, complete with everyone's favourite sexstrument, the saxophone.

Just to mark how far we've come from the small-c conservative country days – for instance, 'asking God if he could play it again' ('Our Song', *Self-titled*) – 'False God' is faintly irreligious. And for clarity – it's not that Swift has become some Cradle of Filth-alike profaner of Christianity; rather that there's a sense of sexuality here that's faintly anti-religious. Hence the title 'False God'.

> *We might just get away with it*
> *The altar is my hips*

The move into sexual territory is complete then; it's possibly crude to dictate this euphemism but it's definitely about the below-the-waist genitals. If you're looking at the altar (the hips) from underneath then it's likely that the euphemism is for cunnilingus.

The complement to this strophe replaces the 'altar' line with 'Religion's in your lips' – each of them dealing with a different element of sacral practice.

The religious element of this is ironic, in a sense – while the chorus is a setup of a religious practice-sex metaphor, the pre-chorus tells us that '...the road gets hard ... / When you're led by blind faith' – that is, any religiosity is undermined by the assertion that the ecstatic/religious experience of (presumably oral) sex.

> *Even if it's a false god*
> *We'd still worship this love*

The split of ev-en in the second part of this couplet is interesting – Swift could have made it one beat but makes it two instead. There's not a massive reason for this except to accentuate the swiftly delivered 'we'd still worship this' and extended 'lo-o-o-o-ve'. The song is relatively downtempo so this is adding contrast to the two lines – ensuring that the second line, the terminal line of the chorus, is felt most keenly. While *Lover* is less obviously production-heavy than its predecessor, there's still a huge amount of detail that's been absorbed into it.

'You Need to Calm Down'
This was the second single off the album; the video ended with text imploring readers to sign a Change.org petition in support of the Equality Act. While this song is only just explicitly in support of queer rights ('shade never made anybody less gay') this is still a significant and important contribution to international dialogues with regards queer rights. And for that we need a bouncy, fun song with a vividly bright video full of drag queens and associated queerabilia.

> *I ain't tryna mess with your self-expression*
> *But I've learned a lesson that stressin' and obsessin' 'bout somebody else is no fun*

Swift's lyrics have long had a substantial rap influence and here it is again – a couplet that's full of sibilant stresses that move the emphasis of the beat and run faster than the underlying rhythm – raising the heart rate, building up tension to the chorus. The chorus itself is a simple sentiment – 'You need to calm down'. Which is to say, it's a very pop chorus, and not a typically Swiftian one – simple, repeatable, memorable but not verbose. That's in service of the political attachment to the song – sometimes, when delivering political statements, what's needed is a simple phrase.

> *snakes and stones never broke my bones*

Again, here we have a sibilant run of sounds and a classically country inversion of a pithy aphorism. Swift might be a long way from sounding like country music – and pro-queer statements in country are fleetingly rare – but this pattern from the earlier works is clearly still present.

'Afterglow'
Afterglow is perhaps the song on *Lover* which is most vestigial of *reputation* – it's got a smidge of autotune on the vocals, the production is very present, with big reverby drums and a noticeable dynamic switch between verse and chorus.

It might well be the case that Swift's subtlety is too much here – the chorus opens with

> *Hey, it's all me, in my head*
> *I'm the one who burned us down*

and there's another five lines between that and the payoff 'Meet me in the afterglow'. It's a great metaphor – burning down the relationship and then asking the antagonist to meet in the afterglow – the dying embers of the burnt-down relationship. 'Afterglow' may also evoke the post-coital state, the intimate moments of exhaustion.

This is another song where it perhaps shouldn't be read as indicative of Taylor Swift, the person – despite the fact that the narrator has fucked up the relationship, she's still pulling back on the antagonist – 'I need to say, hey, it's all me, just don't go'. As Swift has said, there's nothing like a mad woman and this is, perhaps, an exaggerated vision of someone who wrecks relationships then tries to stitch them back together.

'Me!' featuring Brendon Urie

Urie is the vocalist and sole remaining original member of Panic! at the Disco. While that band ultimately ended up very much in a pop rock world, they were for part of the 2000s one of the key emo bands. Or for the emo hardcore, one of the pop bands that people said were emo.

His emo credentials are important insofar as Swift's music, while never actually *sounding* emo, has always been very close to it; emotionally overwrought, over the top, and very much inclined towards expressing it. The big difference between Swift's music and emo is that she took a circuitous route towards 'indie' music while pretty much all of the emo bands started off on the underground circuit, playing basements and doing tours in crapped out old borrowed cars.

No real signs of anything emo in this tune, though – it's a straight-up celebratory love song, a pop song with a big brassy chorus. Both singers take turns at self-deprecating verses – Swift: 'I know that I went psycho on the phone'; Urie: 'I know I tend to make it about me' – before a mutually celebratory chorus of 'I'm the only one of me / Let me keep you company'.

The video is very bright and bouncy and full of dancers. It's also the first time Swift met one of her cats, Benjamin Button. It's a peculiar song because in spite of the self-deprecation, this is atypically happy in a very 1930s musical film or Broadway show way.

Urie takes the line 'And you can't spell awesome without me'; it's not humanity's most astonishing line but it does remind me of another line from UK Grime artist JME, talking about himself and Ed Sheeran:

> *Everybody totally loved mine & Ed Sheeran's track*
> *Maybe because GINGER is an anagram of BLACK*

Which is arguably the final word on self-aggrandisement in song.

'It's Nice to Have a Friend'
This is a wee two-and-a-half-minute number and it's fairly distinct from most of Swift's material. It's a lot more simple than her usual fare. Two chords, verse/chorus and a wee instrumental section. The chorus is just a repeated 'It's nice to have a friend'. The backing is a steel drum tapping out a couple of chords on the beat, the solo is a bar or so of cornet.

It may well be that this is Swift's first effort towards the kind of lyrical parity that she delved into quite strongly on *Midnights* – where usually her lines are conjugated, whole sentences, here the verse is a series of ephemeral sentence fragments. That's not to say that nothing is connoted with these words but that there's a real economy of words to get the point across.

> *Light pink sky, up on the roof*
> *Sun sinks down, no curfew*
> *... Something gave you the nerve*
> *To touch my hand*

Just a simple framing of a where and a when in a few words jumping between minimal sentiments. A few skeletal insinuations and nothing to say what happened after the hand was touched. Except the third verse has:

> *Church bells ring, carry me home*
> *...*
> *Call my bluff, call you 'Babe'*
> *Have my back, yeah, every day*

That is, the song jumps from different times of life; childhood, teenhood, adulthood, and how 'It's nice to have a friend'. It's unusual in Swift's canon but it's also sweet and warming in a way we haven't seen since maybe 'Never Grow Up' on *Speak Now*.

'Daylight'
The closing song for this album and it's one that's chock full of those extended aphorisms and witty inversions that are the mainstay of Swift's writing:

Luck of the draw only draws the unlucky

This line is almost antimetabole, where a sentence is repeated in a different order to give a different meaning. Such as John F. Kennedy's 1961 inaugural address: 'Ask not what your country can do for you; ask what you can do for your country.' The skill here is in finding a commonplace phrase and satirising a gap in its logic; relying on luck is kind of a weak position to be in.

Threw out our cloaks and our daggers because it's morning now

The point of these acerbic inversions is to realise the importance of a brand-new day. Implied but unspoken above is that cloaks and daggers are only necessary by cover of night. The chorus of this strongly leans into the daylight concept as renewal, epiphany – pacific and revelatory as a counterpart to the verse's wisecracking. It's a neat and warming closer for an album which has been mostly positive, a sunny disposition for the complexity of emotional stuff.

folklore

Another about-face into other forms, this time pushing towards the cool, arch world of indie songwriting. While she's still playing classic songforms, there's now the confidence of a songwriter who's spent a lifetime writing. We're in the realm of lowercase song titles and telling a story with a minimum of means. Production craft now honed to the point of exquisite delicacy.

If in her past Swift had an anxiety about 'some indie record much cooler than mine', she's now progressed to define what a successful indie record sounds like, and upped the lyrical game in indie with panache.

'the 1'
Coming on the back of *Lover*, *folklore* is somewhat more demure. The artwork is all soft focus and wooded hipster in a distant lodge. By and large, *folklore* is the point where that line from 'We Are Never Ever Getting Back Together' becomes prophetic – Swift is strongly into the realm of 'some indie record *much* cooler…' Except, of course, Swift is massive and as such loses underground credibility. But also the arbiters of that credibility are, typically, appalling idiots.

Where *reputation*'s dips into or borrowings from hip-hop were somewhat clumsy, here those affectations are delivered with a lot more self-effacing humour: 'I hit the ground running each night / I hit the Sunday matinee' – this is putting those clichés of 'the grind' into a more Swiftian context – gentle, calm.

> *In my defense, I have none*
> *For never leaving well enough alone*

We've seen this pattern previously, where Swift refers to a previously declared grammatical subject in a way that is kind of abrupt, jarring – 'All the liars are calling me one' from 'Call It What You Want', *reputation*. It's arguably more effective here – shortening the line and arresting doubts. If the earlier tone in this song was self-effacing, here that tone is shifting to acceptance, taking responsibility. The song is a 'the one that got away' type song, and rather than that theme producing feelings of petulance (see 'Gorgeous', *reputation*) Swift's narrator is plaintive and observational – 'But it would've been fun / If you would've been the one'. It's difficult to pin this on 'maturity' – different songs will have different outcomes and if these are *stories* then they are merely reflecting whatever the story is – but the protagonist here is a lot *cooler*, in keeping with the louche indie cool of *folklore* in general.

The next repetition of that stophe:

> *In my defense, I have none*
> *For digging up the grave another time*

Which is one of Swift's typical overloaded metaphors. Digging up graves – that is, raking over the past – is extreme enough as a metaphor when done once; the notion of repeating it makes it all the more ghastly and exaggerative and *extra*.

'cardigan'
As with *Lover*, *folklore* is a super-produced, proper pop production that tends to elide that production – it's subtle rather than in-your-face. The piano on this album is exquisitely recorded – close-miked and with plenty of detail. This song features a clip-clop rhythm, like high heels on cobblestones, and conveniently enough there's a lyric of 'high heels on cobblestones'.

It's almost as if the penultimate track on *Lover* ('It's Nice to Have a Friend') was lyrically paving the way for 'cardigan'. Minimal words for maximum impact.

The verse carries a pattern of a simple statements, evoking but not detailing a situation. Short clipped fragments like vintage tee, brand-new phone, fancy shoes tell us that it's a prestigious situation; the 'when you are young they assume you know nothing' line intimating that this is a old situation, and that the protagonist knows full well what she's doing...

It's revealed to be a bad relationship; the minimum amount of words to reveal that the antagonist gives not enough emotionally or in personal time. There's a repeating line, 'I knew you...', that becomes like the gasp of desperation, holding onto that knowledge of a person as the relationship decays.

And when I felt like I was an old cardigan

This is the chorus and it's used with a degree of ambiguity. Two senses of 'old': old as in familiar and comfortable, or old as in easily neglected. And both are true, potentially – if we read the song as about being 'the other woman' or a relationship that wasn't being committed to properly, then it's negligence; but in that negligence there's the intimacy which stokes the relationship.

The smell of smoke would hang around this long

This in verse three; verses one and two have given lie to the notion that young people are assumed to know nothing. So that sentiment is being qualified here – what the younger person lacked in what we might regard as 'worldly smarts' she made up for with her intense understanding of *dread*. 'The smell of smoke' *feels* descriptive as in 'I could still smell his cigarettes in the house' but it's more likely in the sense of lingering, and it being smoke it's easy to read this as a metaphor for the smouldering decay of intensity which is heartbreak.

What Swift is pushing is that the younger person may have been foolish when she 'tried to change the ending' but ultimately she knew that the repercussions would linger for a long time – that the intensity of feeling was an intensity that would persist.

Leavin' like a father

This is a grim line. The 'like' is doing an amount of lifting – the inclination is to say that leaving 'like' a father is intimating a pattern of 'leavingness' that fathers inhabit; but the more sensible, secondary reading is that the leaving had the *impact* of a father leaving. The next line compares the leaving to water – a very particular thing to run like. Not running like Mo Farah but rather in a gushing and nebulous way, disappearing down the sink.

This song occupies a fairly standard place in Swift's canon, insofar as it's describing a failed relationship and the lingering emotional difficulties afterwards, but it's equally a terse, dense rendering of teenage infatuation and deflation.

'the last great american dynasty'

The album is ostensibly called *folklore* because it's about storytelling. And so for 'the last great american dynasty' here we get a rare instance of Swift shifting from first person to third person, temporarily. Rebekah is painted as a money-grabbing woman who's joined a rich family by marriage.

Rebakah's bad taste is drawn out in citational sentence fragments – described as 'a little gauche' and 'new money'. This is a succinct citation of the kind of off-handedly shitty way 'old money' is. The new/old money distinction is a familiar classist trope. The idea is that there's two types of rich people – generational wealth, as in those who are born into money, and those who acquire wealth suddenly. The former are considered to be more proper, orthodox than those who arrive at it suddenly (in the space of a generation). Swift conjures the kinds of stuffy dickheads who objected to Rebekah.

This story of Rebekah principally details a house that Swift actually bought – one previously owned by Rebekah Harkness, famed ruiner of the wealthy Harkness family. The protagonist Rebekah is a real woman, someone who lived out her days 'Pacing the rocks, staring out at the midnight sea'. And the house sat empty, 'Free of women with madness, their men and bad habits / And then it was bought by me'. As in the actual Taylor Swift, at which point the song switches to first person.

The key here is that Swift's detailing of the story is in order to associate herself with Rebekah, the bad taste new money horror. This is presumably self-effacing on Swift's part – whether or not Swift's family are old or new money (see business for a bit on that), it's kind of *cool* to buy a house that was previously owned by a latter-day witch. That is, witch in the sense of being a woman on the edges, disliked and disrespected by the chattering classes of her day.

Given that this song is about the actual house that Swift lives in, it's a bedfellow to the songs 'My New House' and 'Paintwork' by the Fall. Fine company to be keeping in my book.

'exile' featuring Bon Iver

The use of metaphors invoking the drama of the stage is well-worn. Legendarily, the monologue by Jacques in William Shakespeare's *As You Like It* opens with 'All the world's a stage / And all the men and women merely players'. In the context of theatre, it becomes a kind of meta-analysis – a fourth-wall breaking sentiment where the act of watching is referenced by those being watched.

I can see you starin', honey
Like he's just your understudy

This line is delivered by Swift. An understudy is someone who's hired to learn the lines of a part as a backup if an actor (usually a lead role) is unable to do a performance. The sense in which this is a *cutting* insult is that it's a person with the same lines but who is secondary. Someone who does the same job but is less preferential. It's a great, viciously acidic line, and all the more cutting for being an inference from a dark stare. Later on, there's a line delivered by Vernon about using the side door to leave – most likely a reference to the stage exit. In theatres there's typically a door which is considered less prestigious – the side door which allows for a quick and discreet exit without being seen by the audiences.

The music is very similar to the hocket form – in which two voices take turns articulating a melody. So each part observes a different element of the relationship, or rather, each voice articulates a different side of the shared hurt. The music builds around plaintive chords, Swift and Justin Vernon (of Bon Iver) each detailing their character's hurt. Until the denouement (a very theatrical term) neither side's grievances are made clear. The chorus has matching sentiments – I never… / you never… until the culmination:

Vernon:

> *Cause you never gave a warning sign*

Swift:

> *I gave so many signs*

It's a very classy reveal – both mirroring the other's sentiment until the final moment, where Swift's character reveals that the injustice lies with Vernon's character for not reading the signs. Classically tragic, in its way. And also feminist, in a modern sense – being emblematic of the ways in which relationships can be coloured by a lack of emotional responsibility by one partner (typically the male in heterosexual relationships) – not reading the signs that are, to Swift, apparent. And of course, one of the key elements of storytelling in theatre is that the tragedy of the relationship is blindingly apparent to the audience.

And that denouement reveals details about earlier on in the song – in one of the verses, Swift's character sings 'Balancin' on breaking branches' – to describe the precarity of the relationship being discussed. It would be more typical to say 'balancing on breaking bridges' – which would retain the alliteration. But the fact it's *branches* gives rise to the idea that those aren't precarious tree branches but the olive branch of peace – the precarity is within the abuse of the affection Swift's character has afforded Vernon's character.

It's perhaps a high-water mark in Swift's writing – a real shame that besides this and 'The Last Time' (*Red*), there are minimal instances of two-way dialogue duets in Swift's canon.

'my tears ricochet'

This is possibly the song to point to with regards the subtleties of production for this album; while it may seem to be intimate and acoustic, there's a degree of phasing keyboards, background horns, some vocaloid-like vocal effects like interpuncts or dressing to the main vocals.

It's also the song which appears to be Swift's entry into the goth canon, insofar as the protagonist seems to be quite literally dead:

> …*I swear I loved you*
> *'Til my dying day*

There's a tendency in Swift's lyrics to nominally over-reach a metaphor – extend it just so far so as to ensure the metaphor is *felt*. This marries up with *extra* – as in, going too far, being unnecessarily extravagant. So where this song perhaps goes into full goth territory is that the protagonist isn't *like* being dead, they are quite literally dead. This also means is that this song is very funny. In the way that goth is usually at its best when it's kind of high camp meets graveyard.

The main chorus is 'look at how my tears ricochet' – that is, look how futile, look how self-defeating my tears were. Exactly the kind of sentiment you're likely to hear from beyond the grave, a corpse addressing how much value there was in crying at a boyfriend who is now on the other side of death.

Some readers' mileage may vary as to whether this song is detailing an *actual* dead person speaking from beyond the grave or merely just over-investing the 'I wish I was dead' metaphor. The lyrics are ambiguous – it's not imperative that the narrator be actually dead for the intensity of the self-immolation metaphor to work, insofar as it describes a high-intensity which is dangerous to be in proximity of.

> …*aim for my heart, go for blood*
> *But you would still miss me in your bones*

A powerful of *selfhood* here – home is our core, a huge part of our identity. Heart, blood, bones are central to our being. The alienation from home is a terrifying metaphor, a feeling of absolute rootlessness. The strata, the hierarchy of the next is astonishing – it's not good enough to speak of our hearts, which keep us alive, the blood which is the stuff of our existence – the protagonist would be missed at a deeper level still, in the very architecture of our bodies which is 'bones'.

All in all, it's Swift in her most grievous mode and, if we choose to read it that way, humorously so.

'mirrorball'

Swift's singing voice here is atypically subdued – seemingly in the lower register. It's not so much that her voice is weaker in this register but there's a certain breathy distance that's atypical for her delivery.

> *I'll show you every version of yourself tonight*
> *I'll get you out on the floor*
> *Shimmering beautiful*
> *And when I break, it's in a million pieces*

The mirrorball metaphor is turned over, squished and turned several ways here – it's reflective, it's part of the semiotic of discos, it's creating light effects and it's blisteringly complex when broken. Functionally the mirrorball is more typically connoted as the stuff of slightly tacky discos. It's nice for once to see it elevated to the status of Swift-like.

The mirrorball-narrator is a pathetic one – desperately and precariously trying to do too many things to get the antagonist's attention. Balancing on a tightrope, desperately clamouring for attention. So the mirrorball is a luscious metaphor for that fizzy desperation – they're these odd glimmering object with thousands of facets that are quite difficult to look at. They usually overload onlookers by shooting light in every direction.

There's a sideline here that explains why the mirrorball is such a pitiable and a kind of crappy signifier – it's too complex, it does too much and it absorbs too much attention without actually being something you can focus on.

The lyrical tone Swift strikes on this and the successive albums is increasingly elusive – whether by more opaque, dense metaphors or by more transparently using storytelling devices, Swift slowly recuses on the invitation to her private life that was allegedly a presence earlier on. The mirrorball which the narrator occupies is consistently reflective, evasive.

'seven'

While the album's title *folklore* doesn't appear in this album, we do get allusions to folklore, talking about stories that are exchanged 'like folk songs'. Folklore for this song is about a love which extends beyond the length of a human life.

Which is, in some senses, what folklore is – the relationships whose stories far outlast their owners.

The imperative characteristic of folklore, folk songs, folk tales, is as a means of preserving a truth. Not truth in the sense of factual, historical documents, or truth in the sense of brutality as with some buildings or statues, but truth in the sense of *felt* history.

> And I've been meaning to tell you
> I think your house is haunted
> Your dad is always mad and that must be why

This tercet is also spoken of in tropology (see 'The monsters turned out to be just truths') but to speak briefly on it here – this story, of a house haunted by a father's bad moods, is probably not one of a haunted house; but the tale of the haunting contains a truth in it, it holds those emotions that are difficult to express. Haunting doesn't describe – let's extemporise – that the dad is losing his job or ill, but it does describe the presence of an unspoken problem.

'august'

This is a song straight from the 'illicit affair' drawer – 'August slipped away into a moment in time / 'Cause it was never mine'. Memory is an odd thing and there's a moral dimension here. Part of the way we form memories is by repetition – we tell stories about that time we drank too much, we show pictures of that holiday, we laugh at how our dead friends got confused by TV remotes. The process of repeating the story, in whatever form, is also the process of memorising it. And of course one of the things that we *can't* do with illicit affairs is talk about them. So their memory becomes weaker.

Second time around, the 'moment in time' turns to 'bottle of wine'. We take a little bit at a time and before we know it's gone, and we're drunk on August and our bladders are full of August. August also has a life as an adjective, but I don't think Swift is alluding to having nobility slip away through the course of the affair. It does fit, but it's still a stretch.

With a sense of changing styles, Swift's dealing with the lost dalliance in 'august' is more lament than rage (unlike, for instance, 'Dear John' on *Red*). There's a plaintive pathos to 'Cancel plans just in case you'd call' – not so much irate at the lost time but saying 'it is what it is' in the face of 'you weren't mine to lose'.

> Back when we were still changin' for the better
> Wanting was enough
> For me, it was enough

Here there's a lovely switch in the near-repetitious lines – 'wanting was enough; for me, it was enough'. From the declarative to the passive – in the gap between the two there's a shadow of an implication that it wasn't enough, that Swift's narrator was belittled by the gap in understanding.

'this is me trying'

Although *folklore* is nominally a kind of wooded indie record, there's a wide breadth in the arrangements. For 'this is me trying' there's a warbling church organ sound and some lovely brass arrangements decorating the distanced, austerely reverbed vocals.

The chorus here is relatively spare – a single repeated line of 'I just wanted you to know that this is me trying'; all of the semantic work is happening in the verses, where the feelings of regret are detailed.

> *They told me all of my cages were mental*
> *So I got wasted like all my potential*

The regrets that the narrator details here are primarily metaphors for psychic states. It may well be that one of the keys to Swift's broad appeal is that she's typically unspecific. Regrets are not like 'because in June I drunkenly insulted your mother'; rather regrets are immanently relatable.

There are two acts here – getting wasted and being curt ('my words shoot to kill'). Not everyone drinks but most can relate to anxieties over not fulfilling potential; pretty much anyone can relate to mis-speaking. The beauty of this pattern, really, being that each individual can fill out their own backstory to these lyrics.

The payoff line 'I have a lot of regrets about that' is inspired in that sense – Swift hasn't detailed *anything* about which she has regrets, in terms of concrete actions or behaviours, and yet it's given as read that the feelings she outlines were inimical to a relationship.

> *Pouring out my heart to a stranger*
> *But I didn't pour the whiskey*

Here again the 'late Swift' trope – we could also say mature Swift – where a lot of the work, the narrative building, is done in allusions and ellipses. Taking the line 'I didn't pour the whiskey', collocating it with 'my words shoot to kill when I'm mad', and what's left is an image of an argument where the narrator may have gotten mad but she didn't pour the whisky, didn't instigate the situation, is in some ways not responsible, again bookended by the modest, plain 'this is me trying'. So while there's an amount of soul-searching and owning up, there's still a sense of not quite fully taking on responsibility. The tone of the 'at least I'm trying' (itself whispered almost as if it's a background vocal) reads two ways: is it passive, so as to leave the space for blaming the antagonist? Or is it defensive, an act of self-protection?

These ambiguities are more common to Swift's writing as it goes further on – self-reflection mixed with terse writing that is a lot less declarative than the good guy/bad guy of the earlier material.

'illicit affairs'
In which Swift creates the archetypal 'illicit affairs' song, one of her more common song subjects. It's a gorgeous number – a sweet merging of some very studio, reverby oohs, a frittering, bright guitar figure and some brilliantly close-miked vocals. Structurally this is shorter than Swift's usual pattern – verse/chorus/verse/chorus/bridge. It's like the lament of assassins – get in, do the damage, leave.

The song details the souring of illicit relationships – the way in which the initial face of it, all excitement and 'beautiful rooms' ends in the less salubrious environs. This song is a mapping of that souring – the way illicit affairs cause so much restriction and self-denial, the way illicit affairs are acts of self-negation:

When this song's choruses say '…it dies and it dies and it dies / A million little times' it's a sense of personal death. The death of self-expression, where the narrator can't even do nice things for her affairee. The death of *presence* because she can take only memories, leave no footsteps. The economy of affairs is exchanging *personhood* in return for immanent ghosts of trysts.

The song culminates with the bridge, including the line 'You taught me a secret language I can't speak with anyone else'. The rage here focused on the condescension but arising from the dehumanisation – the grievances listed previously in the songs are all to do with losing humanity during illicit affairs.

'Godforsaken mess' is one horror to face but again the dehumanisation is pushed with the user-group-of-one language. Language cuts right to the core of who we are as people – we feel affinities with speakers of the same language, especially when that language is a minority one; to remove the capacity of communication is once again a dehumanising effect. It's not so much that an illicit affair is a 'pain in the arse' in Swift's schema but that it has hugely deleterious effects.

'invisible string'
A very different song to 'Invisible' from *Self-titled*. That 'Invisible' detailed the teenage anxiety of not being seen by the boy you liked; 'invisible string' is about the ephemeral connections we feel between ourselves and those we're affectionate

towards. Although this is a banjo-led track, which does tie it together – perhaps with an invisible string – to the instrumentation on that self-titled record. Despite the homely folky sound of this track there's a distant ebowed guitar – a kind of tonal sentinel stretching across several bars, never quite interfering but adding a kind of soloistic colouring that's unusual for Swift's songs, especially during this period.

Hyperbaton is an inversion of the expected grammar of a phrase and is used extensively throughout this tune. Each line in the verse's two tercets begins with an adjective which is subsequently qualified:

> *Cold was the steel of my axe to grind*

For this line, the emphasis is given to 'cold' rather than the 'axe to grind'. It's odd to describe the material (steel) of the axe to grind but in describing that steel as 'cold' the effect is emphatic – bringing to mind 'revenge is a dish best served cold' and giving the grudge of 'axe to grind' a temperament and a delivery. Later the stanza describes how the narrator sends her ex's children presents. It's lightly self-effacing – to paraphrase Irish freedom fighter Bobby Sands, Swift's revenge will be the laughter of her ex's children.

By comparison to the lighter songs of *Lover*, 'invisible string' is a much more *poetic* approach to writing love songs. Where *Lover* was cute but perhaps less meaty, 'invisible string' has a raft of clever word play to bolster a simple description of affection.

'mad woman'

If there is a failing to Swift's songs which are fundamentally a 'fuck you' to someone else, it's that they don't feature Swift actually saying 'fuck you'. There are those who will say that swearing is not big or clever; to them I advise shutting the fuck up. Swearing is great.

The first instance of a 'fuck' on *folklore* – and in fact, in Swift's albums in general – comes in first verse of mad woman:

> *Do you see my face in the neighbor's lawn?*
> *Does she smile?*
> *Or does she mouth, 'Fuck you forever'?*

The song is in the vein of a few songs on *reputation*. Unlike, for instance, 'Look What You Made Me Do', Swift has here elevated the song about snide, acerbic put-downs with wit and, dare I say, élan. Important to note also that the fuck comes with no small amount of absurdity. It's not just seeing the narrator's face in a lawn; it's not just that lawn-face smiling – it's that lawn-face mouthing 'fuck you forever'. Because a lawn-face would, of course, add 'forever' to a fuck you for additional petulance.

That is also to say that where *reputation*'s put-downs were perhaps a little over-serious, here Swift has managed also to telegraph a sense of humour with the put-downs. 'They say "move on", but you know I won't'. Petulant and childish and at all points refuting the maturity that would 'rise above' this kind of song.

> *Every time you call me crazy, I get more crazy*
> *What about that?*
> *And when you say I seem angry, I get more angry*

There's also a sense here of a popular feminist analysis dangling over. One of the problems of women's rage is that it's typical dismissed, rendered as 'woman's problems'. Of course, that has a compounding effect. Some women are told they're angry when they're not. Some are told they're angry in a belittling way.

'epiphany'

In spite of the title 'epiphany', this is not a celebratory or exultory song. It's also not referencing the Christian commemoration of the baptism of Jesus. This may well be one of Swift's darkest songs, elliptical and bleak.

> *Just one single glimpse of relief*
> *To make some sense of what you've seen*

The epiphany of the title, then, is the thing that's yearned for. Some context or revelation or *something* which justifies an awful situation.

It's a song about war, and the sort of psychological effects of it – especially post-traumatic stress disorder (PTSD). 'Keep your helmet … / … here's your rifle', connoting the military process, and the diminutive way young male soldiers are spoken to.

For all the valorisation of active troops in popular culture, there is always a human cost. I'm not saying that Swift is anti-war – I'm sure she would be smarter than to say that explicitly in the US – but I can't help but read songs like this as making the case for the unbearable suffering wrought from wars as being a cost too high.

> *Holds your hand through plastic now*
> *'Doc, I think she's crashing out'*

The line 'holding hands through plastic now' – conjures that desiccated, antiseptic hospital environment. The plastic sheet as a necessary, physical mediation for human contact. Principally this is the human cost of war – not just the adversary's 'collateral damage' (which is as sick a euphemism as imaginable) but also the PTSD and similar catastrophic effects on the active soldiers, and the families thereof.

There are two elliptical lines here which push to the notion that war generates impossible memories – memories that are too harsh to consider or experience. '…some things you just can't speak about' and the '…you dream of some epiphany / To make some sense of what you've seen'. Epiphanies are exceptional, once-in-a-lifetime events, or at least fleetingly rare. In the face of impossible suffering, PTSD-like states, the only possible *escape* is that supernatural intervention, that shaking revelation. And as most of the content lives in inferences and ellipses – the war, the injuries – it's presumed that the tragedy of the song is that that epiphany is eternally out of reach.

'betty'

Despite Betty being an old person's name, this song also features a healthy use of the word 'fuck'. It's also home to two other rarities – a regrettable mouth organ (an appalling mess of an instrument) and a key change (the first since 'Paper Rings' on *Lover*).

The song presents a story of a mistake the narrator made at 17. Depending on how we read the identity of the narrator, there's potentially different subtexts – if the narrator is female then this song might be a little gay; if not then Swift has moved into narrating male subjects – or potentially, this is the first instance where the male subject is obvious (making more than a few earlier songs potentially very gay).

It's not really necessary to resolve this but it's interesting that either case is a step-change for Swift's writing. Knowing also, at this point (released 2020), that Swifties pore over lyrics to a high degree, there's every chance that the narratorial ambiguity was entirely deliberate.

In context: Betty is typically a female name; 'Will you kiss me on the porch' – platonic kissing is eminently possible, but it's the ambiguity that's important to queer readings. 'Slept next to her … / I dreamt of you …'. The 'you' of this is presumed to be Betty.

The queer-woman-narrator reading is scotched by:

> *I was walking home …*
> *when she pulled up*
>
> …
>
> *She said James, get in'* …

James is most typically a masculine name. So this is pretty comprehensively painting the narrator as a man named James and the situation as that of a teenager cheating on someone called Betty.

But here's the thing – it's always been popular, with queer readings, to conveniently misread situations. The dearth of proper queer representation in popular culture leads to a situation where narratives are easily queered. The interpretation of songs in general are made up of multiple interpretations; for 'betty' there's a strong case to be made that one of those interpretations is gay.

> *If you kiss me, will it be just like I dreamed it?*
> *Will it patch your broken wings?*

As with elsewhere on *folklore*, the specifics of what was done by the narrator to Betty are not made clear; what is transparent is the profound remorse felt by the narrator. That they are investing a meeting with the power to 'patch your broken wings', that the remorse-led dream can be made real. The song is less about whether that action – showing up at the party – was one of reconciliation and more about the severe mental blocks that the narrator put in front of themselves prior to going there. As ever with Swift's writing, it's ambiguous but it's occupying and storytelling around a very precise, very particular, emotional state.

'peace'

Another song here which breaks with established musical form – verse, chorus, verse, chorus. In Swiftian terms, it has a massively extended intro, long instrumental breaks, and an extended outro. In more general terms, those instrumental sections are not significant. It's a relative thing. This is practically prog in Swift's terms.

It's also a relatively restricted form – like 'The Archer', this piece has a continuous note which persists throughout; unlike 'The Archer', this note is a semiquaver or sixteenth note pulse. That pulse is usually faster than the rhythm of the lyrics – two or four beats to each syllable. So the harmonic pulse gives the impression of speed underneath the lyrics. Until the line 'Give you the silence that only comes when two people understand each other', which roughly matches the pulse, one semiquaver per syllable. It's not quite an exact fit but it's an interesting pacing of the lyrics – the underlying pulse marks the fastest point in the lyrical rhythm and the lyrics catch up to it, then fall behind. Ultimately giving the effect of adding a holistic shape to the song – we can see it as four discrete sections (verse one, chorus one, verse two, chorus two) or we can see the whole as a wave shape.

Swift's narrator is described as embodying 'danger' ("Cause it [danger] lives in me'. Broadly the song is about the ways in which the narrator is insufficient for the antagonist – detailing her foibles that alienate the couple from each other.

> *But I'm a fire and I'll keep your brittle heart warm*

Again, a strongly embodied metaphor – it's not 'I'm like a fire', it's 'I am a fire'. I am a state of permanent combustion. It's a song which is expressing humility on the part of the narrator, a humility which results in humiliation, to draw from that word's etymology.

That humility may be read as self-effacing; there's another option insofar as it could be read as the kind of psychic self-awareness which comes from work and maturity. '…the rain is always gonna come if you're standin' with me' is a profoundly noble thing to say about a relationship that's volatile insofar as the narrator and the antagonist have negative reactions to each other. So finally the terminal line 'Would it be enough if I could never give you peace?' is rhetorical; the song has strongly detailed the ways in which it would not be enough.

It's a very different break-up song to Swift's by now substantial break-up catalogue insofar as it's telegraphing not a tragic *situation* but a tragic *coupling*. The focus isn't on actions but on the way different personalities or psychologies interact with each other. And again, there's little that's *specific* about that relationship. In a psychological sense, Swift's gift for describing relationships is less about creating or articulating settings for relationships so much as she articulates *archetypes* of relationships.

'hoax'

A sparse piano and vocal arrangement that matches the parity of the lyrics, although there are very subtle touches of strings, percussion and double tracked vocals under the surface. This is another with the pattern of terse, fragmentary, almost iterative lines:

> *My only one*
> *My smoking gun*
> *My eclipsed sun*
> *This has broken me down*

In poetic terms this is four metrical feet, two iambs. 'My on/ly one'. Contrasted with some of Swift's more dense lyrics, this is supremely taut. And of course with less poetic material to work with the lines carry a sense of weight, however elliptical. Each line is articulating the antagonist as in the centre of Swift's being:

'only one', 'eclipsed sun' and the final line in the stanza is a plain articulation of despair.

In a lot of ways this is a profoundly *dark* song – the narrator is threatening suicide in the chorus – the longest line syllabically 'Stood on the cliffside screaming, "Give me a reason"'. Followed by:

> *Your faithless love's the only hoax I believe in*

It's a line dense with twisting allusions – faithless love, the love which is impure but substantial. That love is a hoax and is the only thing that's apparently holding back the narrator from suicide – that's a desperate and a pathetic situation to be in. To have predicated a miserable existence on a falsehood, an artificial love. And then to predicate it so strongly as to be a condition of existence: 'No other sadness in the world would do'.

A beautiful and beleaguered close to Swift's most mature album to date.

evermore

As near as damnit to a companion piece for *folklore*, *evermore* emerged as a surprise in late 2020, at a time when the world was still shell-shocked from Covid-19. Still in the realm of lowercase song titles, it's a return to the cabins, a return to introspective lyrics.

It includes some of her most acute storytelling and shows a confidence with writing that she can chuck out two albums in a year without breaking a sweat.

'willow'

This album is nominally very similar to its predecessor, *folklore*. Given that they were released very close to each other, it's tempting to say they might work well as a double album. On the other hand, this is pop music – as Shakespeare says, brevity is the soul of wit. Or in more commercial terms, it's easier to sell two discrete albums if they're of more typical length.

This song is immediately similar to *folklore* – acoustic instruments, wooded indie vibes – but there's also a lot more instruments, a degree of building to the arrangement. Electric guitars, handclicks, feather-light drums all join in by the end.

The story is of another bad boy. Since *Red*, Swift has been pretty close to the vogue of the time; 'willow' is peculiar in that it's alluding to falling for a bad boy on one hand and the stuff of real murder podcasts (stereotypically loved by middle-class white women the world over). '...take my hand / wreck my plans...' is a delightfully louche expression of falling for a wrong guy.

> *Wait for the signal, and I'll meet you after dark*
> *... Now this is an open-shut case*

Here is the real murder podcast allusions – 'open-shut case', artful 'bait-and-switches'. Swift writing an 'I fell for a bad boy' song is by this point fairly predictable but finding new metaphors to plough that furrow lends it a certain humour:

> *Life was a willow and it bent right to your wind*
> *But I come back stronger than a '90s trend*

In 2020 coming back like a 1990s trend was very on point (terrifying as that is to say considering I became an adult in the 1990s). And there's a neat play on words here – rather than the expected 'bent right to your *will*', we get wind – a force of nature and a physically powerful thing rather than the individual tenacity and mindpower.

'champagne problems'

To speak again of a very 'produced' intimacy – there's a load of lush touches here. Shuffling pages, adjusting a creaky chair. Connotations of folksy from high production. The structure of the song is in many ways *very* country – there's a story that unfurls and it's not properly articulated until just before the final recap of the chorus. The song circles around an event that's only really disclosed with the line 'She would've made such a lovely bride'.

And the context of the preceding is arrived at; the story is of turning down someone's marriage proposal at a fancy family event. Now this pattern is very country – where the listener re-listens and picks up the hints from earlier on. It's a really effective storytelling technique. My favourite instance of this is Dolly Parton's 'Down from Dover', which the final verse reveals that a pregnancy was stillborn, 'And dying was her way of telling me he wasn't coming down from Dover'. It's absolutely brutal but it's the structure, the slow and steady 'gotcha!' of the reveal that's most impressive. And despite 'champagne problems' being much closer to folk in sound, it's a pattern of very dramatic storytelling that's a lot more like country. And most important of all, the peak of country, which is Her Imperial Majesty St Dolly Parton.

It's a song where the rhyming scheme is so strong you'd easily mistake it for natural speech. One verse has speech/speechless/slipped/reaches/reason as rhyming nodes – complementing euphony but shifting rhythms. Throughout the choruses – each of which has slightly different lyrics – there's the phrase 'champagne problems' at the end of each stanza. Sometimes it's a droll 'boozy parties have problems' idea of champagne problems; sometimes it's inferred that the narrator has drinking issues. It's an anchoring motif that shifts meaning based on the preceding lines.

The earlier lyrics, once the payoff has been revealed, subtly intimate the outcome, such as 'I dropped your hand while dancing'.

> *How evergreen, our group of friends*

As ever with Swift her capacity of intimate details, for *emotional* details, is astounding. When a relationship fails it's not merely a sadness for two people, it comes with a profound social impact. A phrase like 'our group of friends' ceases to have any currency – in many cases a scramble to take sides in a social group. All this is elliptically pointed at by Swift.

> *Sometimes you just don't know the answer*
> *'Til someone's on their knees and asks you*

While it's never explicitly said that the narrator said no to a marriage proposal, it's heavily implied; and with this line we learn that it's not (yet) possible for the narrator to articulate why she said no. It's indicative of the way that emotional traumas – in this case double-sided – are impossible to speak of directly. Suddenly the opening lines, talking about booked trains, make good sense. One of Swift's greatest tunes.

'gold rush'
If there is a middle point between *1989* and *fearless*, it'd be this song. It's got blissful, ethereal backing vocals, a driving bass drum like *1989* but it's got the soft-focus vocals and folksy harmonies of *folklore*.

The gold rush of the title is about the problems of a partner with a choice of suitors – 'I don't like a gold rush' as in 'I don't want to compete with loads of people'. It's a tune where it's important to distinguish between exaggerative storytelling and autobiography – there's a sense in which the narrator of this is highly paranoid and distrusting.

If we needed to draw a wedge between earlier Swift and this material, we might want to point to this song – lines like 'I don't like that falling feels like flying 'til the bone crush' are much more intensity-averse than earlier, especially teenage, Swift. The vertigo of love is all well and good but it comes with a cost when we're crushed. This song is painting an image of being unable to cope with someone whose '…hair [falls] into place like dominoes', someone effortlessly attractive. This is in contrast to an earlier iteration of Swift whose narrator's response to attractive people was more petulant and irked by someone's good looks (see 'Gorgeous', *reputation*).

At dinner parties, I call you out on your contrarian shit

But as ever with Swift there's a sense of intimacy that's formidable. This observation is crisply delicate – while on the one hand it's saying 'I get to call you out on shit' it's also in another sense showing that the narrator is intimate with the antagonist such that she's *allowed* to take the piss. It's a privilege that many of us only have with our favourite people and our family.

'Cause it fades into the gray of my day-old tea
'Cause it will never be

Ultimately the narrator of 'gold rush' avoids diving into a relationship with the antagonist – the last line 'So inviting, I almost jump in' says as much. This is again in contrast to Swift's earlier narrators. I'm loath to describe this as maturity but it is illustrative of more self-reflective narrators and stories. Not 'the one who got away' but 'having the foresight to avoid certain relationships'. Fading into day-old tea is a quaint image – that cooling off that becomes dingy and unbearable given enough time is a perfect encapsulation of learning to withhold oneself from bad decisions.

'tis the damn season'

More in the realm of 'very carefully produced' music. The fourth beat has a hi-hat and what sounds like a very reverbed tom (drum). It's likely not a 'natural' reverb and if it was, it's not the same room as the vocals. Careful and dramatically driving.

The story is of one of those relationships that may just be a Christmas holiday hook-up; allusions to calling each other 'babe' for a brief weekend. But there's detail to it that revolves around false equivocation, which may as well also be a comment on the lack of balance in relationships in general. It doesn't mean that there's equality; it's more to do with cutting losses, making a decision to mutually end without tallying up the economy of the relationship.

There's an ache in you, put there by the ache in me

That relationship economy – not all aches are made equal (to paraphrase *Animal Farm*). In fact (of course) relationships are not reducible to economic terms because of the intense complexity of its modes of exchange. Both parties share in the 'ache', whether given or received, but neither experiences the same ache – doting on the homonymy or potential implications of 'ache'. And ache is to be horny, to be lonely, to love someone despite their being a long way away, to be frustrated (etc.). That both share the state of aching has minimal bearing on the lived experience of that ache. Both parties agree, presumably, that the ache is *bad*.

The old relationship patterns are affirmed; the real equivocation is actually an impasse. 'I won't ask you to wait if you don't ask me to stay', in which again the waste of imbalance is voided rather than measured and equivocated.

> *And the heart I know I'm breakin' is my own*
> *To leave the warmest bed I've ever known*

This in the bridge before the final chorus – that equivocation now entirely broken. Neither party satisfied, and the narrator clear in her own-foot-shooting behaviour. The sense of intimacy is clearly resigned and defeated. The relationship still burns and both are powerless to it and both are aware that it's not 'the same to you as it is to me' and yet both cringingly recognise they can't level the books.

> *And the road not taken looks real good now*
> *And it always leads to you*

Ultimately then there's a sense of teleology to this terrible habit – the narrator can't resist while at home and she knows she's breaking her own heart with it but it still feels inexorable, unstoppable.

'tolerate it'
Despite 'tolerate it' being largely piano-led, there's a background rhythmic section that's influenced by the kind of ambient, drum 'n' bass-ish sounds of so-called Intelligent Dance Music (IDM). That music is by no means radical in the 2020s (there's an argument to say it wasn't radical in the 1990s) but it's certainly a production flex. It's almost so far in the background that it's unnoticeable – which is to say it's secondary – but it's still pretty uncharacteristic of Swift's music. It may well be the case that commercial concerns prevent Swift from chucking out blistering gabber versions of her songs; it may just be better judgement on her part. But at least there's the insinuation that Swift could be pushing in different directions with her production.

If we wanted to describe 'the Swiftian lyrical project' we might say something like the idea is to write a song which quite precisely describes relationship problems; one song per emotion. That's a substantial enough project for a lifetime.

That's not what she's doing and it's dismissive of the breadth of her writing to suggest it, but if it *was* the case, then we'd describe 'tolerate it' as describing the emotions surrounding being belittled by your partner.

It's established early that the relationship has an age gap. And by now there's a kind of thematic trope that younger people might lack for social sophistication but make up for it with emotional clarity (see also: 'cardigan', on *folklore*). 'I know my love should be celebrated / But you tolerate it'. This is the kind of sentiment that is strongly therapeutic – not merely in the sense of being a result of guided self-reflection but also in the sense that asserting oneself, asserting the value of one's own *love*, is an important dimension to mental well-being.

> *I wait by the door like I'm just a kid*
> *Use my best colors for your portrait*
> *Lay the table with the fancy shit*
> *And watch you tolerate it*

The picture here is one of severe condescension; the narrator's own description of the events are jejune, infantile. All of these are acts of affection, acts of valorisation. And importantly, the narrator herself regards them as unimportant, or at least of secondary importance. 'The fancy shit' implies a dispassion, a disinterest. And the antagonist isn't impressed, doesn't take on board the younger narrator's acts but merely tolerates it.

To be tolerated in that context, to be treated as tolerable in a romantic context, is such a severe, diminishing thing. To be tolerated is to be the subject of complacency. It's a simple song but no less powerful for expressing the simple agony of being a diminished partner in a relationship, in both age and stature.

'no body, no crime' featuring HAIM

The second guest on this album – this time with HAIM, US rock sister trio. This is once again something in the realm of true crime podcasts. The story is of sisterly affinity – doing detective work around a friend's husband who's having an affair. The motif of 'no body, no crime' is around a disappeared friend in the mid-song and then, ultimately, a disappeared man.

It's a charming enough song that's, again, very true crime podcast. I'm not sure there's much more to it than being *fun*. A noble enough aim. But also, this is a fairly strong contender for songs that might well have been better delivered by other people. It works, but it might work better if it could be delivered with something more like a hysterical tone (with due apologies for using a distinctly un-feminist word there).

A good example of this is 'My Mama's Broken Heart' – the well-known Miranda Lambert version is all over the top, flouncing prima donna, which very much suits the 'I wish I could be just a little less dramatic' of the lyrics. Kacey Musgrave's version is more demure and doesn't quite marry up with the madness of the song, in spite of the fact that Musgrave wrote it. So perhaps 'no body, no crime' should be sung by someone like Miranda Lambert for maximum vitriolic delivery.

'happiness'

As an arrangement 'happiness' builds out of a simple few chords on a gentle church-like organ and builds, acquiring arching guitars, keyboard, long droning synths, drums, glistening bright sounds. It's an odd one insofar as, if you removed Swift's vocals, you could easily mistake it for some lusciously recorded demure indie rock – like later Yo La Tengo or similar.

There are two repeated lyrical motifs here – 'there is happiness' and 'You haven't met the new me yet'. Both 'happiness' and the 'new me' are maintained as promises:

> *Sorry, I can't see facts through all of my fury*
> *You haven't met the new me yet*

That well-balanced first line with the strongly stressed f-sounds is delivered very drily. So you get the sense of its delivery being coolly acerbic. The 'new me' who hasn't been met belongs to the after-state – the person who is capable of being calm and measured and who isn't bubbling over with rage.

For a narrative caprice it's magnificent – at a glance, the chorus is calmly beatific, and says 'there is happiness'. But looking at the lyrics more closely, the song is not talking about happiness, it's talking about a state of abject frustration and anger.

Perhaps the oddest state in the song is that, despite the narrator's extreme emotional debilitation, she is still able to foresee an after-state of forgiveness. Not yet, but soon – the line 'you haven't met the new me yet' is alluded to as future-forgiveness.

Swift's songs are typically gendered, and they typically come from a female perspective. That's not to say that they are alienating for men (I am one, I can assure you they're not) but that their voice comes from a female experience. There are exceptions – if we read 'betty' on *folklore* as being a male narrator, for instance. And with happiness there's a possibility we see a gendered narrative as a subtext – it's common for women to do the emotional labour in a relationship, doing the emotional work for two people. Here the narrator is *both* experiencing her own emotional state during a break-up but also able to envisage her emotional stability in some promised future. It's very much like the sort of emotional sophistication that characterises a lot of women in relationships, and genders those relationships accordingly. So that is to say that happiness is a thoroughly emotionally *sophisticated* song.

'dorothea'
This might be the closest Swift comes to jaunty, in that the piano part is skipping around stresses in the verse, rolling back and forth. That's also to say that for all Swift's lyrical sophistication, she's most typically regular and metrical in musical arrangements. There's no reason any of her songs couldn't be made to swing in a jazz style but for now the arrangements are simple, as per the typical demands of pop audiences.

It's perhaps fitting that a song which is closest to jaunty is also lyrically quite base – the character Dorothea is someone who's left town, and the narrator only sees her through a mobile phone now ('A tiny screen's the only place I see you now').

There's an outside sense that something wasn't right with Dorothea's childhood – 'When we were younger down in the park / Honey, making a lark of the misery' but it's never quite developed. Dorothea is now a 'queen sellin' dreams, sellin' makeup and magazines' and it's not clear if she's 'still the same soul I met under the bleachers?'

That is to say, it's an odd narrative for the song. While Swift has developed her capacity for storytelling outside of ellipses, for creating dark gaps for her listeners to fill, 'dorothea' doesn't quite get to that darkness. It's a cute little song about looking back at a childhood relationship but unlike even 'Never Grow Up' (*Speak Now*) – which has a similar pattern of talking across generations – it does manage to develop a dramatic tension in the song.

'coney island' featuring the National
Another guest vocal, this time from Matt Berninger of the National. And, the National being closer to indie music (whatever that means in 2020), the references move from emotional states to suburban evocations.

> *'Cause we were like the mall before the internet*
> *It was the one place to be*

Indie music is probably too broad to reduce to a few themes but there's often a vibe that sneaks in – nostalgia. Here we've got the 'world before the Internet', that age of innocence, the childlike evocation of the arcade lights.

> *Were you waiting at our old spot*
> *In the tree line*
> *By the gold clock*

Here those specific *places* bring out the memories of childhood. It's perhaps not so notable insofar as it's the stuff of very typical songwriting but it is notable insofar as it's not quite aligned with Swift's writing more typically at this point. Swift's incisive writing tends to be doing away with specificity, in terms of time and place, and goes for emotional evocation; as soon as another writer is involved, we get these atavisms which conjure youthful relationships, the follies of pissing about before the Internet.

> *Wondering where did my baby go?*
> *The fast times, the bright lights, the merry go*
> *Sorry for not making you my centerfold*

And again with childhood references. Centrefold is an odd veneration to give someone – it's strongly associated with the 'do they still do that?' of *Playboy* and associated porn mags. It feels like a very twentieth-century reference. This has the oddly stunted 'merry go', where one would typically expect 'merry go round' but its abruption draws us in, like a sentence fragment or an interruption.

Perhaps the most remarkable thing is that the lyrics here don't feel like Swift's lyrics. Typically for any given Swift lyric, even if it's with another singer, you can nail the song as Swiftian. It's not so much that this song is radically un-Swiftian but rather that its references and place sit oddly in her canon. That is to say that the remarkable thing may be Swift's loosening of the lyrical reins here.

'ivy'

The arrangement here is a lovely bubbly banjo-y number. It's very much back into the realm of Swift's usual fare.

Petulance has been a tool of Swift's before but in this latest incarnation it's much more sedate or cool. A war is described and an antagonist is accused of starting it. This 'you started it' is in the context of an affair and it's a war to which the narrator has succumbed.

> *My pain fits in the palm of your freezing hand*
> *Taking mine, but it's been promised to another*
> *… Stop you putting roots in my dreamland*
> *My house of stone, your ivy grows*

The metaphor of being in an affair being like a war is revealed to be more from the perspective of succumbing. It's not so much that Swift's narrator is an active combatant but that they are an annexed state. This chorus is rich with metaphors pinging in different directions – to hold someone's pain in a freezing hand; freezing in the sense of emotionally distant? The enjambment '…hand / taking mine…' where unbroken 'hand taking mine' has a very different stress to the stressed 'freezing hand' and 'taking mine'. It's the kind of chorus that pushes and pulls in many directions – the hand that's promised to another is very much a marital metaphor but it's also a container for the narrator's pain. There's a lack of resistance to 'roots in my dreamland' – and that's not a homeland, that's a different core-self-home which is being annexed in this 'war'. My house of stone, if it is a person-house-metaphor, is stone as in cold, unrelenting, but covered in ivy is a kind of usurping of control and ownership.

That's a lot to take in but what it means really is that Swift is metaphoring *a lot*. It's an impressive style and kind of unusual in its density and it's possibly the sort of thing that is more writerly than it is to be taken in in the length of time it takes to sing it. Put another way – if there was a song that illustrates Swift's capacity for poetry proper, this would be it.

'cowboy like me'

It's almost disappointing that a song called 'cowboy like me' isn't a full-blooded return to country-era Swift. There is a guitar motif that is tantalising close to 'Tim McGraw', the opening song on her very first album. But the cowboy of the title is more a sense of a swindler, a con-artist, than it is a down-home, Southern belle vision.

The song's structure is well off-piste for Swift – it could be verse x2, chorus, verse, chorus, post-chorus x2, chorus refrain, post-chorus x2, bridge, verse, chorus, outro (at which point it's more sensible to say something more abstract, like giving each part a letter – AABABCBCDAB). However it's described, it's a lovely and a gently sinuous song – no one part overstays its welcome but there are a lot of them.

Whatever the structure, it's another 'damn you boy' song, this time centred around protagonist and antagonist being hustlers.

> *And the skeletons in both our closets*
> *Plotted hard to fuck this up*

Re-use and punning on common idioms hasn't been so prevalent on this album so it's nice to see that evergreen lyrical technique making a reappearance. It's lush to see that something usually passive and overbearing like a skeleton in a closet can be afforded the agency of malice. The effect is to describe two people whose complex past is so pernicious as to overwhelm and undermine a current relationship that has already been described as two bandits.

> *Never wanted love*
> *Just a fancy car*

The exquisite indifference to relationships – perhaps influenced by those mendacious skeletons – is manifest in the narrator just wanting a fancy car. There's a sense of deprecation or humiliation in this narrator, this materialistic hustler, being embarrassed by her affection for another person. It's one of those reveals that unfurls slowly to show that the narrator is, in fact, a cloistered person whose self-protection has been undermined by falling for someone who's living a similarly distanced cowboy life.

> *Now you hang from my lips*
> *Like the Gardens of Babylon*

This line is particularly difficult to parse – hanging from my lips seems to imply a play on the double meaning of lips as synecdoche (or metaphor) for speech and also the organ for kissing; but the 'like the Gardens of Babylon' is unqualified, insofar as we're left guessing why the Gardens of Babylon are being spoken of or what properties they have, except perhaps that we are to intimate that they are resplendent yet remaining mythical. It's potentially just a simple 'you hang on my lips timelessly' but it's perhaps one of Swift's most ornately opaque metaphors. And more power to her for it.

'long story short'

It might well be the case that *evermore* is the album on which Swift has most *fun*. The album, like *folklore*, was written during lockdown, a period when people were mostly spending time indoors baking bread. It would make sense if Swift ended up writing a bunch of songs in the vein of *folklore*, and elected to try out some new ideas – writing songs with non-female narrators (arguably 'betty', *folklore*), writing relatively lightweight songs based on true crime podcasts ('willow' and 'no body, no crime' on this record). Lightweight in the sense that the songs aren't addressing eternal truths about emotional states. Like most pop music does.

The most striking element of 'long story short' is the expansion of metre – verses start with couplets of two syllables long rest/longer second line; after two such couplets, it's five syllables slightly shorter rest/longer second line. This is for two couplets. The chorus in turn has irregular syllables but no musical rests at the end of the lines – meaning that the lines are full and continuous. The upshot is that there's a push and pull with intensity – the chorus draws in the attention and hammers away at the rhythms, and the verses offer respite. Long musical rests are not common for Swift, so it's nice to see her playing with her own form here.

The lyrics themselves are largely affectionate towards a current beau, while referencing previous relationship mistakes – 'No more keepin' score'. And within that it's leaning on the kind of extended aphorisms that have been a mainstay of her lyrical style since the beginning:

> *I tried to pick my battles 'til the battle picked me*

Having this massive stock of aphorisms to pick from is also a useful critique of habitual language. Swift is very good at taking those aphorisms and deflating or perverting them. The reason I've consistently used the term 'aphorism' is because the definition for that is something like 'a pithy phrase expressing a general truth'. There's a sense in which aphorisms can be obstructive or oppressive, that their repetition is to present an insurmountable counterargument. For instance, the Bible's 'Let he who is without sin cast the first stone' (John 8:7) works well for articulating hypocrisy but can have a paralysing effect when direct action or criticism is needed. Swift's undermining of aphorisms is frequently cheeky and fun – I don't think she's mounting an intellectual attack on linguistic devices – but it does have the consequence of destabilising habitual truisms.

'marjorie'

Another song that builds to a quiet storm. There's a background keyboard that bears a striking resemblance to the keyboard in the Who's 'Baba O'Riley' (1971) – perhaps Swift has a rock opera in her waiting to come out.

> *Never be so kind*
> *You forget to be clever*
> *Never be so clever*
> *You forget to be kind*

There's a small irony here insofar as this is an aphorism that is delivered nearly free from changes, unlike most of Swift's wordplay. It's technically an example of antimetabole – transposing the order of words (as in 'one for all, all for one'). It's an effective way of showing the obverse of a phrase, and ensuring a holism to the advice, or at least exposing two sides (life is rarely simple enough to have only two sides…).

The lyrics are those of mourning – 'You're alive, you're alive in my head'. And the expression is that of the scattershot way that mourning bears down on a person. The difficulty with mourning – besides the absence – that it takes many forms, profound and facile:

> *I should've asked you questions*
> *I should've asked you how to be*

The absence of a person is an absence of access to their wisdom. An aspect of grief is that it highlights a failing on the part of those who remain – questions that go un-asked. 'How to be' is quite an enormous question, existential in scope. And by contrast, Swift's narrator also regrets that they 'Should've kept every grocery store receipt'. That receipt is a kind of existential synecdoche, the person's effect which stands in for their absence. The small, asinine details are negligible during life and are exploded, filled with *meaning* when their absence is eternal.

> *What died didn't stay dead*
> *You're alive… in my head*

And of course ultimately what we keep of a person is what we remember, and the objects we inherit that bring those memories to mind. The process of mourning is a calibration of memorialisation.

'closure'
Like 'tolerate it', this has some backgrounded drum figures, flicking through effected EQ like a rapidly rotated radio dial. Again, it might want to point to the potential that Swift might do something more radical with her arrangements in the future.

The song's story is about a reaction to an ex reaching out for closure, to be friends after an acrimonious break-up, and Swift's narrator basically telling him to fuck off.

> *Don't treat me like*
> *Some situation that needs to be handled*
> *I'm fine with my spite*

Where previously petulance was more often presented as bratty and reactionary, here it's louche and cool. The narrator is not in need of resolving the relationship.

She's happy to rest in spite. It's a marked difference and arguably a lot more affective for its cold delivery. It's always better to not care when telling someone to fuck off. Being fine with her spite also means having a sense of emotional fidelity, realness – 'Staying friends would iron it out so nice / ... / But it's fake and it's oh so unnecessary'.

There's two instances here where the relationship problems are referred to in terms of fabric – 'I can feel you smoothing me over' in verse two and 'I know I'm just a wrinkle in your new life' in the bridge. It's a neat way to express the sense of the antagonist's framing the lack of closure as *inconvenience* rather than an emotional imperative. Whether or not the narrator is justified in her spite, she's certainly clear that she doesn't want the closure to be a result of social impropriety. Incidentally, in Bristolian English, what is usually called 'stroking' – as in to run one's hand over the fur of a pet – is called 'smoothing'. In that context, I find that the sense of condescension with 'smoothing me over' is amplified thought I doubt Swift is aiming for a (gurt) Bristolian register (mind).

'evermore' featuring Bon Iver

Another guest which makes this Swift's most guested-on album. To speak again of Swift using this record to explore different aspects of her form, there's a bridge on this which has a key *and* a tempo change – when Justin Vernon's falsetto part comes in it speeds up into a new range. It's quite a jolting effect, ensuring the listener is paying attention like kicking their chair out from underneath them.

It's an odd-shaped song with an odd-shaped sentiment – the solo Swift vocal seems to be one of lament: 'I had a feeling so peculiar / That this pain would be for / Evermore'. And then the Vernon-Swift extended bridge reveals that the lamented antagonist was present, which fulfils the restitution of the final 'This pain wouldn't be for evermore'. As a form, it's perhaps like two songs wedged together. Thematically it might be closer to lieder than pop songs, though pop is a broad enough church to accept this as its only errant relative to Swift's usual fare.

That lament is fairly depressive – minimal articulations expressing the inordinate futility of this pain which is for evermore. 'Writing letters / Addressed to the fire'. It's not clear if these letters' recipient is dead or unavailable or if the writer is simply incapable of sending them but the result is that same, that of a futile act. Although of course the act of writing in itself suggests that writing has some sort of cathartic function, even if the intended reader is terminally absent.

> *And I was catching my breath*
> *Staring out an open window*
> *Catching my death*

This line 'catching my death' is a great play on 'catching my death of cold'. It's not merely that the narrator is cold here but also that she is occupying futility (as in the letters to the fire) – catching death in the sense of seeking oblivion or rushing towards a murky end.

> *I had a feeling so peculiar*
> *That this pain would be for*
> *Evermore*

The enjambment for the final line of the chorus here does a great job – like a deep breath in for a final shout only to be a minor, thwarted, deflated 'evermore'. A long rest to allow that 'evermore' to carry through, jangling in its depressive resonance.

It's almost a disappointment that Vernon's bridge appears to announce the presence of the lamented antagonist ('I swear / You were there') – it lends the final chorus, with its payoff that inverts the earlier lament ('This pain wouldn't be for evermore'), a sense of happiness. And that's fine. It reminds me a little of how Billie Holiday recorded a version of 'Gloomy Sunday' (Hungarian: 'Szomorú vasárnap'; Holiday's version recorded 1941) but was obliged to tack on a happy ending – 'Dreaming, I was only dreaming' – that repositions the maudlin and macabre lyrics as unnecessary worrying. Swift is, of course, a much better songwriter than me so I'll let it pass but personally my gothometer has space for more misery.

Midnights

Swift's last album, at the time of writing (early 2023) and a cool, shimmering electro-pop album that's blinking through its own lavender haze. Swift at her most opaque but no less compelling for that. Despite selling enough to dominate the charts, she's still experimenting with her form and writing at the peak of her game.

Despite some of the darker moments in Swift's songs, there's a lightness to this album – or perhaps a light exuding from within this album's core – that makes for peerless pop music.

'Lavender Haze'

Straight off the bat, a different record to the preceding two – there's a lot more (apparent) vocal production, there's more (obviously) electronic sections. That is to say, the instrumentation and arrangements are closer to the electro-pop of *1989* than *folklore/evermore* – the sound for *Midnights* is more transparently 'produced'.

> *I'm damned if I do give a damn what people say*
> *No deal*
> *The 1950s shit they want from me*
> *I just wanna stay in that lavender haze*

This is a very heavy allusion to feminist ideas. In many ways, the sort of values that women are held to in the public eye in the 2020s is not so far different to the 1950s. Be sexy, not too sexy; don't speak out too much, and so on. For all the progress that has been made, there's still a strong conservativism that haunts gender relations, conversations about sexuality etc. 'Lavender haze' is apparently to reference the state of being in love but it sounds a lot like drugs. There's a distinctly soft, distinctly muted drift to the backing – there's a loop in the background that is like voices in the next room. It's very *druggy*.

The song dotes on preferring the lavender haze of love to the barbs of public life. Whether this is a reference to Swift's own public persona, it's easy to read it as about the ways in which relationships, especially new relationships, carry a pull that's often greater than the desire to have a public life. The way new relationships cause us to hibernate into each other's beds. It's a gorgeous pop song and it's got a drifting, opiated haze to it that's very *luscious*.

But most significant about this song is one of the details that I've outright ignored when considering Swift's work – the music video. The character in the video who's playing Swift's love interest is played by a trans man, Laith Ashley. It shouldn't be the case in 2023 that having a trans man in a video is significant, but sadly it is. Sadly, trans folk are still dying, sadly trans folk are still under regular attack (especially in the British press), trans folk's identities are still under question, trans access to healthcare is still lacking, dating while trans is still a bloody nightmare. One of the things that needs to happen is normalising trans and cis partnerships. Another thing is that the public needs to see more trans bodies, in all their wonder, in a normal fashion and not just in the fetishised frame of pornography. World-famous children's authors showing solidarity with fascists and people who seek to remove the identities of trans people is not the way forward, but it does have a strong enough standing to be front-page news, still. In this context, Swift's hiring of a (really hot) trans man is significant and necessary – and when history takes account it'll see that Swift was on the right side of history when she did it.

'Maroon'

There's some more of those helicopter synths and they're more present here, and across the album, making it a kind of successor to *1989*. 'Maroon' has a lush, sultry, soft pulsing throb to it.

Having had a foray into what's principally a straight-up love song, we go back to the intricate storytelling:

> *Your roommate's cheap-ass screw-top rosé, that's how*

This line follows a question of how some people ended up on a floor (presumably sleeping there, presumably drunk). Poetically this has a lovely euphony – the spondees of 'Your roommate's cheap-ass screw-top rosé', where every syllable is stressed, stresses the rhythm for the second line only for the substantial rest of the third to dissipate it. The assonance of '*ch*eap… *scr*ew', the assonance of '*scr*ew… *r*osé'.

Giving rosé the quality of being a *cause* is very much part of contemporary vernacular. The listener fills in the gaps to surmise that, consequent to cheap booze, bad decisions were made that ended up with sleeping on the floor (with a possible subtext of also sexing on the floor). Another substantial gloss helps the narrative jump from the initial bad decisions into an embedded, ongoing relationship. Musically as well, that substantial gloss of drinking to habituation is prepended by a substantial rest.

> *The mark they saw on my collarbone*
> *The rust that grew between telephones*

The quick stresses, strong rhyming scheme here that builds a tension released by the simple and plain 'so scarlet it was [pause] maroon'. And again the (now far darker) insinuation of an unexpurgated story with 'the mark they saw on my collarbone', the metaphor of the dropped communication – suddenly the fairly typical Swiftian 'lyrics about lipstick' is thrown into question – when lips are later described as scarlet-maroon, is that as a result of bruising?

> *And I wake with your memory over me*
> *That's a real fucking legacy…*

Yes, Tayls. Good swear. Almost tmesis. It's such a great swear in that it is gratuitous, but it's also lazy (the two best qualities for swearing) – given we've (hopefully) established that Swift can really write a song, the fact that she's stuck an emphatic but semantically value-less 'fucking' here, just to make the line longer for the musical phrase, makes it arguably the most important swear in Swift's lyrics.

For the last chorus, where previously the melody had a few notes, it's now reduced to one. It's repeating the same lyrical content but the melody is now restricted to an incantation; it's a really effective way of connoting a lyrical story in music without changing the lyrics; the dynamic and bright melody (even if minor key) suddenly turns grave and dirge-like, lending the lyrics a newly bitter and soured quality.

'Anti-Hero'
Something that's perhaps more true for *Midnights* than elsewhere is that what is typically framed in euphemistic or metaphorical terms now becomes candid and explicit. This is a minor problem for wanting to read Swift without also inferring autobiographical detail; nevertheless, there's nothing to say that the candour doesn't belong to the *narrator* rather than the *author*.

> *When my depression works the graveyard shift ...*

It's fairly atypical, in pop music, to refer directly to depression; much more so in the more confessional modes of emo, heavy metal traditions (especially Black Metal), or some of the more exposed emotional indie music. That isn't so much a statistical assertion about what has happened, but rather an assertion about the nature of lyricism which codifies the form. Pop music may accept darkness and introspection but typically in the form of euphemism and metaphor (as previously with Swift); emo (in particular) as a lyrical genre had a habit of avoiding lyrical *affectation* – meaning there was a drive to elide lyrical euphemism; that isn't to say it's devoid of poetry but rather that its 'authenticity' was measured relative to the distance from the core of the expression – the shorter the better.

For a writer who's so often used metaphors of demons, ghosts, hauntings, monsters (see 'The monsters turned out to be just truths' in tropology), Taylor's reference to 'ghosting' people in this song has a kind of sedimented history. While 'ghosted' in contemporary vernacular means 'to fail to respond to a person', in Swift's usage it acquires (or reaffirms) a spectral presence. If there is such a thing as Swiftology, I can, at least, imagine schistmatic tribes forming to say 'no, it just means to ignore' and another who focus on the spectral thread when taking Swift's lyrics as a whole.

> *I should not be left to my own devices*
> *They come with prices and vices*

Here we have a technique likely borrowed from hip-hop, strong repetitious internal rhymes (or multis, for multisyllabic rhymes). It's not the first time Swift has graced the edges of hip-hop culture(s) but it'd be foolhardy to intimate that she's particularly endeavouring towards the dense and complex lyricism of hip-hop cultures. 'Devices… prices and vices' all happening in a short space of time such that the stress of the rhyme is shifting at a kind of meta-level within the larger stanza; the effect is very much one of disorientation. This is far from being anything like the sort of multis that proliferate in hip-hop but it's an interesting development considering the relative parity of rhyming schemes elsewhere in Swift's corpus.

The chorus here is also fully in confessional mode. An over declared statement of culpability:

> *It's me, hi*
> *I'm the problem, it's me*

Where 'it's me' is a simple sentiment of responsibility, this sort of over-declaration functions to self-deprecatingly insert oneself; no escaping from who the problem is as it's been repeated for absolute clarity.

It's possible that *Midnights* is Swift's most effective use of semi-opaque or atypical usages. The rhyming, musical phrase 'teatime' seems oddly unkempt, or atypical; it's difficult to pin down what is it specifically being insinuated.

This is a jam-packed chorus, maybe the most exciting of Swift's career. The narrator is unafraid of risks to their personal health but incapable of self-reflection – there's a line about never staring in the mirror. The payoff is an assertion about how exhausting it is supporting the anti-hero. It's not clear *who* is doing the rooting for the anti-hero – and autobiographical readings will probably point to a relationship between Swift and her fanbase – but the result is that the effective self-deprecated person functions as the anti-hero; given that we've already directly affirmed a depressive mindset here, this anti-hero is given as the depressive, the person who might be the centre of the story but never the driving positive force of the hero.

Immediately after that we have this blinder of a stanza:

> *…I feel like everybody is a sexy baby*
> *And I'm a monster…*

Initially my response to the first line here was bafflement. 'Sexy baby'. 'Baby'? Sure, infantilism or innocence. That's fairly predictable. What is that qualifier 'sexy' doing, and what is it doing *there*?

There's a point within some artists' work where they break with the given tradition; a good example of that is James Joyce's *Ulysses*, in which he elected to abandon many of the proprieties of writing but maintain a laser focus on storytelling refracted through an impossible lens. Utterly singular and bold.

But the point for me is that Joyce came to that having cut his teeth on some inviting and high quality storytelling; to change the form, he first came to know it most intimately. And that's how I intuitively wanted to frame this peculiar term, as outrageous and opaque.

I'm not quite looking to insinuate that Swift is comparable with Joyce – not least because that's very much a 'comparing apples with oranges', disingenuous proposition. But Swift's increased use of unusual opacity does, for me, indicate the kind of confidence and surety in her own craft that comes from having very much nailed 'being a songwriter', however narrowly we describe the area of songwriting she has occupied.

However, further down the line I realised that it's most likely a reference to 'sexy baby voice' – an affected way of speaking that is adopted by women whereby the voice is artificially high-pitched; it's a parallel to the 'valley girl' voice or other ways of speaking that carry specifically feminised connotations. 'Sexy baby' is a very 'girly' way to speak, hyper-feminine and juvenile. It carries fairly negative connotations, not least for being simultaneously a very childish way of speaking whilst also being sexually alluring. Within this context, it's more likely used to intimate that the women around the narrator are all inauthentic, performing a version of femininity that, by contrast, makes the narrator appear like a 'monster', an expression of the self which is alienated from excessively performed femininity. In that sense, it's obliquely addressing issues around femininity and performance – not to say that Swift is doing the same work as a Judith Butler (whose book *Gender Trouble* is widely cited as a key work that helped improve public understanding of the notions of 'gender roles') but the narrative lives in a similar space to psychoanalytic-feminist thought.

Even without the tropological notion that Swift strongly collocates location with self-identity, or that this building-self-identity gets haunted and grown around, this has a keenly psychodynamic bent – not insofar as it alludes to the therapeutical practice but the sort of post-Freudian notions of magic and fantasy and how they relate to the self. While I've typically avoided talking about the visual support for a song – that is, the promotional video – in this case we've got a substantially compelling image of a grotesquely large Swift stomping around invasively, unable to curtail her enormity. Within *that* context, the sexy baby suddenly becomes more hypnogogic, where the rational logic of awakeness is elided and perhaps a baby can be described as 'sexy'; this in turn is compounded by the 'midnights' which are established as the setting in the opening line. Or in tl;dr form – if it's a dream, then everything's weird; why not *sexy* babies?

That's been quite an intense ride; just to return to the usual pace, there's a lovely piquant, simple and unequivocal metaphor about the narrator's heart getting pierced, but not fatally. Which is also to say that for the opacity which has triggered my verbosity, Swift is well capable of steering us back to comfortable territory.

Similarly the next section:

> *Did you hear my covert narcissism I disguise as altruism*

Which alludes to the of a kind of overly-therapised vernacular (think US sitcoms of the last twenty-five years, especially *Frasier*) and a quick one-off about congressmen and their truculence as a wee salve of witticism.

'Anti-Hero' again uses the technique we spoke of in 'Maroon' of flattening out the melodic curve so as to turn the lightness into a battery, or emphatic dirge. Drilling home the sense that the self-responsibility of 'it's me' is less revelatory and more dread. It must be exhausting always rooting for the anti-hero.

'Snow on the Beach' featuring Lana Del Rey

The only collaboration on *Midnights* and while it's great to have Lana in the house, her vocals are not quite front-and-centre. Rather the arrangement is very lush, all glacial reverbed vocals and classy pizzicato.

> *And it's like snow at the beach*
> *Weird, but fuckin' beautiful*

Because Lana is in the house, it is obligatory that both show off their bad girl credentials and what better way to do that than a gratuitous swear? There isn't a bad Swift swear in her canon to date (early 2023) and this has all the right qualities: it doesn't really add much to the content but it is big, hard, *and* clever.

> *I don't even dare to wish it*
> *But your eyes are flying saucers from another planet*

It's tempting to stretch a little here and read 'snow' as the old euphemism for cocaine – 'eyes [like] flying saucers' implying the pupil dilation of coke but… despite the presence of Lana's classic rock vibes, it doesn't add much to the narrative. Nevertheless, this is Swift's most transparent allusion to drugs – incredibly circumspect as it is.

The vision here is less a setting of dramatic tension and more an isolated snapshot of the weird moment where it was snowing, and they were on the beach. 'You wanting me / tonight feels impossible'. All we get is an articulation of odd relationship. Whatever detail is revealed is just to say 'this is a weird situation'.

> *This scene feels like what I once saw on a screen*
> *I searched 'aurora borealis green'*

Gorgeous and somewhat goofy euphony here. 'Aurora borealis' operates as an internal rhyme, while screen/green defines the outer rhyme. The song is certainly cool and lush sounding. It's also a very well-matched song for Lana, in that it's very much her *vibe*. It is, however, probably one of Swift's more lightweight songs – we're in the realm of cool vibes rather than dense prosaic form.

'You're on Your Own, Kid'
If *folklore* and *evermore* were two slices of wooded indie, this is much closer to the more conventional, riff-leaden indie of yore. Most of the song rides on a rhythmic pulse from a guitar, ostinatoing away until the full band which ploughs in later in the song.

Oddly enough after the (potential) reference to coke in the preceding song, there's a second here – 'I hear it in your voice, you're smoking with your boys' – one assumes that social smoking typically denotes weed rather than tobacco.

There's another instance here of how *Midnights* seems inflected with a kind of psychoanalytical self-analysis:

> *I search the party of better bodies*
> *Just to learn that my dreams aren't rare*
> *You're on your own, kid*
> *You always have been*

Where Swift is definitely at home with high vim and drama, this is more a case of self-identity with banality – 'my dreams aren't rare'. This is an understated approach for Swift, and its relevance isn't obviously revealed. Which is to say that this isn't so much Swift in storytelling mode (most obvious on the preceding albums) as it is Swift in confessional, psychodynamic mode – a reflection on self-reflection itself.

I've said that *evermore* was an experimental record for Swift in terms of the structure and form of the songs, and also the lyrics. *Midnights* is perhaps more experimental in terms of the arrangements, which are closer to the *1989* model, doting more on synthesisers than 'organic' sounds. But more importantly, the lyrics list towards passivity and indistinction. Where antagonists, spurned lovers or objects of affection have typically been very sharply outlined, *Midnights* leaves us with a woman doing something akin to making arrangements out of a dream diary or notes from therapy. And insofar as that seems to be the case, it's an oddly *flat* exegesis; the narrator's notions typically ambiguous. Which is compelling in the case of Swift and produces some amazingly opaque or peculiar metaphors.

Flat possibly seems mean-spirited, but I don't mean it in a qualitative sense – I mean in the sense of having an ambiguity which is nondescript. There's a plaintive 'stated-ness' to 'You're on Your Own, Kid' – like the outcome of therapy where someone accepts a problem and is able to articulate it as such but is yet to act on it; to begin to change is to recognise the problem in objective (or objective-like) terms.

'Midnight Rain'
The opening of this is notable in that it's possibly the most obviously synthetic voice on a Swift record; where *folklore* and *evermore* had a lot of close mics, breathy and transparent vocals, here we see this record's ambiguity mirrored in the vocal production – the sound isn't hyper-artificial but it is obfuscating and uncanny, occupying a sonic territory perhaps closer to synths than vocals.

There's a danger with my assertion that Swift is ambiguous or opaque on this record because what detail is insinuated is done so relatively circumspectly, and is no less sharp for that:

> *He wanted it comfortable, I wanted that pain*
> *He wanted a bride, I was making my own name*

The story is a thematically familiar one of the break between small-town affections and a more mobile narrator (see ''tis the damn season', *evermore*; 'Dear John', *Speak Now*, etc.). Here we've got a great pairing of oppositions – comfortable-pain, bride-name; the sense in which 'bride' is the opposite of 'name' is circumstantial (i.e. women often take their husband's name in marriage) but also, there's a sense that the narrator would elide their hard-won identity in the case of changing their name. He stayed the same, he also gets to stay the same (typically men don't change their name in marriage).

Again, we see the ambiguity – the story of the song is fairly plain, the narrator went out in the world, the antagonist did not. There's less in the way of qualitative detail – like how the narrator feels about it – but there is a kind of plain-spoken observation of:

> *I guess sometimes we all get*
> *Some kind of haunted, some kind of haunted*
> *And I never think of him*
> *Except on midnights like this*

So this is again less about declarative statements and more about describing a paralysed moment in time; thematically, for this record, that time is always midnight. There's clearly an air of melancholy but it's less an exposure of *pain* in a direct sense, and more a kind of passive exposition of *aching*.

'Question…?'
There's some great cheap (or more likely, faux-cheap) electronic drums on this one – a striking contrast with the cheap snare on the second and fourth beat and the blissy, dreamy reverbed keys and vocals swimming around elsewhere.

> *Fuckin' situations, circumstances*

The great thing here about each successive swear is that they're slightly different, yet equally perfunctory. This swear is properly over it, the kind of swear you do when the weight of describing *things* (in this case, situations and circumstances) is too great and you just want to make it clear that those situations and circumstances are filthy and wrong.

'Question…?' leans quite heavily into the not-quite-declared situation at the end of the ellipsis. Allusions in a variety of modes. 'Half-moon eyes' suggesting perhaps an emoji, something from the textual realm of telecoms.

> *Did you realize out of time?*
> *She was on your mind with some dickhead guy*

This couplet is difficult to parse in terms of who is what in relation to the narrator. Perhaps 'did it cross your mind later that you were thinking about her with a dickhead'. The situation is articulated with 'one drink after another', so it may be that the logic of the song in general is the skewed logic of alcoholic haze, perhaps as a complement to the hypnogogic logic of 'Anti-Hero'. The stanza is then a discombobulated re-telling of a night out, a faint allusion to tensions that 'got swept away in the gray' on a night out. The grey in this case being the fuzzy haze which surrounds nights of heavy drinking, the memory failure.

The chorus also is wittily opaque. It is is a series of questions – a story about someone being kissed, then everyone in the room making fun, and then everyone clapping. It's a peculiar set of assertions. The stanza closes with a deflatory 'it's just a question' at the end, which does nothing to recant the preceding. The bits before 'can I ask you a question' are so specific as to render the effect of 'it's just a question' moot – that specificity indicates that there's a very particular point being sought. It's a hilarious thing to say – ask a series of specific questions then try and act like it was an off-hand comment. Later in the chorus 'Do you wish you could still touch her?' gives a sense that there's a very real relationship that's been scotched but there's such unspecific language surrounding it it's not clear if the 'her' is the narrator or a third party.

So again, with the ambiguity and faintness, it's more like a snapshot of a moment in time, the midnights of drunken confusion and tensions. Emotions alluded to but never declared.

The wit of this tune, and the tenor of the wit on *Midnights* more generally, relies on self-effacing understatement. The bridge features a line that's overly formal, stilted and non-familiar: 'I'm sure that's what's suitable'. It rubs against the broadly intimate tone of the rest of the song. Given that this is Swift and we know her songs are often about trysts, breakups, romances-that-never-were, we can insinuate that the 'her' of the song is the narrator. That the story is that of trying to hide a very specific situation, a very specific 'boy who got away' moment in 'It's just a question'.

'Vigilante Shit'
With the changing of the guard in pop music there's some odd artefacts; one of the biggest impacts in the last few years has been that of Billie Eilish. Consequently, something resembling Billie Eilish – electronic, low tempo, trap-like hi-hats, spare near-spoken lyrics – appears in all sorts of places. The last few years of Eurovision have featured Eilish-esque tunes. 'Vigilante Shit' feels strongly like Swift's entry into the Eilish-esque.

So far as the narrative of the song goes, it's a story about the solidarity of women scorned by the same lover. While I say it's Eilish-esque, it's also very much the kind of tone that we've last heard on *reputation* (2017, five years earlier).

Once again, we have a reference to drugs:

> *While he was doin' lines and crossin' all of mine*
> *Someone told his white-collar crimes to the FBI*

This touches on the true crime podcast vibe – the notion of the women who are exacting revenge on men in solidarity with each other: 'Picture me thick as thieves with your ex-wife', 'Someone told his white-collar crimes to the FBI'. It's possibly disingenuous to describe it as too close to Eilish – Swift has dipped into these lyrical fields many times. It's the arrangement that's potentially Eilishian, and it's also fair to say that it's a style that was all over pop in 2022, when the album was released.

'Bejeweled'
There's a lovely expanding synth chord in the intro which sounds oddly like 8-bit computer games from a long time ago. Atypically for *Midnights*, this tune is classic Swift: self-assertive, clear, confident and bright:

> *Best believe I'm still bejeweled*
> *When I walk in the room*
> *I can still make the whole place shimmer*

This is a kind of bittersweet assertion:

> *Sapphire tears on my face*
> *Sadness became my whole sky*

That sadness isn't dwelled on, though; keeping with the theme of self-reflection the chorus is the counterpart to this sadness – given that the 'sadness became my whole sky' we might read this tune as ironic. 'I can still make the whole place shimmer' is contrary to that sadness. But perhaps ironic is less important – given the tone is so ambiguous throughout this record, suddenly 'Bejeweled', in the last quarter of the record, potentially appears as the consequence and result of the therapeutic self-reflection – 'Diamonds in my eyes / ... I polish up real nice'.

'Labyrinth'
An organ sound that's not so far from the heavily tremeloed *1989*. We're in the realm of very produced pop – there's so much detail in this production, from the gentle caress of plain guitar sounds to the squiggly rush of noisy synth complements and the bass drum holding the pulse steady like it's waiting to break into disco.

It's a spare and a witty song; it may be that it's noticeably more 'produced' because it's a relatively simple pop song:

> *You know how scared I am of elevators*
> *Never trust it if it rises fast*
> *It can't last*

The self-doubt and reservation measured against the 'uh-oh, I'm fallin' in love again' makes the euphoria of the arrangement precipitous; again dealing out ambiguity, it's not clear the ohs of the chorus are worry or pop-phatic.

'Karma'

Karma can be a precarious sentiment; it's typically taken in the English-speaking West to mean the sense in which actions have consequences. In its originary India it has similar associations, but there's a complex range of philosophies and theologies surrounding it; dharma and adharma are not facile adjuncts to the concept of karma. Or put another way – karma is not a facile concept. Without putting my theology hat on, suffice it to say that karma does not simply or uncomplicatedly correspond to an idea of 'cosmic justice' in its religious context for many of the religions of South Asia. Swift's conception of karma is somewhat less nuanced.

This song dotes heavily on its chorus, repeated three times with one stanza/ bridge of an altered form:

> *…karma is my boyfriend*
> *Karma is a god*
> *Karma is the breeze in my hair on the weekend*
> *Karma's a relaxing thought*
> *…*
> *Me and karma vibe like that*

The joke of this song really is that karma is all manner of things for the protagonist – there's a single line to suggest that it's directed at someone with negative intent – 'Aren't you envious that for you it's not?' and the remainder of the song is gleefully gloating in an over the top fashion. The notion being that the protagonist is blessed, is intimate with, and benefits from karma.

It wouldn't be too overwrought to say that this is a hilariously overwrought and ornately petty dig at its antagonist.

'Sweet Nothing'

A disarmingly simple song – the arrangement doesn't lack for complexity but the bulk is around a jaunty rhodes-esque piano line. It's the kind of simple that we've not seen for a while, possibly since *Fearless*.

> *Outside, they're push and shovin'*
> *You're in the kitchen hummin'*
> *All that you ever wanted from me was sweet nothin'*

It's an assertion of a kind of domestic simplicity; to have a relationship devoid of expectations or drama.

> *On the way home*
> *I wrote a poem*
> *You say, 'What a mind'*
> *This happens all the time*

The second verse details the idea of a compliment as worth noting; those sweet nothings are the solidity of the relationship; the first verse details a rock that was picked up in Wicklow (a town on the south-west coast of Ireland). This is a plain but not unique notion – Swift has played on humdrum observations countless times; rarely have those humdrum observations been *un*invested with meaning – here the nothings are quite nothingy, but also emblematic and symbolic of the relationship free from trammels and problems.

It is, for a record marked by ambiguity and cryptic notions, somewhat disarming to realise that the track least ambiguous is the one which details the relief of lacking expectations; again, building on the idea that the record has a broad theme of self-analysis in a therapeutic (or pseudo-therapeutic) context it reads like a self-assertion of what is imperative to the protagonist – that they not be stressed or called upon.

'Mastermind'

Another lovely synth opening in the *1989* mode; this time accompanied with a driving bass drum.

Mastermind is again something of an ironic song; for all the self-doubt and ambiguity of this record, to suddenly paint a picture of a controlling narcissist ('Anti-Hero' from the same album speaks directly about narcissism) or at least deluded narcissist:

> *What if I told you none of it was accidental?*
> ...
> *And now you're mine*
> ...
> *'Cause I'm a mastermind*

but elsewhere:

> *No one wanted to play with me as a little kid*
> ...
> *I'm only cryptic and Machiavellian*
> *'Cause I care*

It's not so much that the 'mastermind' assertion is therefore convincing but rather that this is a portrait of a sad person who's asserting their dominance to counteract their childish loneliness; in which view it becomes easier to see the 'mastermind' assertion as covert narcissism (though probably not disguised as altruism).

Ultimately then there's something *pathetic* (in the sense of pathos) about the narrator here, but it's richly woven into a tapestry of someone bigging themselves up.

Coda

What's next for Taylor

This coda is already on shifting grounds – between the time of starting this book and submission date, Swift elected to release *Midnights*. No great trouble, but it also meant that I had to amend my plans in order to accommodate it. I'm not saying that she's selfish but just to say that I'd appreciate a bit more warning before the next album if you're reading, Big T. Between *folklore* and *evermore* being released there was a mere four-and-a-half months, so there's every reason to suggest that between me finishing this book and you reading it, there's been another album or two released.

The business essay discusses the (alleged) confrontation between Spotify and Swift, whereby Swift withheld her music from the platform. I say 'alleged' because it's difficult to know what is merely differences in business practice and that which carries animosity. It's worth noting that those differences are not so grievous as they might seem.

There is a narrative fallacy here, combined with the fact that, obviously, some artists that used to do well in the past may not do well in this future landscape, where you can't record music once every three to four years and think that's going to be enough.

> The artists today that are making it realise that it's about creating a continuous engagement with their fans. It is about putting the work in, about the storytelling around the album, and about keeping a continuous dialogue with your fans.
>
> Daniel Ek, CEO of Spotify[4]

What Ek is talking about here is also succinctly Swift. The key to the Swiftie fanbase (see 'Swift for Swifties') is that they have a strong relationship to Swift, and there's a feeling of a continuous dialogue with the fans. Swift has a strong hand in her brand – it's now typical for her to direct her own music videos. Swift has a release schedule that's substantially quicker than 'every three to four

---

4. https://musically.com/2020/07/30/spotify-ceo-talks-covid-19-artist-incomes-and-podcasting-interview, accessed 22 January 2023.

years'. Whether those frequent releases are of quality (and I'd argue they are), the point is that Swift is the model for commercial pop music in the 2020s, at least according to Ek's rendering.

What this means is that Swift speaks to a specific generation. One which uses Spotify for music, and Instagram for social media. Instagram was released 2010, millennials are born (roughly) in 1981–1996, so in 2010 they were 14–30 (i.e. somewhere between school and starting a family). In terms of the social media of millennials, Swift is fifteenth most popular overall and fourth most popular musician on Instagram, seventh most popular overall and fourth most popular musician on Twitter, thirtieth most popular overall and sixth most popular musician on Facebook. By contrast, newer social media is less Swift-ly inclined – she doesn't feature in the top most-followed TikTok accounts. TikTok is largely contemporary with Generation Z, so younger musicians – such as Bella Poarch, Loren Gray, Billie Eilish – tend to proliferate there.

The overlap between contemporary media and popularity of an artist is related to Ek's point – social media allows the audience to feel a proximity to their favourite artists. For some artists, this has allowed for a resurgence – Cher is rightly notorious for being hilarious on Twitter. Dolly Parton (less than a year older than Cher) has long since cultivated a fairly intimate relationship with her fanbase and social media has only amplified that. But there's an adjacent point that, as the younger generations migrate to new social media, so too does the vogue of popular music shift. Even though she's only in her 30s, Swift is regarded as 'older'. Which makes sense, she's a clear decade-and-a-half older than an 18-year-old.

The next step in this is when Taylor Swift passes from 'current vogue' to *older people's music*. As inevitably happens. And while plenty of musicians come in and out of favour – I've probably witnessed five Madonna revivals in my lifetime – there comes a point when 'most successful musician in the world' passes to 'still successful but not dominating'. What happens to Swift at that point? Well, she'll probably continue releasing records. She's still liable to be enormously profitable. Most musicians do just carry on – there's plenty of acts – for instance, U2 – whose career best is twenty-plus years ago. There's plenty of acts who continue to develop their form to produce impressive but less-appreciated work later in life. Leonard Cohen, for instance – who never had Swift levels of popularity but certainly persisted with improving and exploring songwriter form. Another example is Prince, who continued to turn out impressive and surprising works right up until his passing.

Prince feels like the model for Swift's music. Not necessarily in terms of style – Prince's work was most typically somewhere between funk and pop, with a few ventures into more 'musicianly' avenues – such as the jazz jams of *N E*

W S (2003). Prince also had a seemingly insatiable appetite for work – there's notoriously an enormous backlog of unreleased work in his Paisley Park studios. Prince's issue in the 1990s with his label Warner Bros was complex, but one of the critical details was that Prince wanted to release material more frequently than the 1990s pace of 'an album every two years'; shortly after disentangling himself from Warner Bros, he released the *Emancipation* box set, three CDs of new or unheard material.

That is to say – Prince was very much the kind of musician Ek would appreciate, someone who can provide a steady flow of quality material for music platforms – though Prince, like Swift, was not keen on having Spotify host his music, and it was largely absent from the platform until after he died.

The critical commonality with Prince and Swift – or at least, potential-future-Swift – was as songwriters for other people. In 2019, there was a posthumous release of *Originals* – songs written by Prince, recorded by other people (including 'Manic Monday', as recorded by the Bangles, and 'Nothing Compares 2 U', as made famous by Sinéad O'Connor.

Swift has also penned (or co-penned) the lyrics for 'Better Man' by Little Big Town, 'You'll Always Find Your Way Back Home' by Miley Cyrus (as Hannah Montana), 'Best Days of Your Life' by Kellie Pickler, 'Babe' by Sugarland, 'Both of Us' by B.o.B and 'Two Is Better than One' by Boys Like Girls. Swift also used the pseudonym 'Nils Sjöberg' for 'This is What You Came For', by Calvin Harris featuring Rihanna. That is to say, there's an *Originals*-worth of material just waiting to be recorded. Some of them have reappeared as part of the re-recording project.

There's other precedents for taking more of a backseat into songwriting. Mylène Farmer is one of France's most successful popstars. In English-speaking territories, she's often described as like a French Madonna, but that does a disservice to Farmer's work – rich and sumptuous but also fun and pop and with a lyrical bent that's incisive and queer (in several senses). Farmer also had a strong hand in producing her music videos, many of which extend the 1980s pop music video format massively to something much more expansive and opulent – check out the 8m+ video for 'Sans contrefaçon'.

By the turn of the 2000s, Farmer turned to acting as songwriter for Alizée – at the time an unknown young singer, twenty-three years Farmer's junior. Using a younger performer allowed Farmer to explore certain aspect of youth and sexuality that would've been less authentic for a woman in her 40s. That's not to say that a woman in her 40s cannot express sexuality, but rather that sentiments like those of 'Moi… Lolita' are more convincing when coming from a younger woman.

One suspects that Swift is more likely to explore lyrics as a means to express her changing self as she gets older; nevertheless, we've seen that she's an adept storyteller and there have been glimpses of writing outside of her own experience (e.g. 'Mary's Song' on *Self-titled*); one can imagine that an adult life spent largely in the limelight would result in seeking out ways to retreat from view – as many very famous people do (think Prince, Michael Jackson, Enya, etc.). So no reason she couldn't make a Farmer-like turn and take on a protégé.

Another option that we might see developing is her turning to directing. Swift's later music videos are typically directed by Swift. That, coupled with her proven record for storytelling in general, could easily result in her turning her hand to directing larger projects – film, TV. It follows also that a different form of writing like prose would seem a predictable complement for her skills. Although perhaps poetry would be a more seemly match for her capacity for taut, expressive parity.

But, in the short term, the most likely thing is that she'll carry on at whatever rate she will; the themes will follow her adult life. It may be that she pulls another turn in terms of musical styles but it seems that the two threads of her music are well established – the storytelling folklore of (ahem) *folklore/evermore* and the sparse electro-pop of *1989/Midnights*. Swift's management of her own career, and the important steps she's taken for retaining copyright of her own material, probably mean that she's less likely to go down a route of exploring her love of something left-of-centre – whether that's big band music or drum 'n' bass. But who knows, she's done plenty of guest spots on TV shows doing very faux white girl rapping so perhaps there's still gas in the tank of embarrassing miss-steps. It's been quite clear that she's into dance music and rap music so perhaps there's something preposterous and atypical just waiting round the corner. I'm hoping she doesn't decide to take up a left turn as a drill rapper but it's not for me to say. She's got previous with London musicians so maybe there's a guest verse from Kay-O or Digga D just waiting to happen.

Whatever happens, though, I'm sure it'll all be perfectly adult and compellingly honest, as always.

What's next for Swiftology

So this book could never promise to be exhaustive, comprehensive. I've very deliberately limited the remit of what I'm talking about to talk about Swift's songwriting. What have I left out? A lot.

There's a lot about Swift's visual brand that's hugely interesting. Not just the red lips (see the lips section in tropology) but the broader visual image. How does the album artwork relate to the videos? What are the visual themes in the albums? It's clear that the *Midnights* videos all have a similar visual feel, and by design – not least because Swift is also her own director. One of the more interesting things for me is the typography – by the time of *Midnights*, the typeface is a solidly elegant sans serif (Neue Haas Grotesk) – and its age and standing make it classic. Clean and taut but subtly more readable than the more recognisable Futura or Helvetica. What can we get from the differences between Neue Haas Grotesk and Tungsten Bold (*Red*)? Is there a correspondence between the music and the typeface? Or whether it's a handwriting typeface (*Self-titled, Speak Now, folklore, evermore*) or a print typeface (*Fearless, Red, 1989, reputation, Lover, Midnights*)?

There's a heap of music that I haven't looked at. With ten albums of material, there's enough to be getting on with. There's a lot to be said about the apocrypha – the songs that didn't make it onto albums, or the tracks that were included on the re-recorded albums. There's a lot of juvenile work floating about on the Internet – and there's definitely a lot that could be said about those works that show Swift in her most nascent form.

I've primarily focused on the details that are *not* Taylor Swift's private life, how one maps her biography onto the songs. I'm personally averse to gossip column writing – it's at best invasive, and tends to perpetuate the worst of sexism. Women can fuck or not fuck whoever they want and, assuming it's consensual, it has no bearing on them as people, on their art, and it's not interesting to speculate about that. Speculating on women's sex lives is something we can leave the fuck behind in the twentieth century. And maybe then we can, as fans of pop music, have more mature conversations about sex. Or at least more songs as banging as 'WAP'.

Having said that, I imagine there is potentially a more 'Swiftie'-centric version of this book – one that sympathetically draws out the personal biography without drifting into sleazy schoolyard bullshit. There's also a fascinating ethnographic study in the Swiftie fandom itself – it's a very active community and one with some surprisingly coherent politics; moreover, there's a very strong relationship between Swift and her fanbase – at least in terms of how she speaks about them in her interviews.

Swiftology was a term I used in a kind of self-deprecating way to describe being a bit *extra* about Swift. But it's also worth saying that what we see in Swift – the musician, director, celebrity, cat-lover, feminist, etc. – is important insofar as it tells us stuff about life in the early twenty-first century. She is a case study in the pop art of millennial culture. All these ideas, and probably lots I haven't thought about, doubtless tell us about ourselves and our relationship to this weird and increasingly on-fire planet. Plus she's a whole banger machine.

Finally, then – I hope I've given you new ways to listen to Swift, and things to think about along the way.

Dear Reader,

We hope you have enjoyed this book, but why not share your views on social media? You can also follow our pages to see more about our other products: facebook.com/penandswordbooks or follow us on Twitter @penswordbooks

You can also view our products at www.pen-and-sword.co.uk (UK and ROW) or www.penandswordbooks.com (North America).

To keep up to date with our latest releases and online catalogues, please sign up to our newsletter at: www.pen-and-sword.co.uk/newsletter

If you would like a printed catalogue with our latest books, then please email: enquiries@pen-and-sword.co.uk or telephone: 01226 734555 (UK and ROW) or email: uspen-and-sword@casematepublishers.com or telephone: (610) 853-9131 (North America).

We respect your privacy and we will only use personal information to send you information about our products.

Thank you!